Pineapple Maids

A Pineapple Port Mystery: Book Nineteen

Amy Vansant

Vansant Creations, LLC / Amy Vansant
Annapolis, MD
http://www.AmyVansant.com
http://www.PineapplePort.com

Editing/Proofreading by Effrosyni Moschoudi & Meg Barnhart

CHAPTER ONE

Darla held a glass of white wine aloft to examine its color against the light. She swirled it until the Pinot Grigio sloshed over the edge and brought the stemware to her nose. She inhaled like a vacuum, punctuating with a snort.

"I detect notes of oak and peach," she announced with authority.

Her friend Mariska arched an eyebrow.

"I think you have to *taste* it to *detect notes*." She took a sip from the glass in her hand and swished it around her mouth, sounding much like a clothes washer. "I detect notes of lavender and ear wax."

"Hm. *Really...*" Darla sipped. "Yes, I see that...and day-old donuts. And...*lizard feet*."

Mariska nodded solemnly. "Yes. That's how they crush the grapes, you know. Trained lizards."

"You don't say?"

Darla held her serious expression a second longer and then gave up.

The women dissolved into giggles.

It wasn't their fault. They'd been at the wine tasting for a good hour.

Make that a *great* hour.

A notice promoting the wine tasting had appeared on the Pineapple Port fifty-five-plus community bulletin board. They decided to go because the event benefitted a good cause—though they'd forgotten what it was.

They'd tried a dizzying array of bottles for ten dollars.

Not a bad deal.

The only downside was the function's location was in a rented rustic barn—known as The Barn—a popular spot for weddings and corporate events. It made for a charming setting *and* a great place to collapse from heat prostration.

As a rule, local Floridians like Darla and Mariska did their best to avoid unairconditioned barns—unairconditioned *anything*, for that matter. They'd broken a rule attending the wine tasting, but an hour in, it seemed worth it, even if their grinning faces were shiny as a licked lollipop.

A breeze generated by one of the large standing fans cooled their cheeks, and the ladies turned toward it like petunias to the sun.

"I love that fan," sighed Mariska.

"I'm going to marry it," agreed Darla.

The lofty barn—all beams and weather-aged slats—had been swept clean and dotted with decorative haybales and a smattering of sawdust sprinkled around the tasting areas. Twinkling fairy lights covered tables, booths, and seating like a swarm of glowing locusts. Long tables draped with white tablecloths and topped with rustic floral arrangements lined the room's perimeter while people milled in the center, chatting, sipping, and sweating.

"They did a nice job with the barn," said Mariska, fanning herself as the breeze from the fan meandered away. "It's a real barn, you know—when they aren't renting it."

"I figured. It smells a little like horses," said Darla.

Mariska motioned to the nearest wine station. "Have we tried them all?"

"Reds, whites, rosés, and back to white. Judging by the look that the last pourer gave us, I think we've been around once or twice."

"What look?"

Darla shrugged. "Maybe it was less the look and more the way she said, *you again*."

She could tell Mariska wasn't listening by the way she scanned the tables. She was probably thinking about food.

"We should probably hit the cheese trays again," murmured Mariska.

Darla nodded.

Yep. Food.

"The cheeses are long gone," she said.

"Bread and olive oil?"

"Good luck. They were gone before the cheeses."

Mariska pouted. "I should have taken some extra."

Darla took the last sip of her glass.

"I think they frown on people bringing doggy bags."

A short, older gentleman with a waxed mustache curled at the edges approached them. He wore a summer suit the color of a light Pinot Noir.

"Ladies, hello. I'm Bernard Boyle. You can call me Bernie. Have you enjoyed the evening?" he asked, holding out his hand.

Even in the heat, he looked as cool as a polar bear's toenails.

"We've had a great time," said Darla, shaking his hand.

Even his palms weren't sweating. It made her feel like a swamp critter by comparison.

"Maybe a few more fans," suggested Mariska.

Bernie nodded. "It *did* turn out warmer than we expected."

"Florida does that," said Darla. "It's what it does best, really."

Bernie paused to take a sip of his wine.

"How did you hear about us?" he asked.

"We live in Pineapple Port. There was a flyer there," said Darla.

Bernie pressed his lips into a grim line.

"Ah, we hoped to get a few more of you from there, but you two are the first I've met."

Darla put her flat hand to the side of her mouth and leaned in to stage-whisper.

"You made the mistake of not making everything *free*."

She tittered, and when Bernie didn't join her, she worried she'd been too bold with the little man. Then he cocked his head like a robin eyeing a worm, and she realized his mind had wandered elsewhere. Maybe he was obsessed with the missing cheese, too.

"I don't suppose you two know anything about that detective agency on the outskirts of Pineapple Port, do you?" he asked.

"Do we?" asked Mariska, her chest puffing. "It's owned by our Charlotte."

Bernie's eyebrows bounced upward. "*Your* Charlotte?

Granddaughter? Daughter?"

"Neither, but we raised her when her grandmother died. It was a community effort," said Darla.

"She stayed in her house, mostly, but we were there every step of the way," said Mariska.

Bernie pursed his lips. "Isn't Pineapple Port a retirement community? They let the girl grow up there?"

Darla scoffed. "We made sure she stayed. My husband's the sheriff."

She eyed Bernie as he nodded. He looked like he wanted to say something but hadn't found the nerve, and she wondered if he planned to turn them in for keeping Charlotte out of the orphanage twenty years ago.

She took a phantom sip from her empty glass to keep her hands busy.

"What did you want to know about Charlotte?" asked Mariska.

Darla heard annoyance in her friend's tone. She'd also noticed Bernie's odd behavior and shifted into Mama Mode.

"Oh, nothing..." he said, taking another sip.

"It doesn't look like nothing," pushed Darla.

Bernie sighed. "I have a problem."

"The sort that requires a detective?" asked Mariska.

He nodded. "Maybe. Increasingly, I think so."

Darla slapped her hand on her chest, relieved the little man's pained expression wasn't trouble, *and* he might be a customer for Charlotte's new Charlock Holmes Detective Agency.

"I'm sure Charlotte can help you," she said.

"You can't do better than Charlotte," gushed Mariska. "She's the *best*. She's partners with her fiancé, Declan, and he's no slouch either."

"And he's handsome," said Darla.

Mariska looked at her.

Darla shrugged. "Well, he is. I mean, not for *me*, I'm a thousand years old, but for Charlotte..."

Mariska frowned. "I don't think that's what makes him a good detective, though."

"No. Mostly not." Darla bobbed one shoulder. "Maybe a little. Good looks never hurt."

Mariska turned her attention back to Bernie. "Do you have a case for them?"

"I do. I think." He pulled at his mustache and then leaned in to whisper. "It's sensitive."

"Charlotte's very sensitive," said Mariska.

Darla agreed. "She's a girl. I mean a *woman*. We're better with sensitive things. In general."

Bernie seemed interested.

"Do you have a card for her?" he asked.

"I *do*." Mariska put her empty glass on a wine barrel table and rooted through her purse. She removed a chunk of baguette and placed it next to her glass.

Bernie scowled at it.

"I brought that from home. Just in case there weren't snacks," she said.

He nodded and sipped his wine as Mariska pawed through her bag.

Darla motioned to his glass.

"What do you taste?"

Bernard smacked his lips.

"A flirtation of black cherry and... pencil shavings?"

Darla nodded. "You're good at this." She glanced behind her. "I should get some more..."

Mariska pulled a business card from her purse. "Here it is."

She handed the card to Bernie.

"Thank you," he said, putting the card into his pocket.

"You can't tell us what it's about?" she asked.

He grimaced and took the last swallow of his wine. "I own an assisted living manor. There's been some...*oddities*."

"What sort of oddities?"

"People have been—I mean, they're *supposed* to die. They're old, but..."

Darla straightened. "You think someone's bumping off your residents?"

His eyes popped wide, and he scanned the area as if looking for eavesdroppers. "Whoa, I didn't say *that*—"

"Why else would you need a detective?"

Bernie cleared his throat. "I, uh, it was nice meeting you."

He grabbed Darla's hand, shook it, shook Mariska's, and hurried away in a less-than-straight line.

Mariska slapped Darla's arm.

Darla snapped her attention to her.

"*Ow.*"

"You scared him away."

"No, I didn't, and what's up with that bread? I thought you forgot to steal some for later."

Mariska shrugged. "It's not as good without the cheese."

Darla stared off in the direction Bernie had left and clenched a fist. "We have to get Charlotte that job."

"We *definitely* do, especially now that you maybe ruined her chances by being so nosey."

Darla gaped. "I did *not.*" She huffed and then had a thought that smoothed her bunched shoulders. "Hey, I think she needs our help for this one."

Mariska scoffed. "I don't know if she wants our help."

"That's just it. Normally, she'd be afraid to let us help, but we're *naturals* for this one."

"What are you talking about?" asked Mariska, scowling like she was processing long-division.

Darla held out her hands, her wine glass dangling between two fingers. "Isn't it obvious? *We'll pose as residents.* Get the inside scoop."

"You want to pose as residents in an assisted living home where people are *being murdered*?"

Darla brushed away her concerns. "He's imagining it. They're just *old*. Charlotte will get paid for putting his mind at ease."

Mariska tapped the edge of her empty glass against her chin. "It does sound like fun—"

Darla produced her phone and started a search. "I'll look up local nursing homes and people named Bernard Boyle and figure out which one he owns."

"Smart. Good idea. Ooh, look at *that*," said Mariska, peering at a large white mansion on Darla's phone screen. "That's pretty. Is that it?"

"I think so. Elderbrook Manor—yep, here's his name. This is the one."

Mariska grabbed for the phone.

"I want to check out the dining facilities. Oh—look at that *carrot cake*."

Darla groaned. "I love carrot cake. I could use some right now. It would go really well with that playful, fruity white we had over there at that booth."

Her attention drifted through the open barn doors.

What the—

She gasped and pointed with all the urgency of a little girl spotting a live unicorn.

"Look—there's the jitney. Let's go. We have work to do."

"We have to get a carrot cake," muttered Mariska.

They hustled outside to catch their ride and groaned with pleasure as they entered the air-conditioned jitney.

"Bernie's place looked really nice," said Mariska as they took seats. "Though, I don't know if carrot cake is worth getting *murdered* for."

Darla shrugged.

"Depends on the icing."

CHAPTER TWO

Charlotte stood staring through the Charlock Holmes Detective Agency window, watching cars whiz by on the main thoroughfare bordering the edge of the Pineapple Port retirement community.

Her fiancé, Declan, left his place at his desk, flipping through the junk mail, to arrive beside her.

"Penny for your thoughts?" he asked.

She shook her head. "I need at least a buck. Inflation."

"Make it two."

"Deal. I'm working on marketing ideas to get us business."

"How's it going?"

"Not great. I keep getting distracted, thinking about what to have for lunch. I'm too hungry to be a brilliant marketer right now."

Declan slipped his arm around her waist and pulled her to him. Charlotte felt her breath catch in her throat as the heat of his body touched hers.

"I know what *I'd* like to have for lunch," he murmured.

She swallowed. "Sir, I'd like to remind you this is a place of office—"

"*A place of office?*" he echoed, chuckling.

"A, uh, office of work— *Place of work.*"

He took a step away to peer into her eyes.

"Miss, have you been drinking?"

"*No—*" She giggled as he grabbed her and kissed her neck. "My brain just isn't working right—"

"Why is that?" he murmured in her ear.

Charlotte spotted a flash of movement outside.

"*Mariska.*"

Declan's playful kisses stopped.

"You can't think because of *Mariska*?"

"No—Mariska is headed for our door."

"Oh, jeez—"

Declan spun away from her as the door opened to the tune of their wonky bellringer.

Mariska and Darla burst into the office with their usual perfect timing.

Declan dropped his adorable tush on the corner of a desk and picked up a book on poisons she'd been reading.

"What are you doing here?" asked Charlotte.

Both women looked animated.

Suspiciously animated.

Frighteningly animated.

"We have some good news—" Mariska's head tilted. "What's wrong with your chest?"

Charlotte glanced down. "Hm?"

"You're all blotchy, your chest and neck?"

"Am I?" Charlotte's hand fluttered to her throat. "I don't know."

She noticed Darla's attention had locked on the book Declan was pretending to read. She looked to see what she found so fascinating.

Declan had the book upside down.

Evidence is piling up.

She plucked the book from his hands and put it on the desk beside him.

"So, what brings you here?" she repeated, returning to their unexpected visitors.

The ladies exchanged a look that made Charlotte want to crawl under her desk.

She braced herself.

They are definitely up to something.

"We have a job for you," said Darla.

"*You* do?" asked Declan, standing.

Charlotte glanced at him. Her poor fiancé hadn't known Darla and Mariska for as long as she had. He was still naïve enough to think they'd escape this visit unscathed.

Foolish boy.

The ladies nodded like bobbleheads, but Charlotte noticed a blip of concern in their eyes. Declan's eager response hadn't gone unnoticed—it had exposed how desperately they needed new business.

"We might be able to fit something else into our schedule," Charlotte said, trying hard to look casual.

Declan scoffed.

"You *think*? We could fit a dozen—"

He noticed her glare and caught on.

"—uh, maybe *one* more. Right. *Maybe*," he corrected.

"You have other cases?" asked Mariska.

"Always," said Charlotte.

The ladies seemed relieved.

Mission accomplished.

That would keep them from worrying about her for five minutes.

"What are you working on now?" asked Mariska.

Make that five *seconds*.

Charlotte and Declan exchanged a look, and she could tell he expected her to come up with the lie.

"Um, a couple of things. I can't really talk about them. There's patient—er, *client* confidentiality and all that."

Darla grinned. "Well, I hope you have some spare time because we've got you a *good* one."

"Yes? What is it?"

Darla put a hand on Mariska's arm before continuing.

Charlotte scowled.

"What's going on? Why are you being so weird?" she asked.

Darla sniffed. "We have a caveat."

"What's that?"

"It means we have a stipulation."

Charlotte sighed. "I know what *caveat* means. I mean, what *is* your *stipulation*?"

"We have *conditions* we need you to meet in exchange for our *very important* information," said Mariska.

Charlotte pinched the bridge of her nose.

"Should I get the thesaurus so we can keep this up all day, or are you going to tell me what you want?"

"We want to *help*," blurted Darla.

Charlotte blinked at her. "Help with what? The case?"

The ladies nodded in unison.

"You're saying you won't give us the case unless you can help us work it?"

The ladies nodded harder, like a pair of eager labradors.

Charlotte looked at Declan.

He shrugged. "Why not?"

She put a hand on his chest. "You're adorable. Remember this moment."

She turned back to the ladies.

"*How* involved do you want to be?" she asked.

"*Totally*. We want to be part of solving the case," said Mariska.

"Can you be more specific? I can tell you're already brewing a plan."

Darla crossed her arms against her chest. "That's just it—you have nothing to worry about. We've got it all figured out."

Charlotte winced. "Oh no."

"I'm serious. You'll *want* us to be involved. You'll see. We'll be an *intricate part of the process*."

"Uh-huh. So, what's the case?"

Darla took a deep breath and gathered herself as though she were preparing to give a State of the Union address.

"Last night, at the wine tasting—"

Mariska touched Darla's arm to stop her story, but her eyes remained locked on Charlotte. "It was at The Barn. You know that old barn you can see off seventy-five? The one they use for events?"

Darla jerked her arm away from Mariska's touch.

"The *venue* isn't important."

Mariska shrugged. "I know. I was just wondering if Charlotte knew it."

Darla huffed and returned her attention to Charlotte and Declan.

"The important part is that at the wine tasting—"

"At The Barn," interjected Mariska.

"—we met a man named Bernie, who owns an assisted living home."

"A *manor*," corrected Mariska.

"A *manor*," agreed Darla. "Elderbrook Manor."

Mariska's eyes rolled back. "You should read their *menus*. The carrot cake looks *amazing*."

Darla side-eyed her and continued.

"Bernie has a problem—"

"His people are dying," said Mariska.

"His *people*?" asked Declan.

"His residents. He says they seem to be dying too much, but he isn't sure."

"He isn't sure people are dying?"

Darla shrugged. "Well, it *is* an assisted living home. They're old, but he's worried they're dying *too much*."

"He thinks something's up," said Mariska.

Charlotte nodded. "And he wants us to look into it?"

Darla crossed her arms against her chest. "Yep. If you let us help."

"*He* said that? Or that's *your* caveat?"

"Both," said the women together.

Charlotte sighed. "Now, you're lying in stereo."

"Do you agree?" asked Darla, thrusting out her hand to shake. "Agree, and we'll call him right now."

"It's the only way you'll get him. He really wants to work with *us*," added Mariska. Her nostrils flared—a sure sign she was lying.

Darla opened her mouth to continue the pitch, but as she sucked in her breath, the agency door opened, and the ladies shuffled aside to avoid being struck by it.

A short, older gentleman with a gray waxed mustache entered. He met Charlotte's gaze and then turned to Mariska and Darla.

"Oh, hello, you two," he said, smiling.

"We were just about to call you," said Darla.

"*Me*?" he asked, looking confused.

Charlotte squinted at the ladies and then turned her focus to the man.

"Hello, welcome to the Charlock Holmes Agency."

She paused and tried not to wince at the silly agency name they'd chosen. When the man didn't fall over laughing, she continued.

"I'm Charlotte Morgan, and this is my partner, Declan

Bingham."

"Bernard Boyle," said the man, shaking their hands.

"You've already met Mariska and Darla?" asked Charlotte.

He smiled. "Yes, at the wine tasting. It's funny they're here because I told them last night I might swing by to talk to you about a problem I'm having."

Charlotte pointed at the ladies. "And you want to work with *them*?"

Bernie's brow knit. "With *them*?" He turned to eye Darla and Mariska. "Do *you* work here?"

The ladies' cheeks flushed red.

"Charlotte's in charge. We should probably give you your privacy," said Darla, pushing Mariska toward the back.

Mariska nodded. "We'll talk later."

"We just have to get something over here," added Darla.

Charlotte watched them go.

"Have a seat," said Declan, motioning to their little sitting area.

Bernie sat and twirled the end of his fancy mustache like a nervous villain fresh from tying a lady to the train tracks.

"I have an assisted living home. Maybe you've heard of it? Elderbrook Manor?" he asked.

"Rings a bell," said Charlotte, though only because Darla had just mentioned the name.

"Laura Scarpetta went there," said Mariska from the corner. "Do you remember Mrs. Scarpetta? She left Pineapple Port when you were still young."

Charlotte twisted in her seat.

"Did you find what you were looking for?" she asked.

Darla, who'd been standing beside Mariska, squatted behind the desk.

"Not yet," she called.

Charlotte turned back to Bernie.

"I'm sorry. You were saying?"

Bernie paused to compose himself, his expression grim.

"Lately—and I hope this is all a strange coincidence—manor guests have been dying at an unusual rate."

He whispered the last part of the sentence.

"What's an *unusual* rate?" asked Declan.

"Well, we usually lose one resident a year, maybe two, to the usual reasons—age, illness, a need for a home with more nursing support than we provide—but over the last twelve months, we've lost *five*."

"Has there been anything unusual about the deaths?" asked Charlotte.

Bernie pulled at his mustache again. "No, except that some of them were our healthiest residents beforehand. There was no warning."

"Were there autopsies?"

Bernie squirmed. "No, it would be up to the families to request those."

He looked away, and Charlotte nodded. She understood his discomfort. Requesting an investigation would cause alarm or maybe even be used as an admission of guilt should he ever be sued.

"Have you taken any steps to investigate before coming to us?" asked Declan.

Bernie released a deep sigh. "I have. You have no idea. I've looked into everything—the food, medications, cleanliness, things the deceased had in common—nothing at the manor explains the deaths. There are never any wounds, no falls—I'm baffled."

"How were you thinking we might help?" asked Charlotte.

"I was thinking you could talk to the staff and patients?"

"Have *you* talked to them?"

"Yes, of course, and I've narrowed down the list of people I think *could* be involved; that is, if anyone is."

"How?" asked Declan.

"The deaths have happened too frequently to feel normal but too far apart to feel on purpose. Since they happened over time, *if* someone is responsible, it has to be someone who's been with us for at least a year. Those are the people I'd like you to investigate. I thought maybe you could get more out of them than me."

"I think they'd be *less* likely to talk to us, especially if they knew something," said Charlotte.

Bernie cocked his head. "Not if *you* were staff..."

Charlotte perked. "Oh—you want us to go undercover?"

He nodded and looked to Mariska and Darla, who'd run out of ways to pretend they were looking for something and now stood in the corner like a pair of grandmother clocks gawping at the meeting.

He pointed at them, and their necks retracted as if he'd poked them on the nose.

"Now that I know *they* work with you, I could introduce them as residents. It's *perfect*."

Charlotte turned in time to see Darla fist-pump while mouthing the word, *Yes!*

"You're the perfect people for this," said Bernie, hammering home his point.

Charlotte sighed. She couldn't argue with his logic.

"I guess we are," she admitted.

"They *do* work for you?" he asked, eyeing the ladies.

Charlotte nodded.

"Apparently."

CHAPTER THREE

Charlotte drove Declan, Mariska, and Darla to Elderbrook Manor in her old Volvo wagon, still wondering if she'd lost her mind allowing Mariska and Darla to work the case with them. She knew the ladies meant well and would try their best to be helpful, but that wasn't always the recipe for success.

"I don't know how you two managed to wedge yourselves into this investigation," she said, pulling off the highway toward the manor.

"Even you have to admit we're coming in handy for this one," said Darla.

Charlotte grunted. Having insiders who could move seamlessly among the residents would be handy, but she couldn't let Darla *know* that.

"Just be careful," said Declan. "It'll all probably be nothing but a coincidence, but if someone *is* killing the residents, you don't want to be next."

"Of course, we'll be careful," huffed Mariska as if she'd never ignored good advice.

"Tiniest little oddity, and you let us know. Don't try to investigate yourselves," added Declan.

"Don't be those *I wonder what's down this dark hallway* people," said Charlotte.

The ladies giggled, and in her rearview mirror, Charlotte saw their warnings had had *zero* effect on their giddiness.

"I hope they have cornhole," said Darla. "We could make some money sharking the locals."

"Do *not* shake down the residents," said Charlotte.

"*Or shuffleboard*," she heard Mariska whisper.

Before she could object again, Charlotte spotted the sign for Elderbrook and pulled down the property's winding drive. Acres of manicured lawns dotted with lush flowerbeds of pink and white had all four wide-eyed.

"When I can't live alone anymore, I want to come here," said Darla.

"We'll share a room," agreed Mariska.

Declan twisted in his seat. "Where are Bob and Frank in this scenario?"

"At the cheap home," said Darla.

The ladies cackled.

As they rounded a patch of oak trees, the manor house appeared—a square, three-story structure with east and west wings, a gray stone facade, and endless windows.

"*Luxury assisted living*," said Charlotte, quoting the brochure as she pulled into the paved parking area.

As she shifted the car into park, she spotted several structures scattered around the property—a gazebo, shed, and pool house—each designed with the same aesthetic as the main residence. At the back of the property, a pond shimmered in the sunlight, its edges lined with coconut and traveler's palms. Walking paths wove from the manor to the lake, back yard, and other unknown destinations.

She had to admit, the place was impressive.

They climbed broad steps flanked by stone urns overflowing with more cheery flowers to pass through massive double doors and enter the lobby.

"Hello, how can I help you?" asked a young, smiling brunette with a nametag reading *Luna*. She wore a light blue and white uniform that felt more *maid* than *receptionist*.

"We're here to see Mr. Boyle?" said Charlotte as Mariska and Darla wandered the room, oohing, aahing, and touching everything they could reach.

"There's a *store*," exclaimed Mariska, tugging on a locked door beneath the sign *Manor Mementos*. She pressed her face against the glass to peer into the darkened room. "I want to buy something."

"Perfect timing," said Bernie, appearing from a door next to the store's entrance. "Leave your bags there. I'll have them taken to your rooms. The residents are at lunch. Come to my office."

He led them into a small square office. A bulldog sleeping beside a dark wood desk looked up at them when they entered, but only with its eyes—its head never moved.

Charlotte couldn't help but notice the dog wore the same maid uniform as the receptionist.

"That's Apple. She's our mascot and one of the maids," explained Bernie, motioning to the dog.

"She seems very calm," said Darla, squatting to pet the animal. "Must be nice."

"*Her* dog is a nutcase," said Mariska with a chuckle to Bernie, pointing to Darla.

"Take a seat, please." Bernie motioned to chairs facing his desk as he sat behind it.

"Nice place," said Declan.

"Very *grand*," chirped Mariska.

Darla nodded. "*Grand.* That's *exactly* what it is."

"Thank you." Bernie turned to Charlotte. "So, I've arranged for you to be one of our maids."

Charlotte nodded. She'd requested the position. Maids had access to the rooms and residents and probably talked amongst themselves.

Bernie stood to grab a familiar uniform in plastic hanging from the wall behind him—a light blue dress with a white apron around the middle and a crisp white collar. She guessed the hem would land at or below her knee.

The phone on the desk rang, and Bernie thrust the dress at Charlotte.

"Just a second."

He answered and turned away from them to talk.

Charlotte held up her uniform for Declan to see.

"I think this would look better on you," she whispered.

"*Duh*," he said.

She chuckled. "I can't hope to wear it as well as Apple."

Bernie hung up and returned his attention to them. "I've Yasmine on her way. Sorry. Lots of things going on today. Declan, my boy, you'll be a house manager shadowing Dana."

"Does that mean I'm in charge of her?" he asked, bobbing his head in Charlotte's direction.

Bernie nodded. "Technically."

Declan smirked. "That would be a nice change."

Charlotte rolled her eyes at him and turned to Bernie.

"Does it matter that the receptionist saw us together? She won't think it's odd a new maid, manager, and two residents came in together?"

Bernie shook his head. "That's my granddaughter, Luna. She knows who you are. I had her meet you."

He picked up his landline, dialed two numbers, and spoke to someone before hanging up.

"Yasmine will be here in a moment to give Charlotte a tour, and I've got Oksana coming for the ladies. Declan, I'll show you around as soon as I get everyone else settled."

"Tell me again the people we need to keep an eye on?" asked Declan.

Bernie frowned. "Yasmine, Dana, and Oksana are the three staff members who've been here for the full period in question—and the residents—though I can't imagine them being involved."

"What about your granddaughter?"

Bernie scowled. "Luna? She's nineteen. She's my *granddaughter*."

"I just mean, has she been here long enough? Maybe she's seen things?"

It wasn't what she'd meant, but she realized now it sounded better.

"Oh." Bernie paused. "Yes, she's been here almost a year—much to her mother's chagrin. She hoped to have her off to college by now."

Charlotte nodded and made a mental note to watch Luna, too, granddaughter or not.

"What about the cooking staff? Landscapers?" she asked.

"The grounds are kept by a third-party company, as is the catering. A lot of the same people work every day, but there's shuffling." He sighed. "If someone from those groups is involved, it will be much harder to figure out *who*."

"Is there anything we should know about Yasmine, Dana, and Oksana? Anything that leads you to believe they'd wish the residents harm?"

Bernie frowned. "No. Yasmine's been a bit short-tempered lately and always strict, but that's what makes her so effective. Dana and Oksana are just—*normal*."

A woman entered wearing the same housekeeper uniform Charlotte held in her hand.

"Here's Yasmine, now," said Bernie a little too loudly.

Yasmine appeared in her early sixties, a thick woman with large hands and a brooding air. She paused at the doorway to scan the room over her hawk-like nose. Threads of silver streaked through her jet-black hair. Every strand was pulled so tight toward the bun at the nape of her neck that Charlotte suspected she ripped out errant strands cheeky enough to escape—maybe tortured them with a hot curler before tossing them away.

As the woman's steely grey eyes locked on Charlotte, they narrowed in synch with her pressed lips.

"*Guilty*," she heard Darla mutter.

Charlotte elbowed her.

Beneath his mustache, Bernie's lips danced a nervous cha-cha before finding a way to smile.

"Charlotte, this is Yasmine Lambert, my head of housekeeping. She'll get you settled."

Yasmine nodded to show she'd heard and ran her hand over the bodice of her uniform. It looked like she'd pulled it from the dry cleaners—crisp, neat, not a stain marring the apron. Charlotte couldn't help but think hers would look like modern art ten minutes after starting work.

She stood as Yasmine motioned for her to follow.

"This way."

She offered a smile that didn't quite reach her eyes but avoided looking at Charlotte. Her gaze, instead, locked on a pile of brochures sitting on the desk. She leaned in to straighten the stack and then proceeded to the lobby.

"See you later," said Charlotte to the others. She gathered her uniform and followed Yasmine out of the room.

"Have fun!" called Mariska.

Charlotte winced. *Undercover* wasn't really Mariska's thing.

"Beautiful place," she said, hustling to keep up with the head housekeeper's lengthy stride.

"It is. Welcome to Elderbrook Manor." Yasmine said the phrase with all the enthusiasm of a mortician. "You've been a maid before?"

Charlotte nodded. "Sure. Long time. I've got a passion for cleaning."

She swallowed a smile, knowing anyone who knew her would fall over laughing to hear her say she had a *passion for cleaning*.

They passed an art room filled with A-frame easels. Inside, a man with curly gray hair painted alone. The grin on his face made Charlotte curious about his art, but she couldn't see the canvas as she whizzed by and couldn't stop without losing speedy Yasmine.

The housekeeper made a sharp right into a staff locker room before motioning to the adjacent bathroom.

"Go change."

Charlotte looked at the door leading into the bathroom and glanced at her watch. It was past two p.m.

"Now?" she asked.

The head housekeeper scowled at her.

"Maybe you want to start next week?"

"No. No, of course. Sorry."

Charlotte took the uniform into the bathroom and changed, wondering how she'd get any investigating done with Yasmine's watchful eye on her. She certainly wasn't going to get any meaningful work done so late in the day; that was for sure.

She re-entered the locker room a few minutes later with her street clothes balled beneath her arm.

Yasmine shook her head and held out her hands.

"Give me those."

Charlotte turned over her clothes, and Yasmine folded them with a precision Charlotte couldn't comprehend. She'd never folded a handkerchief half as flat as her shirt now lay.

She'd heard about mythical women who could fold fitted sheets but never believed they existed. Yasmine had to be one of them.

A folding *unicorn*.

When her clothes sat in a perfect pile, Yasmine turned her terrifying attention on Charlotte, straightening her uniform until everything clung how she liked it. As she jerked and jostled while being handled, Charlotte recalled a prom gown fitting with Mariska and Darla. Her adoptive mothers had a similar way of adjusting clothing without regard for the body inside.

Another minute of this, and I'll have internal injuries...

"It's too tight in the chest, and your shoes are too flashy," grumbled Yasmine with a final tug that threatened to break a rib.

Charlotte glanced down at her sneakers. She'd thought her morning walkers would make good cleaning shoes but hadn't considered the violet logos and soles might clash with Elderbrook's color scheme.

"I can get plain shoes?" she offered.

"Yes, you will, and I'll get you the next size uniform tomorrow."

Charlotte offered a tight smile. Nothing made a girl feel more warm and fuzzy than hearing she needed a larger size.

Yasmine took a step back and considered her with unabashed dismay.

"Move on," she said softly. Charlotte suspected she wasn't talking to her.

"I'm sorry?" she asked.

Yasmine shook her head. "I'm going to give you a rundown of the daily routine."

"Okay." Charlotte cocked her hip, looking for a comfortable way to stand for what promised to be a long story.

"Stand up straight," said Yasmine.

She did. The stitches on the side of her dress groaned.

Oblivious to the overstuffed turkey in front of her, Yasmine continued.

"Bed linens are to be changed and smoothed every morning—no wrinkles. Think of the bed as a freshly ironed suit."

"Suit. Got it."

"Bathroom next. No spots, no streaks, or you'll hear about it. If not from the residents, then *me*. Straighten their items. Half the people here are pigs, and it is up to us to save them from themselves."

Charlotte opened her mouth to comment and then shut it. She couldn't agree the residents were pigs, and she couldn't argue.

Yasmine continued.

"Once around the room, dust, vacuum, straighten—in that order—on to the next room. Got it?"

Charlotte nodded. "Should I report anything odd to you?'

Yasmine scowled. "What do you mean, *odd*?"

Charlotte shrugged. "I don't know. If someone looks ill—"

Yasmine was already shaking her head. "None of that is your responsibility. You need to get in and get out while they're at breakfast. They want their rooms clean, but they don't want to see how it's done. *We're invisible*."

Charlotte nodded. "Got it."

Yasmine motioned to an open locker. "You can put your clothes in there."

Charlotte moved to the locker and put her clothes inside. Yasmine handed her a padlock with a keyhole in the center and removed a springy plastic bracelet from her arm, from which several keys hung. She held the collection by a gold key, which she handed to Charlotte.

"Turn the key and set your combination."

Charlotte took the key and reset the combination to something she'd remember before returning the bracelet to Yasmine.

Yasmine glanced at her watch.

"You can change back into your clothes now."

Charlotte blinked at her.

"I just got dressed."

Yasmine nodded. "The day for you ends at two-thirty. It's two-thirty now. I'll see you here tomorrow at *six*-thirty—*a.m.* Don't be late."

She left the locker room, leaving Charlotte behind and feeling like she'd been mugged.

"You have got to be kidding me," she grumbled, changing back into her street clothes. She couldn't wait to get back to Declan so she could tell him about her fantastic, understanding, *sweetheart* of a boss.

She opened the door to the locker room to leave and froze on the threshold.

Yasmine stood a few doors down the hall.

Oh no.

The last thing she wanted to do was catch that woman's eye and end up having to run drills or pass some kind of cleaning challenge.

Yasmine knocked on a door, and when no one answered, she looked both ways as if she were making sure no one was watching.

Charlotte tucked back and peered around the corner.

There was no way to describe the maid's behavior other than *suspicious*.

She leaned forward a fraction more to get a better view.

What is she doing?

Yasmine punched a code into the door lock and slipped inside. Charlotte waited, and five minutes later, Yasmine reappeared, eyes darting back and forth, looking as sneaky on the way out as she had on the way in.

Charlotte prepared to slip back into the locker room, but Yasmine headed in the opposite direction. She strode down the hall and disappeared.

When Yasmine disappeared around the corner, Charlotte jogged down the hall to the room she'd entered. It had the name *Edward* on the door, but other than that, it looked like any other resident's room. Each had the resident's first name on a hand-printed card hanging from a plaque. Some doors sported additional decorations like seasonal wreaths or other knickknacks, but most, like Edward's, didn't.

Charlotte tried the knob to find it locked. She turned and looked down the hall where Yasmine had gone.

Hm.

What were you up to?

CHAPTER FOUR

Darla watched the maid lead Charlotte away, and a moment later, another appeared in an identical outfit as if stamped by a cloning machine kept somewhere in the back.

Though her hair was pulled into a similar bun, this one was platinum blonde. She stood taller than the last and was younger and slimmer with large blue eyes.

Bernie stood as she entered. "Ah, here's Oksana, ladies. She'll take you to your room."

The maid smiled and nodded, which set her hoop earrings, large enough to serve as parrot perches, rocking.

Bennie frowned.

"Oksana, I told you these earrings are too much. It upsets the residents."

Oksana's hand fluttered to her ear to stop the earring from swinging.

"Oh, silly me. I forgot to change them. I will do it."

"See that you do. Yasmine will have a fit if she sees those."

Oksana turned to Darla and Mariska and welcomed them with outstretched hands.

"Ah, my lovely ladies—you like to come with me?"

The maid led the way, and they followed, waving goodbye to Declan and Bernie as they walked.

"How many maids are there?" asked Darla when they entered the foyer. "Even the dog is wearing one of those uniforms."

Oksana laughed. "It is our nickname—Maid Manor. Dressing everyone as a maid is Bernie's idea of marketing." She leaned toward them and lowered her voice. "It is very silly. He says older people like being waited on by maids."

"I think everyone does," said Mariska.

Oksana touched her ear as she led them into the elevator. "Do my earrings bother you?"

"No, I think they're very nice," said Mariska as the doors closed.

The maid grinned. "See? Upset the residents?—*bah*. Thank you. I think *you* are very nice. Ready for the grand tour of your new kingdom?"

The elevator doors opened on the second floor, and she led the way.

"This is the parlor for this floor," she said, gesturing toward a sitting area outside the elevator. Several padded chairs and a plush sofa lined the perimeter. A huge bay window with cushions offered additional seating.

Oksana sighed as the ladies peeked through the window at the view.

"This spot is perfect for afternoon tea. Do you like tea?" she asked.

"I love tea," said Mariska.

Darla nodded in agreement.

Oksana grasped her hands together and bounced on her toes. "I *love* tea. I make my own. I will bring you some."

They continued down the hall, Oksana again in the lead, walking with a sailor's swagger. Ahead, a woman stood watching them approach, smiling.

"Hello," said Mariska as they grew closer.

"Hello—" The woman stopped, her attention drawn somewhere behind them.

Darla twisted to see a woman wearing a bright pink and blue scarf staring at them from the sitting area they'd left. She smirked when Darla noticed her and disappeared around the corner toward the elevators.

Darla scowled and turned to find the smiling woman had retreated into a room with the nameplate *Gail* on the door.

"What was that about? Did you see that woman behind us?" she asked.

Mariska glanced over her shoulder. "No. The Gail lady seemed like she wanted to talk, and then she ran into her room and shut the door like we're a couple of grizzly bears."

Darla clucked her tongue. "I don't think it was *us* she was afraid of."

Mariska stopped in her tracks. "It wasn't a ghost, was it?"

Darla squinted. "What are you talking about? Why would it be a ghost?"

"Big houses full of old people always have ghosts," said Oksana in a flat tone, her expression haunted.

Darla and Mariska blinked at her.

"*What*?" asked Darla.

Oksana's expression brightened. "Okay, ready to see your room, ladies?"

Mariska held up a hand. "Hold on, about the ghosts—"

Darla pointed behind her. "Who was that woman?"

Oksana's brow knitted. "Miss Gail? In that room?" she asked, pointing to the plate with that name on it.

"No, the woman at the end of the hall."

"I didn't see her."

"She was staring at us, and Gail seemed scared of her."

Oksana lowered her voice. "Was she wearing old-timey clothing?"

Darla gaped. "*What*?"

"She still thinks it was a ghost," whispered Mariska.

"Yeah, I get that," snapped Darla. "Oksana, didn't it seem like Gail was going to talk to us? Why did she run away?"

Oksana shrugged. "She maybe remembered she had something on the stove?"

Darla sighed. The girl seemed sweet but maybe wasn't the quickest bunny in the field. Either that, or the place was riddled with ghosts, and poor Oksana was barely holding it together.

Darla was about to give up when she gasped, remembering a detail that might help.

"The woman down the hall was wearing a *scarf*," she said.

"A scarf?" Oksana's expression changed to something resembling disgust.

"*Hm*," she grunted.

Oksana punched a code into the lock and swung the door open

with a flourish. She didn't expound on her grunt, but Darla suspected she knew the mystery woman's identity and wasn't a fan. Maybe she didn't want to speak ill of the residents.

"*Voila*, ladies. Your piece of Elderbrook Manor, complete with an en-suite bathroom and view of the community garden."

Mariska and Darla made a collective *Oooh* noise as the door swung open. A large picture window bathed the airy room in light and pulled them to the view like a magnet.

"You can see for *miles*," said Mariska.

"This is so much nicer than my house," murmured Darla.

"I am right? You'll be sharing this room?" asked Oksana, motioning to two full beds.

Darla nodded, one eye still on the view of a pool she hadn't seen from the front when they arrived.

"We put the beds apart, but we could push them together if you like," mumbled Oksana.

Mariska turned. "Push them—*oh*. No, we're not— We're *married*."

Oksana straightened. "Married? Then, yes? Push them together?"

"No, not to each other. To *husbands*. We're married to *men*," said Darla, realizing the misunderstanding.

Oksana seemed more confused.

"There will be four of you here? You and your husbands?"

Darla and Mariska exchanged a look, realizing their mistake.

They weren't supposed to be married.

"I mean, we *were* married to men. Now, we're just friends growing old together," said Darla.

The confusion cleared from Oksana's expression.

"Ah, I see. How nice for you to have friends. You are both young to be here. Most of the other residents are older."

Darla and Mariska beamed.

"That was nice. It's not often someone calls us young," said Mariska with a chuckle.

Oksana moved to straighten a pillow, and the ladies turned back to the view.

"*Whew*," whispered Darla. "We almost blew that on the first test. We have to be more careful."

Mariska nodded. "Close one."

Darla turned to make a three-sixty scan of the room. The soothing mix of soft neutral colors—beiges, greys, blues, and warm whites, made her want to fall into a comfy chair and read a book for about a year.

She dropped her butt onto the bed's cloud-like duvet.

"This bed is *amazing*." She snatched a controller from the bedside table. "It's a *lift* bed," she added, her voice tinged with awe.

With a soft grinding noise, the head of the bed rose, taking Darla with it.

Mariska sat in a cushioned chair near the window.

Oksana stood smiling at them.

"You two look happy," she said.

"Very happy," said Darla, her eyes shut.

"I will leave you to rest. I will bring you some tea tomorrow. If you need anything, you can push this button here. You see?"

She pointed to a button near the door.

"Thank you," said Mariska.

Oksana waved and left.

The moment the door latched shut, Darla's eyes sprang open.

"How much money do we need to retire here?" she asked.

Mariska frowned. "More than we have."

Darla groaned.

"Charlotte always makes it sound like she works so hard. Turns out being a detective is *heaven*."

Darla's gaze drifted to a counter serving as a sleek kitchenette. It blended so well with the furniture in the room that she only now noticed its tiny sink.

Rocking to her feet, Mariska opened a cabinet that turned out to be a refrigerator stocked with water and juices.

She gasped.

"*We have a minibar*."

Darla leaned forward to see.

"Sweet Mother Goose. Is there candy?"

"No. It's mostly empty, but there are some drinks. I guess we have to fill it ourselves." She grinned. "We should go *shopping*."

"Oh no, you don't. You aren't allowed to go shopping. You go to the store, and we'll be shoving things in there with a crowbar."

Mariska pouted. "You're no fun. I need snacks."

Darla slid out of bed and opened a door they'd yet to investigate.

"Bathroom, she said.

Mariska hustled over. The bath had a walk-in shower, a walk-in tub, and a walk-in closet. She moved through the main bath and into the closet.

"*Everything* is walk-in. I've *dreamed* about closets like this."

"I've lived in closets like this," said Darla.

Someone knocked on the door, and they turned in that direction.

"Who do you think that is?" hissed Mariska.

"I don't know. But I bet if we *answer,* we'll know."

She walked to their door and reached for the knob. Mariska grabbed her arm before she could turn it.

"You don't think there's someone out there ready to shoot us, do you? Don't forget we're here to look into *murders.*"

Darla rolled her eyes. "No one is *shooting* anyone. They said all the people who died could have died from natural causes. Nothing natural about a bullet. Unless there's someone out there waiting to shoot us with a heart attack ray, I think we're fine."

Mariska nodded. "I guess they would have noticed bullets. Fine. Open it."

Darla opened the door.

In the hall, three ladies stood side by side. They appeared healthy, smartly dressed, and somewhere in their mid-seventies. All three had white hair pulled into ponytails.

"You're young," said the one in the center.

She sounded disappointed.

Darla knew this one. She recognized her scarf, light blue golf skirt, and pink polo. This was the woman she'd seen smirking at her from the parlor—the one who'd frightened their neighbor Gail into her room.

"We're new," said Mariska.

"I can see that," said Scarf.

"We heard you're living together. Can't afford your own rooms?" asked the one on the left wearing a similar sporty outfit. Her skort featured vertical stripes, and the collar of her white polo stood popped at attention.

Darla scowled.

Insults already.

These ladies weren't going to pretend to be nice. She had to admire their honesty.

"Did you want something?" she asked.

Mariska looked at her.

"Excuse us a minute," she said, jerking Darla back into the room and shutting the door.

"You're blowing it," she hissed.

Darla rolled her eyes. "What are you talking about? Those three are up to no good—"

"We have to *talk* to them. Remember? We're here to *gather intel.*"

Darla gritted her teeth. "You're right. I'm sorry." She leaned in to whisper. "But don't give them an inch. They're bad news."

Mariska huffed. "Oh, you always see the worst in people."

"They aren't trying to hide it."

Mariska took a deep breath and opened the door.

"I'm sorry," she said in a cheery singsong, stepping in front of Darla. "I'm Mariska and this is Darla."

"What kind of name is *Mariska*?" said the one on the left.

"It's Polish for Mary," said Mariska.

"I think I had a diner waitress named Darla once," said the one in the center, leaning to look around Mariska and lock her gaze on Darla.

Darla glared back.

So far, the one on the right hadn't said a word. She stood beside the others with her hands crossed before her, staring with large green eyes.

The center woman flung out her arms to tap the two beside her on the chests with the back of her hands.

"Ladies, introduce yourselves. I'm Gretchen," she said, smiling with dead eyes. Darla wouldn't have been surprised if a forked tongue slithered out of her mouth.

"I'm Amanda," said the one on the left.

"I'm Muffin," said the quiet one. She wore a floral skort covered with hibiscuses and a baggy linen blouse tied at the bottom.

"*Muffin*?" said Darla. She looked at Mariska. "Remind me, were they making fun of *our* names?"

Mariska squinted at her.

Queen Gretchen ignored the comment.

"I guess we'll see you at breakfast tomorrow," she said.

Without waiting for a response, she turned on her heel and started down the hall, her ponytail swinging.

"See you at breakfast," echoed Amanda before following. Muffin flashed a quick smile and hustled after the others. Darla heard them giggling as she shut the door.

Mariska looked at her.

"I don't think I like them," she said.

Darla shook her head.

"And I thought all we had to worry about were the ghosts."

CHAPTER FIVE

Bernie looked at Declan and then checked his watch.

"I planned to give you a tour of the facilities myself, but I have a meeting in the city, and I'm running short on time." He grimaced and moved for the door. "I'll have Dana walk you around. She's the current manager."

Declan stood. "No problem. Maybe tomorrow morning we can review specifics and any questions that pop up."

Bernie nodded. "That sounds perfect. You're staying at the motel down the street, right? There's a little place down the road from there that no one here ever goes to—Spice Bomb. Could we meet there at six?"

"Sure. See you there."

Bernie looked at the dog.

"You'll have to go to the lobby, Apple."

The bulldog stood, stretched, and waddled out the door without waiting for the men.

Bernie smiled at Declan. "She doesn't do a lick of work after lunch."

"I can see that," said Declan as he watched the dog sploot herself on the cool tile floor of the lobby.

They entered the lobby, where Declan spotted Bernie's granddaughter, the maid-slash-receptionist, talking on the phone. He heard her say something about *money*, but that was the only word he'd caught.

"*Luna*," called Bernie.

The girl turned, her eyes wide. She said something into her phone and lowered it.

Bernie motioned to Declan. "I have to run. Can you take Mr. Bingham to Dana for an introduction to the facility?"

Luna nodded and slipped her phone into her pocket.

"Yep."

"Great. Thank you." He turned to Declan. "I'll talk with you later?"

Declan nodded.

Luna headed for the back door and motioned for Declan to follow.

"I think Dana's at the back garden," she said.

Declan followed Luna through an expansive all-weather porch and then out to the outer porch, where an elderly couple sat on a double-wide bench suspended from the ceiling. A pile of colorful cards lay on the seat between them. The pair looked up as they exited the manor, and the woman's expression perked.

"*Luna*, there you are. We have the party invites for Gladdy's shindig, and I was thinking—"

"Not *now*, Barb," said Luna, hustling down the steps to the patio.

Surprised by Luna's brusque tone, Declan glanced over his shoulder to see the woman's animated expression collapse. She leaned to murmur something to the man.

Luna's pace quickened as they walked around the pool. It felt like she couldn't escape the woman on the porch fast enough.

"Do you plan parties for the residents?" asked Declan.

She scoffed. "*No*. I'm a *maid*."

"And the receptionist. I thought maybe you wore three hats?"

She scowled at him. "What do hats have to do with anything?"

"It's a phrase. *Wearing many hats*, like, you have a lot of different jobs."

She paused to look at him as if he were speaking Martian. "Jobs that need *hats*? What, like a construction worker?"

Declan gave up. "It's an old-timey saying. I guess they wore hats for everything then."

She shrugged and continued walking. "One job is enough, thank you. I'm not the receptionist. Bernie just told me to wait for you guys."

Declan nodded. "Right. So, your grandfather told you why we're here?"

She nodded.

"Do *you* think something is going on?" he asked.

She stopped again.

"You mean, do I think someone is *murdering* people?"

He nodded, and she laughed.

"No. Bernie's paranoid. They're just *old*. Old people die."

"Sure, but he said some were healthy."

She shrugged. "Aren't we all until we're not?"

Declan crossed his arms against his chest.

She had a point.

He spotted a woman across the manicured lawn staring at a garden with her hands on her hips. She also wore a maid's uniform.

"Is that Dana?" he asked, pointing at her.

Luna turned and started walking again. "Yes. Good. I thought she was out here."

"And she's a maid, too? I thought she was the manager?"

Luna huffed as if he were an annoying mosquito she couldn't seem to lose.

"Everyone wears the costumes. Bernie likes us *all* to be maids. He says it makes the residents feel fancy."

"Will I need a uniform?"

"Yep, except you'll look like a butler. Bernie's crazy for that stuff." She cupped her hands around her mouth to create a makeshift megaphone. "*Dana—*"

Dana turned. The manager looked in her fifties, with chestnut hair pulled into what Declan was starting to realize was Elderbrook's trademark bun.

Luna motioned to Declan as they approached. "This is Declan, the new manager. Bernie asked me to bring him to you."

Dana smiled as if she were relieved.

"Great. Thanks."

Luna turned on her heel and returned to the manor without another word.

Dana held a hand out to Declan. "Nice to meet you. I've been *waiting* for Bernie to find someone."

"Oh." Declan nodded, feeling guilty he had no intention of staying.

"I guess Bernie wanted me to give you the tour?" she asked.

"I suppose, yes." He motioned to the large garden with its rows of tomatoes, flowers, herbs, and other green things he didn't recognize. "Are you the gardener, too?"

She chuckled. "No, I was stretching my legs. The residents take care of this. It's a community garden. We have a lot of guests who enjoy gardening." She squinted into the sun. "Let's go back inside before we bake."

They headed back to the manor.

Declan saw Luna on the porch talking to the couple she'd been so short with a moment before. The older woman stood and hugged her. Clearly, there were no hard feelings.

Luna was still chatting with them as they approached the porch, and she stopped talking to wave as they re-entered the manor house.

Inside, Apple remained lounging in the lobby's center, wearing her maid costume.

Declan pointed to the dog.

"Bernie really has a thing for maids, huh?"

She nodded. "He swears the residents love us all dressed like servants. I think his mother was a maid, or his first love, or *something* deep-rooted."

Declan chuckled.

She sighed. "Honestly, it's one of the reasons I'm leaving. I'd like to wear normal clothes again."

Dana made a hard right to head down the hallway toward the manor's west wing.

"This hall is where most of the recreation rooms are. There's a game room, an exercise room, and an art room."

Declan heard laughter coming from the third door down on the right.

"What's going on in there? It's not Wednesday," said Dana aloud to herself.

They turned into a room filled with rows of easels pointed toward the front of the room, where a chalkboard covered half the wall and dry erase the other half. In the back, shelves filled with pottery in varying degrees of completion hung near large folding tables and a kiln.

Declan spotted a cackling man sitting behind one of the easels, his face red and veins bulging on his balding head.

"What's so funny, Ed?" asked Dana.

"I'm painting a gift for Gretchen," he said, though he was laughing so hard he could barely form the words. He pointed at the painting with one hand and placed the other against his chest. He held a paintbrush in that hand and painted his chin light blue as he giggled.

Declan found it odd he didn't seem to notice or care.

Dana looked alarmed. "Ed, you need to calm down—"

The old man looked at her. His eyes popped wide as if a current had run through him, and he lurched a step forward before tumbling off his stool. As he fell, he reached upward, taking the easel down with him.

"Ed!" screamed Dana.

Dana and Declan ran to the fallen man.

Ed didn't move. Lying on his back with one leg still entangled in the stool, he stared at them with his mouth hanging open.

Declan felt for a pulse.

"Come on, Ed, stay with us," he said, beginning chest compressions and CPR.

"Is he dead?" asked Dana.

Declan couldn't find a heartbeat.

"Do you have a defibrillator?"

"Yes—somewhere, in the medical room."

"Get it."

Dana ran, knocking over another easel as she pushed for the door.

Declan continued compressions. When two minutes passed, and Dana hadn't returned, he tried a precordial thump to Ed's chest to no avail.

Dana appeared with Yasmine and a portable defibrillator.

"It's too late. He's dead," said Declan, out of breath.

Dana put her hand over her mouth. "Oh no. I got it as fast as I could—"

Declan stood. "It isn't your fault. I think he was dead when he hit the floor."

Yasmine grimaced. "Not another one. I have to call Bernie. He's not going to be happy."

She strode out of the room.

Dana continued to stare at the man on the floor.

"Are you okay?" asked Declan.

She jumped as if she'd forgotten he was there.

"Yes. I'm sorry." She turned to him. "It looked like you knew what you were doing. Do you have medical training?"

Declan shrugged. "Military."

Really, he'd been *para*-military helping his uncle Seamus during one of his shadow operations in South America—back when his uncle was even shadowier than he was now—but Dana didn't need the gritty details. She didn't look like she needed to hear anything unsettling. Her hands were shaking.

And, whatever his training, it hadn't been enough for poor Ed.

He leaned down to right the easel and placed Ed's painting back on it. The canvas had fallen face down, and as he turned it over, he saw Ed had painted an impressive reproduction of Botticelli's *The Birth of Venus*—with a notable adjustment.

"He painted this for someone named Gretchen?" he asked.

She stepped forward to get a better view. "That's what he said—"

She fell silent, her mouth hanging open.

Declan knew why.

There was one glaring difference between Ed's rendition of the Botticelli and the original. Naked Venus, standing on her seashell, had been replaced by a woman not a day under seventy. Her arm covered her breasts, but instead of using her lengthy hair to cover her nether parts, she held a scarf over her lower half.

Declan looked at Dana.

"Gretchen, I presume?"

Dana nodded.

"Yep."

CHAPTER SIX

"So our only clue is that the man laughed himself to death painting *The Aging of Venus*," said Charlotte, tapping the table.

She and Declan sat in a booth of the Spice Bomb restaurant, waiting for Bernie. She could see why Bernie didn't think they'd bump into anyone there. The building was shaped like an old-time silver-plated diner and featured throwback booths for seating, but the menu and decor were *uber* modern. She didn't imagine most of Bernie's elderly residents embraced menu items like quinoa porridge topped with goji berries, chia seeds, and a drizzle of raw honey.

Declan nodded as he peered at the menu. "The EMTs didn't think there was anything weird."

Charlotte snickered. "They obviously didn't see that painting."

Though she hadn't seen the collapse, Declan sent her a photo of Ed's strange painting, and now Charlotte wondered if she'd ever see the famous Botticelli the same way again.

She ran her finger along the edge of her mug. She wanted to think, but her mind felt fuzzy. She hadn't slept well. They'd spent the night at a borderline seedy motel within walking distance of the manor. The place wouldn't win any awards for *best mattresses*. In addition, Declan returned late after being waylaid by the police—they'd interviewed him as a witness to Ed's passing. They'd stayed up half the night talking about the death and how it might help them crack the case—and if there was a case to crack at all.

Less than a day on the job, and they had an additional victim. People were toppling like bowling pins, and they weren't any closer to proving the deaths *were* or were *not* suspicious—not even when one happened *literally* under their noses.

"I guess it's handy you saw someone die with your own eyes. At least we know people die around here without someone hovering over them, actively killing them."

Declan shrugged. "At least, this guy didn't seem to have any help. It looked like he laughed himself into a heart attack."

Charlotte noticed Declan's brow furrow as he stared into his coffee.

"What is it?" she asked.

He squinted at her with one eye. "I don't know. Something *does* feel weird about it. The painting was funny, but Ed was laughing so hard that the veins in his head were *bulging*. He was red in the face. It seemed over the top—like he couldn't stop himself."

"You think he was drunk or on drugs or something?"

He nodded. "Maybe. That would make more sense."

Charlotte frowned. "We could really use an autopsy."

The restaurant door jingled, and Bernie rushed in, looking flustered and overdressed as usual. He wore a long-sleeved white shirt with a knit vest that made Charlotte sweat just looking at it.

He noticed Charlotte waving to him and trotted to the booth to sit across from them.

"Good morning. Sorry I'm late. It's been a *time*, as you can imagine," he said.

He glanced at the waitress as she approached. "Coffee, please?" he asked.

She nodded. "Could I interest you in some blue spirulina pancakes?"

He blinked at her.

"Some *what*?"

She pumped her arm as if she were rooting for the home team. "It's full of vitamins E, C, and B6 *and* boosts the production of white blood cells."

Bernie nodded. "But what *is* it?"

"They're pancakes colored with natural spirulina, topped with mixed berries, lemon zest, and a drizzle of lavender-infused maple syrup."

The waitress beamed, but Charlotte couldn't help but sense discomfort behind her smile. As for Bernie, he remained scowling.

"I think he means, what is *spirulina*, exactly? It's some kind of seaweed or something, isn't it?" she interjected, hoping to help. She'd read about spirulina somewhere, but the details hadn't stuck in her mind.

The waitress pulled a piece of paper from her pocket.

"It's a cyano*brffffeee*," she read, mumbling the last bit. She looked up to find the three looking no less confused and huffed a heavy sigh.

"*Bacteria*. It's a *cyanobacteria*," she said, looking defeated.

The three stared back at her for a beat, and she thrust the paper back into her pocket.

"I should probably start looking for another job," she said, patting Bernie on the shoulder. "I'll go get your coffee."

"*Hold the bacteria*," he called after her as she strode off. He turned his attention back to the table. "Okay. So where are we?"

"Is there any word back on what happened to Ed?" asked Declan.

Bernie rolled his eyes. "You know more than I do. *You* saw him. You said he laughed so hard he blew a gasket or something? That's what Dana said, too. That's all I know."

"That's what it looked like, but have you heard anything else about what the responders thought? Or his family?"

Bernie shrugged. "They're all assuming heart attack. They don't know."

"Is the family going to have him autopsied?"

"I don't know." Bernie made a soft moaning noise and ran a hand over his head to smooth his hair.

"Would you mind if we *suggested* an autopsy?" asked Charlotte. She suspected Bernie did *not* want them suggesting autopsies, but it didn't hurt to ask.

The little man straightened like someone had run a current through his seat.

"Yes, I *mind*. How could you suggest an autopsy without explaining who you are and what you're doing? They'll sue me on principle."

Charlotte frowned. "Declan thinks there might have been something suspicious about the death."

She darted a glance at Declan, who almost choked on his

coffee. Bernie's eyes popped wide as he locked his attention on Declan.

"Why? What does that mean? How?"

He might have said more, but by the end of his sentence, he'd hit a note only screech owls could hear.

Declan put down his coffee mug. "It's more of a *feeling* than anything solid."

"*Don't*," said Bernie.

"Don't what?"

"Don't have *feelings*. I can't take this." He gripped his vest over his heart with one hand.

Declan chuckled. "You're paying us to have *feelings*."

Bernie's shoulders slumped, and he bent to rest his forehead on the table.

"Fine. What do *you* think happened?" he asked into his lap.

Declan leaned back. "I don't know. I'm not trying to upset you. I was just telling Charlotte his laughter seemed uncontrollable—like he was under the influence of something. Did he drink?"

Bernie sat up. "I've seen him drink at gatherings and whatnot, but I don't know if he was *drunk painting* in the middle of the afternoon."

"Drugs?"

Bernie laughed as his coffee arrived and nodded his thanks to the waitress before refocusing on Declan.

"Strangely, the residents don't report to me about their drug habits," he drawled.

He took a sip and then sat back to peer at Charlotte.

"What do you think? Did you hear anything from the maids?"

She shook her head. "No, but I haven't had a chance to talk to them one-on-one. I couldn't come out of the gate with a ton of questions. You don't want them suspicious."

Bernie sighed. "No. I guess not."

"I'll concentrate on Dana today," said Declan. "I can tell you she seemed as shocked by Ed's death as I was. Maybe I can cross her off our list."

"What about Gretchen?" asked Charlotte.

Bernie's eyes darted up to meet hers.

"What about her?"

"She was his Venus."

His shoulders slumped. "Oh. That painting. She's very—"

He trailed off, and the detectives stared at him, waiting for him to finish his sentence.

"I don't know. She's a terrible flirt. I imagine that's why he used her for inspiration."

"Were they dating?"

"No. I mean, I don't think so."

His gaze drifted across the restaurant. After a moment, he dropped his head back against the booth and sighed.

"This is a nightmare."

Charlotte glanced at her watch. "Speaking of work, I better get going, or Yasmine will fire me on day one."

"If she does, I'll hire you back," said Bernie. "But *go*. Please. I don't want to hear it from Yasmine. The woman is as strict as a Victorian nun, and she's been even worse than usual lately."

"What room was Ed's?" asked Charlotte.

"Three-thirty-three."

Declan fished keys from his pocket. "You take the car. I can walk from here."

Charlotte took the keys and shimmied out of the booth. Bernie offered a little wave as she said her goodbyes, looking like a man headed to the gallows.

CHAPTER SEVEN

Darla and Mariska entered Elderbrook's dining room to the hum of chatter and clinking cutlery. The smell of breakfast meats and toast filled the air.

"Look at this *spread*," said Darla as she and Mariska approached the breakfast buffet and took a deep inhale.

She swallowed to keep from drooling.

"This must be what breakfast is like in heaven," she said, eyeing the line of silver chafing dishes.

Residents occupied most of the white linen-covered tables encircling the buffet. Women and a smattering of men sat in pairs and groups, eating, talking, and refilling their plates. Through arched, tall glass doors, Mariska saw others enjoying breakfast on the enclosed porch's white wicker tables as fans twirled overhead.

"Should we dine al fresco?" asked Mariska.

"Al *who*?" asked Darla, grabbing a large ivory plate from a stack at the end of the buffet. She headed toward a pile of warm waffles without waiting for an answer.

Mariska took a plate to what she hoped would be the pastry area but found only bread, croissants, and bagels.

No donuts. No patisserie. No danish.

Crap.

She made do by collecting a selection of jellies and nibbled a muffin while her croissant ran through a conveyor belt toaster.

"Did you leave any for the rest of us?" asked Darla, walking over with a plate of waffles and bacon.

"They didn't have pastries, so I'm using jelly."

Darla eyed Mariska's stack of jelly containers. "You might want to pace yourself so you don't keel over with diabetic shock."

Mariska ignored her and retrieved her croissant as it dropped from the toaster.

"They have an amazing fruit tray over there," said Darla, piling more bacon from a nearby chafing dish like Lincoln Logs.

"Fruit is fruit wherever you go," said Mariska, her attention shifting to the porch. "Should we eat inside or out?"

Darla followed her gaze to the porch. "I don't know... What do you think? It might be hot out there."

Mariska spotted a table for two at the window and pointed. "Ooh, how about that one? All of the view, none of the heat. Let's grab that spot."

Darla nodded her approval. "Okay. I'll meet you there after I get some fruit."

Mariska wandered to the table and set down her plate. She noticed a woman sitting alone at a nearby table. She looked lonely— like maybe she'd like to *talk*.

Hm.

Mariska strolled to the woman.

"Hello."

The woman smiled but quickly looked away as if she were trying to avoid conversation.

Undeterred, Mariska tried again.

"I'm Mariska."

The woman looked at her long enough to say a single word.

"Ginny."

"Hi, Ginny. We're new. It's me and my friend Darla."

The woman sipped her coffee but didn't answer.

"Did you hear about that man who died?" asked Mariska. She knew death inspired half the best gossip at Pineapple Port and assumed it would also be a hot topic at the manor.

The woman glanced toward the windows again, and Mariska leaned forward to see what caught her interest.

She frowned.

Gretchen, Amanda, and Muffin, the mean girls who'd stopped at their room the previous day, sat on the porch, staring at her.

Gretchen's scarf was black today.

Like her heart.

"Do you know them?" asked Mariska.

The woman stood.

"I can't talk to you," she said.

"Why not?"

"They said I can't. Not until you qualify."

Mariska's chin tucked. "*Qualify?*"

The woman shook her head and scurried away.

Mariska shot a look at the laughing mean girls and sat at the table she'd picked. From there, she couldn't see them, and they couldn't see her.

She stewed.

Darla arrived and took a seat across from her.

"Who put a kink in your slinky?" she asked.

"I was trying to talk to someone."

"I saw that. Who was she?"

"I don't know."

"You didn't ask her name?"

"Her name's Ginny, but she couldn't talk to me."

Darla scowled. "Why? Is she deaf?"

"*No*, she's not *deaf*. She couldn't talk because those horrible women said she wasn't *allowed* to."

Darla paused with a strip of bacon halfway to her lips. "She said that? You said she couldn't talk."

"She talked enough to tell me she couldn't talk. She said Gretchen and those other witches said she couldn't talk to me until we *qualify*."

"Qualify? What does that mean?"

"I don't know—" Mariska bit into a croissant and sucked in a breath. "I think this has a hint of almond. I didn't expect that. I almost made a ham sandwich. They have beautiful baby Swiss over there. You can add jelly and make a Monte Cristo."

Darla crunched her bacon.

"What's the difference between Swiss and baby Swiss cheese?"

"The holes are smaller."

"How come?"

Mariska shrugged. "Smaller mice."

The ladies giggled.

"We need to talk to that Gretchen idiot," said Darla, sobering.

"Go ahead. They're right outside."

Darla leaned back to look through the window.

"Yep. Let's go."

Mariska stared at her jelly stack. "But—"

"You can come back to that."

"But it's almond—"

"*You'll come back*," said Darla, grabbing her arm and tugging her to her feet.

"You need to get your priorities straight," muttered Mariska. "What if you make them mad?"

"We're ten years younger than them. I can take them."

"I mean, what if you ruin our chances of ever getting information?"

Darla cracked her neck as they stepped onto the porch.

"Let me do the talking. I'll be subtle."

"Riiight. That's you all over," said Mariska.

Darla walked to the three ladies, who watched them approach giggling amongst themselves.

Darla approached their table, set her feet wide, and stabbed her hands on her hips.

"Are you telling people they can't talk to us?" she asked.

Mariska groaned without meaning to.

Gretchen's chin lifted. "We don't have to tell anybody anything. They know the rules."

Darla scowled. "What *rules*?"

"It's simple. You have to qualify."

"Qualify for what?"

"We run a test to see if you're worthy to be here."

"If we're *worthy*?" Darla looked back at Mariska, her mouth wide, before returning her attention to the ladies at the table.

"Who the h—"

Mariska grabbed her friend's arm and pulled herself in front of her.

"What do we have to do?" she asked before Darla could finish her thought.

Gretchen smiled. "Five events. Sports, cooking, gardening, art, and cards."

Mariska nodded. "Fine."

"Fine?" screeched Darla behind her. "You're going to let them—"

Mariska kicked behind her and felt her heel hit Darla's shin.

"*Ow*," yipped Darla.

"What's first?" asked Mariska. "Let's get this show on the road."

"Sports," said Amanda. "Pickleball in an hour?"

Mariska grimaced. She'd never played pickleball.

"Can we pick a *different* sport?" she asked.

Amanda smirked. "*No*."

"*Fine*."

Mariska turned on her heel, grabbed Darla's arm, and dragged her with her. When they reached the entrance back into the dining room, Darla jerked her arm from Mariska's grasp.

"Are you *crazy*? We can't put up with this nonsense, and you wouldn't know a pickleball from a *pickle*."

"Does it use a real pickle?" asked Mariska.

Darla scowled. "No. I don't think so. It's like tennis, isn't it?"

Mariska huffed. "We'll have to look it up. We've played tennis. This could work."

Darla crossed her arms against her chest. "Or—and stay with me—we could tell those ladies to take their pickleballs and shove them up—"

Mariska poked a finger at her friend.

"*Shush*. We won't be any use to Charlotte and Declan if we can't talk to the residents, and we can't talk to them until we *qualify*."

Darla rolled her eyes as they headed back to their table. "This is *ridiculous*—"

Mariska sucked in a breath. "*No*."

Darla looked at her. "You don't think it's ridiculous?"

"Not that. They cleared away my *plate*."

Mariska pointed at the table.

Darla patted her arm.

"Just as well. The last thing you want running around a hot pickleball court is a belly full of jelly and baby Swiss."

CHAPTER EIGHT

Charlotte headed to her car, already missing her Spice Bomb coffee. She wasn't sure she wanted a deconstructed vegan omelet, but the odd little place had *great* coffee.

After driving the half mile to the manor and parking in the employee parking area, Charlotte entered the employee locker room to find Yasmine waiting, her dark bun so tight it gave her a makeshift facelift.

"You *just* made it," she said, holding up her watch.

Charlotte smiled. "Just a quick change and I'm ready to get started."

Her taskmaster didn't return the smile. Charlotte changed and found Yasmine in the hall, waiting again. The woman looked at her uniform, grunted, and walked away without a word, pushing a maid cart ahead of her.

Charlotte followed.

"Did you hear about Ed?" she asked.

"Don't gossip," said Yasmine without turning.

Charlotte sighed.

So much for subtle prying.

Gathering intel would be slow going if Yasmine blocked her every attempt.

"We're going to do the first room together so I can walk you through my process," the housekeeper announced as they took the elevator to the third floor.

As they exited the car, Charlotte noticed another maid cart sitting in front of one of the resident rooms. As they passed, she glanced inside the room and spotted Oksana making a bed.

Yasmine grunted as she rolled past the other maid's cart.

Oksana's cart looked typical to Charlotte, but she suspected she knew the source of Yasmine's disapproval. Oksana's cart looked like it was *in use*—a half-dirty rag hung off an edge, a box of fancy soaps sat open, and the dustpan brush had *dust* clinging to it.

Horrors.

In contrast, the items in Yasmine's cart looked brand new and stacked with precision. Charlotte guessed the woman spent twenty minutes a day *cleaning her cleaning products.*

Yasmine stopped at the next door to punch in the hotel's master code. She entered and approached the unmade bed inside with the intensity of a bomb disposal expert.

Charlotte moved to the opposite side to help strip the bed, but Yasmine waved her off.

"Let me do this room—you watch," she said.

Charlotte nodded and stepped back to watch Yasmine strip the bed and replace the sheets with a new set. She left no wrinkles, gaps, or bagging. Even when the bed seemed perfect, Yasmine went over it again, smoothing and tucking, correcting imperfections invisible to the average human.

What a terrible superpower to have.

Charlotte knew she'd never make a bed with such precision. If she *was* a new housekeeper at Elderbrook, she'd quit on the spot to save herself from being fired later.

"Did you know Ed well?" Charlotte asked.

Yasmine answered without looking up from her sheets. "Don't mingle with the guests. They don't want to know you. You're here to keep their lives in order."

Charlotte nodded.

Strike two.

Yasmine proceeded to dust, vacuum, and clean the windows.

"I thought no one ever did windows," said Charlotte, chuckling so Yasmine would know she was kidding. She suspected the woman might need a few breadcrumbs when it came to humor.

"That's ridiculous," said Yasmine, each stroke of her squeegee lining perfectly with the last. When she finished, Charlotte doubted the window remained—it looked like a hole of blue sky hanging where a smudged window used to be.

Yasmine moved on to clean the bathroom, scrubbing each large tile one by one in a pattern that started at the upper left and moved across and down—as if she were reading the wall in braille.

She rearranged the resident's items on the bathroom counter, grumbling.

"I swear, this woman—"

"I'm sorry?" said Charlotte, unable to hear the last bit.

Yasmine huffed. "Sometimes, it feels like I'm at war with these people to keep them organized. I want to *throttle* them."

Charlotte nodded with a good showing of forced empathy, though Yasmine's death threats seemed an extreme reaction to crooked electric toothbrush chargers.

Yasmine finished by thrusting the vacuum to and fro like she was trying to hurt the carpet.

Unsettled, Charlotte looked away and noticed a small clown-themed keepsake box sitting on a hanging shelf.

Her lip curled.

She hated clowns.

When Yasmine turned for another vacuum stab, Charlotte moved the statue off-center.

She couldn't help herself.

Yasmine turned off the vacuum and wrapped the cord.

Charlotte frowned.

Why would she wrap the vacuum cord?

It would take effort to unravel it for use in the next room. Any rational person would loop the cord *loosely* on the hook—if not *always*, then at least until they finished for the day. She hadn't wrapped her own vacuum cord since she bought the thing.

"Think you've got it?" Yasmine asked.

Charlotte nodded. "Yep. Thank you."

"No questions?"

"Nope."

"Okay, you do the next room by yourself, and I'll be back—"

Yasmine's eyebrow arched as her gaze shifted past Charlotte. She moved to the hanging shelf as if drawn by a tractor beam and shifted the clown box to the center.

Charlotte looked away to hide a smile. Not often did she play a prank and get such instant gratification. Yasmine had *issues*. The woman was wound tighter than a submarine's hatch screw.

"Should I go to the next room?" she asked.

Still eying the clown as if she expected it to move, Yasmine snapped out of her trance.

"Hm? Oh. Yes. Don't do three-thirty-three. I'll be back to check."

Charlotte nodded.

Three-thirty-three was Ed's room.

Yasmine left, and a moment later, Charlotte heard her chastising Oksana for the state of her cart.

Yikes.

She moved to the next room and mimicked Yasmine's cleaning style as best she could without losing her mind. Halfway through the process and already sweating, she stuck her head into the hall to listen.

She didn't see or hear Yasmine.

Now might be a good time to talk to Oksana.

Commiserating over their common enemy might create an instant bond that would hopefully have Oksana chattier than Yasmine "The Vault" Lambert.

She wandered down the hall to peer into Oksana's room.

"Hi, you're Oksana, right?"

The blonde looked up from the bed she was making to smile and nod.

"Yes, you are new?"

Charlotte moved in to shake her hand.

"Yep. First day. Charlotte."

"Nice to meet you, Charlotte."

Charlotte put her hands on her hips.

"*Whew*. That Yasmine is pretty intense, huh?" she said.

Oksana tittered, and Charlotte relaxed to find Oksana a tad more human.

"She is too much," agreed Oksana.

"Right? How could anyone keep to those standards? I think she's OCD."

Oksana scowled. "OCD? What is OCD?"

"Obsessive Compulsive Disorder. It means she can't stop herself from doing things, often in a pattern."

"*Yes*," said Oksana, pointing at her. "She *is* this OCD."

Charlotte noticed the same clown box she'd moved to test Yasmine's powers of observation on the bedside table in this room. She picked it up, looking for a logo or stamp, and found one that said *Made in China*, but that didn't help with the investigation.

She opened it to find it empty.

"Do you know what this is?" she asked, holding it up.

"The clown box? It is maybe for keeping jewelry?" suggested Oksana.

"No, I mean, does it have some significance? The other room I cleaned had one, too. Same clown."

Oksana shrugged. "They copy each other. One will get something, and another will get that thing. They are like children in school."

Charlotte nodded. She knew something about that from growing up in Pineapple Port. One resident would plant daisies, and the next week, four other houses nearby would have daisies.

She put the little trinket box back on the table.

"How about that Ed guy? The one who died? Did you know him?"

Oksana frowned. "Yes, very sad. This morning, Mrs. Brown told me he died in the art room."

"Was he sick?"

"I don't think so."

"Do people die here a lot?"

Oksana's brow knit. "No. I don't think so. Compared to my village, they are very healthy for their age here." Oksana cocked her head. "There are much less wolves here."

Charlotte nodded and noted Oksana might not be the best person to quiz about unusual death rates. She'd be a *great* person to ask about surviving wolf attacks, though.

"Is there anything else I should know about this place?" she asked. "Any tips? People to avoid?"

Oksana opened her mouth to answer, but her gaze floated past Charlotte, and she suddenly returned to bed-making.

Charlotte felt a chill run down her spine.

I know what that means.

"Are you socializing?" said a familiar voice.

Charlotte winced.

Hello, Yasmine.

She turned to find her boss glaring at her.

"No. Sorry. I was asking Oksana which way to hang the toilet paper."

"Which way to—" Yasmine's expression twisted with horror. *"There is only one way to hang toilet paper."*

She stormed across the hall to Charlotte's half-finished room and barked for her.

Charlotte exchanged a look with Oksana.

"Guess I better go," she said.

Oksana giggled.

housekeeper's lengthy stride.

"It is. Welcome to Elderbrook Manor." Yasmine said the phrase with all the enthusiasm of a mortician. "You've been a maid before?"

Charlotte nodded. "Sure. Long time. I've got a passion for cleaning."

She swallowed a smile, knowing anyone who knew her would fall over laughing to hear her say she had a *passion for cleaning*.

They passed an art room filled with A-frame easels. Inside, a man with curly gray hair painted alone. The grin on his face made Charlotte curious about his art, but she couldn't see the canvas as she whizzed by and couldn't stop without losing speedy Yasmine.

The housekeeper made a sharp right into a staff locker room before motioning to the adjacent bathroom.

"Go change."

Charlotte looked at the door leading into the bathroom and glanced at her watch. It was past two p.m.

"Now?" she asked.

The head housekeeper scowled at her.

"Maybe you want to start next week?"

"No. No, of course. Sorry."

Charlotte took the uniform into the bathroom and changed, wondering how she'd get any investigating done with Yasmine's watchful eye on her. She certainly wasn't going to get any meaningful work done so late in the day; that was for sure.

She re-entered the locker room a few minutes later with her street clothes balled beneath her arm.

Yasmine shook her head and held out her hands.

"Give me those."

Charlotte turned over her clothes, and Yasmine folded them with a precision Charlotte couldn't comprehend. She'd never folded a handkerchief half as flat as her shirt now lay.

She'd heard about mythical women who could fold fitted sheets but never believed they existed. Yasmine had to be one of them.

A folding *unicorn*.

When her clothes sat in a perfect pile, Yasmine turned her terrifying attention on Charlotte, straightening her uniform until everything clung how she liked it. As she jerked and jostled while being handled, Charlotte recalled a prom gown fitting with Mariska and Darla. Her adoptive mothers had a similar way of adjusting clothing without regard for the body inside.

Another minute of this, and I'll have internal injuries...

"It's too tight in the chest, and your shoes are too flashy," grumbled Yasmine with a final tug that threatened to break a rib.

Charlotte glanced down at her sneakers. She'd thought her morning walkers would make good cleaning shoes but hadn't considered the violet logos and soles might clash with Elderbrook's color scheme.

"I can get plain shoes?" she offered.

"Yes, you will, and I'll get you the next size uniform tomorrow."

Charlotte offered a tight smile. Nothing made a girl feel more warm and fuzzy than hearing she needed a larger size.

Yasmine took a step back and considered her with unabashed dismay.

"Move on," she said softly. Charlotte suspected she wasn't talking to her.

"I'm sorry?" she asked.

Yasmine shook her head. "I'm going to give you a rundown of the daily routine."

"Okay." Charlotte cocked her hip, looking for a comfortable way to stand for what promised to be a long story.

"Stand up straight," said Yasmine.

She did. The stitches on the side of her dress groaned.

Oblivious to the overstuffed turkey in front of her, Yasmine continued.

"Bed linens are to be changed and smoothed every morning—no wrinkles. Think of the bed as a freshly ironed suit."

"Suit. Got it."

"Bathroom next. No spots, no streaks, or you'll hear about it. If not from the residents, then *me*. Straighten their items. Half the people here are pigs, and it is up to us to save them from themselves."

Charlotte opened her mouth to comment and then shut it. She couldn't agree the residents were pigs, and she couldn't argue.

CHAPTER NINE

Charlotte headed down the west hallway to Oksana's cleaning cart. Yasmine was gone, and Dead Ed's room was near. They'd been told not to disturb that room, but she wanted to take a peek.

First, she'd ensure Oksana was busy so there weren't any witnesses.

As she parked her cart, she had to stop to avoid bumping into Apple, who came waddling from the room Oksana was cleaning. The dog wore her maid costume and carried a small wax paper cup in her mouth, which she deposited in the hall's center before toddling back into the room.

Charlotte snorted a laugh.

The dog really *was* a maid.

She approached Apple's pile and squatted to inspect the dog's collection of mostly paper products. Nothing edible.

Shocker.

A torn label sat between the paper cup and a wadded tissue, and she plucked it out to get a better look. What she could make from the design didn't look familiar. It was definitely a *label*—the back had carpet fuzzies stuck to it. She could make out what looked like tiny plants or trees dotting the remaining visible area on the unsticky side. A green edge ran by an incomplete word starting *Mir*—printed in a stylized *Old English* font.

Finding nothing else of interest, she stood and dropped the label into the pocket of her uniform before poking her head into the room where Apple had disappeared.

"Hello?" she called.

Apple walked around the corner from the bathroom with an empty toilet roll in her mouth and took it to the hall to deposit on her pile.

"Hello?" said Oksana, appearing from the bathroom.

Charlotte waved. "Hello, again."

"Good morning, again," said Oksana, wiping her hands on her apron.

Charlotte pointed toward the hall.

"Am I crazy, or is the dog helping you clean?"

Oksana laughed. "Oh yes. She loves it. Watch this. *Apple, bed.*"

Apple clamped the corner of the bed's cover in her mouth and tugged. Oksana stopped her before she could pull off the new sheets.

"She helps me change the sheets and picks up trash. She finds things under the tables I can't see." Oksana giggled. "Of course, she eats what she can, but everything else goes to the hall."

Charlotte was impressed. "Wow. We better be careful. We might lose our jobs."

She tilted to the right to peer around Oksana. It looked as though she'd *just* started cleaning the bathroom, so she'd be busy for a while.

Perfect.

She clapped her hands together. "Well, I guess I better get back to work. I don't have a helper."

She waved goodbye and returned to her room, pausing to be sure Oksana didn't follow with any last-minute thoughts.

Not even Apple appeared.

Perfect.

Now would be the perfect time to slip into Ed's room and look around. Maybe something there could give her some idea of what killed him. She doubted there'd be a handwritten confession lying on the kitchen table, but it would be crazy not to poke around, at least.

She crept down the hall, punched the master passcode into room three-thirty-three, and slipped inside.

It felt like stepping into another world.

While neutral pastels and florals adorned most of the manor, this room's tone leaned toward dark and masculine. Baseball cards hung in frames mounted on the wall, and sports-themed knickknacks cluttered the shelves. It felt very different than other rooms she'd cleaned. The residents were mostly female, and the rooms reflected that gender.

She chuckled.

Maybe that's why Ed was in such a good mood.

Her head cocked as she studied one of the framed sports cards. Since they remained hanging on the wall, Ed's family evidently hadn't come to clear out the room. That made sense—it hadn't even been twenty-four hours.

What *didn't* make sense was that the place was *immaculate*.

Ed had died in the late afternoon. He would have spent *some* time in his room since yesterday's morning cleaning, yet everything looked untouched, down to the vacuum tracks in the rug. Not a single footprint, other than her own, marred the pattern.

She wandered into Ed's bathroom and found everything neat.

Perfectly neat.

She studied the carpet a second time.

The vacuum lines were *perfect*.

That could only be one person.

Yasmine.

Yasmine had cleaned Ed's room after his death.

But why? And why before the following day? It's like she heard he'd died and *bolted* to his room to clean it.

Maybe she wanted it to look nice for the grieving family when they stopped by to pick up his things before the body cooled?

Or maybe she wanted to hide evidence.

But evidence of what?

Charlotte walked around the room, clinging near the furniture and treading as lightly as possible to avoid leaving more footprints. It wasn't easy. She'd probably have to sneak in again to vacuum away her—

She froze.

Clown.

On Ed's dresser, behind a baseball encased in a plexiglass box, sat a clown keepsake box identical to the ones she'd seen in the other rooms.

She picked it up and looked it over.

What the heck is this thing? Why do so many residents have it?

Most puzzling—how could so many people sleep in a room with a *clown* in it?

Ugh.

She shivered and put it down.

The door suddenly swung open, and Charlotte spun.

"What are you doing here?" asked Yasmine, standing in the doorway like a marauding bear.

Damn.

"I was getting ready to clean?" said Charlotte. Even she didn't believe her.

Yasmine scowled. "Get out."

She nodded, hurried back to the room she was supposed to clean, and started stripping the sheets. By the time she finished, Yasmine had appeared. She closed the door behind her. Her face was red.

"Why were you in there?" she asked.

"I was cleaning."

Yasmine stabbed a finger at the ground. "But you're in *this* room. That room is two doors down. Were you stealing from a dead man?"

Charlotte gasped. She'd never considered it might look like she was *stealing*, but of course it did. Dead men didn't notice when something went missing.

"*No*," she said. "I'd never steal from anyone."

"Then why were you in there?"

"I—" Charlotte sighed. "I guess I wanted to see the dead guy's room." She winced. She didn't like sounding like a ghoul, but it was better than looking like a thief.

Yasmine frowned. "Bring your cart in here."

Charlotte wasn't sure she understood.

"What?"

"Never mind."

Yasmine opened the door and wrestled Charlotte's cart into the room. Once the door shut, she searched the cart, checking every possible hiding spot.

Charlotte watched her, her face hot with embarrassment. She knew she wasn't a thief, but having Yasmine search her cart for stolen goods made her feel like one.

Finding nothing in the cart, Yasmine turned to her.

"Raise your arms."

Charlotte did as instructed and submitted to Yasmine's patdown. The woman searched her pockets and pulled out the torn sticker. She crumpled it in her hand and stepped back.

"Take off your shoes."

A flood of anger mixed with Charlotte's embarrassment.

"I didn't *steal* anything," she said, kicking off her shoes.

Yasmine searched through the sneakers and then stared at her chest.

"Do you have anything in your bra?"

Charlotte's teeth clenched. She needed to stay calm and undercover, but Yasmine's accusations were going too far.

"*No*," said Charlotte. "I'm not a thief."

Yasmine pressed her lips tight, her eyes glistening. "We've *never* had a thief here, and there is no reason for you to be in Ed's room."

Charlotte found her emotion unsettling.

"I'm sorry. I am. I was being stupid. Looking for ghosts."

"For *ghosts*?"

Charlotte nodded. "I, um, wondered if his ghost went back to the room."

Yasmine sniffed. "They don't come back," she said, her eyes dropping to the ground. She took a beat and then straightened. "Just know if his family thinks anything is missing from that room, I'll fire you on the spot."

Charlotte watched as Yasmine rolled the crumpled label between her fingers.

She wanted that back.

Yasmine opened the door and pushed her cart into the hall. Oksana peered around the corner of the room she was cleaning. Apple's round face appeared several feet lower, both gawking until Yasmine spotted them.

"What are you looking at? Get back to work. All of you," said Yasmine.

Oksana and Apple disappeared back into their room.

Yasmine stormed down the hall toward the elevator, taking the mystery label with her.

CHAPTER TEN

After coffee at the crazy modern diner, Declan arrived at Elderbrook Manor chanting a list in his head. The day before, Dana had covered his general list of duties as manager. That night, using their motel's complimentary pen and a chunk of a pizza box, he'd made an alternative list of duties most conducive to investigating the manor.

The list of things he'd *rather* do.

He planned to approach Dana and suggest what he'd like to do before she wasted his day with duties that kept him from interacting with the rest of the staff and residents.

He memorized his new alternative list so he didn't have to cart around a chunk of pizza box. He planned to interact with as many people as possible, and after work, he had a case review date with Charlotte in Mariska and Darla's room. Hopefully, all four would have new information from various sources by then, and some pattern for the manor's deaths would emerge.

Declan walked down the hall to Dana's office to find her door open. Inside, she sat at her desk, staring at a laptop, scratching at her wrist, seemingly deep in thought.

He rapped on the door, and she looked up, startled.

"Good morning," he said.

She smiled as she closed her laptop. "You scared me. The staff is usually trying to *avoid* me, not *find* me. Come in."

He entered and sat in the chair in front of her desk when she motioned to it.

"Do you know what you're doing today?" she asked.

He nodded, happy to hear the way she'd phrased the question.

It didn't seem she had a schedule in mind for him, just as he'd hoped.

His legs flexed as he fought the urge to leap to his feet and bolt from the room. He needed to leave before she changed her mind and handed him a stack of papers to file.

"I've got my to-do list up here," he said, tapping the side of his skull with his finger.

It wasn't a lie. It just wasn't necessarily the list she'd given him.

She nodded and scratched at her wrist again. "Sounds good."

He motioned to the angry rash on her arm.

"Are you okay?"

She rolled her eyes. "Yes. I get these stupid rashes all the time. Skin doctors are useless. I have cream in here," she said, jerking open a drawer and pulling out a half-empty white tube. She looked at him and sighed. "I think it's stress-related. I have Ed's family coming to go through his room in half an hour."

He nodded. "Ah. It can't be easy dealing with the death of a resident."

"No, it isn't. I can't point them toward his room and run away, which is what I'd *like* to do. I need to be there for them to answer questions I don't know the answers to." She rolled her neck, and he heard it crack. "I'm looking forward to it like a stick in the eye. This is part of the job I won't miss."

"I bet." Declan was about to stand when he had an idea. *He* should talk to Ed's family. He could ask if Ed had complained about symptoms or said anything odd before his death. Maybe he shared with his family things he didn't want friends or staff at the manor to know.

"Um, I could do it?" he asked.

Dana tucked her chin against her long neck, tilted her head, and observed him like a confused ostrich.

"Really? You'd do that?"

He nodded. "Sure. I can do it. I've dealt with things like this a lot in the past."

That was half a lie. He had *no* experience working with bereaved families but had spent a lifetime apologizing to people his uncle Seamus inadvertently—or purposely—offended.

Close enough.

Dana chewed on her lip as she rubbed itch cream on her arm.

"Wow. Okay—I don't know. You're so new. I feel bad—like I'm throwing you to the wolves on day one—but if you really want to? You don't mind?"

He shook his head. "No problem at all."

She took a deep breath and put the cap back on the tube. "You're a lifesaver. I have so much paperwork to do. I have to schedule shifts, and this itch is driving me crazy—"

He pointed out the door, which was where he wanted to go.

"They'll be here in half an hour, you said? I should meet them in the lobby?"

She nodded. "*Perfect.* You can take them to Ed's room and say some—you know—*kind words*. Make sure they feel taken care of. If they have questions you don't have answers to, don't try to fake it— tell them you'll ask me and get back to them."

He nodded. "In short, make sure they don't sue us."

She tittered. "Exactly. We've had a lot of stuff happen—"

She stopped herself and opened her drawer to toss the tube back inside.

"Whatever. You get the idea."

Declan stood. "I'm going to grab some coffee, make some rounds, and then I'll be back in the lobby in half an hour."

"Sounds good. Thanks. Can you close the door on your way out?"

He nodded and shut the door behind him.

He grinned.

Perfect.

He couldn't have asked for a better assignment. He'd have to be careful talking to Ed's family—he didn't want them to think something was off or imply they *should* be suspicious—but maybe they knew something they didn't even know they knew.

He'd run through a few different approaches before they arrived and planned his attack.

But first, he needed another coffee. He'd been up late the night before—at first, because he was talking about the case with Charlotte and then because he was waiting for a bug or rat to stroll across his face the second he fell asleep.

If the case took too much longer, they'd *really* need to upgrade their motel.

He headed for the breakroom, where he found the blonde maid, Oksana, doting over a steaming kettle on the smallest stove he'd ever seen.

"Good morning," he said as he headed for the coffee machine on the counter beside her. "I don't think we've met officially. I'm Declan, the new manager?"

She smiled and shook his hand. "Good morning. I am Oksana. Would you like some tea?"

He pulled a mug from the cabinet. "I'm more of a coffee guy."

She scoffed. "You don't know what you're missing."

He chuckled and thought it would end there.

He was wrong.

Oksana gestured to the teapot on the stove, speaking in breathy awe.

"Tea isn't just a morning drink. It is a *journey*. Every cup is a ticket to a different part of the world."

He nodded. Her reverent tone made it clear he needed to listen or risk offending her, but all he wanted to do was get moving. He fought to keep from checking his watch.

"Uh-huh. I can see that," he said.

He knew he'd made mistakes almost immediately. First, he'd *engaged*. Second, he'd leaned towards the door a little without meaning to do it.

The maid grabbed his arm with one hand and snatched a container off the counter with the other. She held the tin aloft for him to admire as if it were the Stanley Cup.

"This is my special blend of Ceylon black tea with Russian samovar traditions. It's like a waltz of two cultures in a cup."

He nodded.

Wow. She really loves tea.

"You, uh, make your own blends?" he asked.

Oksana's attention drifted past him, and he glanced over his shoulder even though he knew there wasn't anything there except the sink.

No, Oksana was looking at something far away and entirely in her mind.

She still gripped his arm, and he knew he couldn't move. It felt like the woman could crush walnuts with those paws.

"It started back in my home country," she waxed as if she were narrating a documentary about orphans. "My babushka made a tea very much like this from herbs from her garden. The flavor—it was like nothing else. When I moved here, I missed it and began my journey to recreate it."

Declan leaned to the left to center himself in her faraway gaze. It felt as if she'd forgotten he was there, and he needed to humanize himself before she shattered his ulna bone in her vise grip.

"Yep, I can see how this is more than a morning pick-me-up to you," he said, attempting to tug away his arm.

Spell broken by his movement, Oksana released him and opened a cabinet door. Inside sat a flowered porcelain teapot, which she removed and held against her chest, caressing it like it was a nervous kitten she'd plucked from a tree.

"Tea is a connection to my past, a piece of home. And every time someone enjoys my tea, it's like sharing a piece of that home with them."

She stared hard at him.

Declan swallowed.

Apparently, he hadn't turned down a hot drink. He'd insulted her entire family.

"Um, gosh. Can I have a cup, after all?"

Her expression brightened.

"Yes?"

"Absolutely. You've convinced me. It sounds *life changing*."

"Oh, it *is*."

Oksana released a happy squeak. She scooped her special blend from the container, collecting a portion in a spoon-shaped clip dotted with holes. The clip looked like it was made out of two tiny colanders.

"The residents love my teas. I make special blends for their tastes. I get to know them through their tea choices," she said as she stirred.

"I'm sure they appreciate that. Do you grow it, too?" he asked.

Before she could answer, he suffered a moment of doubt.

Can a person grow tea, or does that only happen in China?

He'd never realized how little he knew about where tea came from. If she told him she picked tea bags from trees, he'd believe her.

"I *do* grow my own tea," she said, her chest puffing. "I have several bushes at home. I have a Schilling's Dwarf."

He chuckled. "Does Schilling know you took him?"

Her brow knitted. "Who?"

"The dwarf."

She remained staring at him, her forehead furrowed with confusion.

He waved her off. "Nothing. Nevermind. Stupid joke."

She shrugged and returned to her tea-making. "I grow other ingredients too, of course, both here and in the community garden out back—ginger, mint, roselle—you might know roselle as the Florida cranberry."

He nodded. "I might. I don't."

She turned, beaming, teacup in hand.

"The cup is my grandmother's," she said, thrusting it at him.

Declan stared at it, his arms refusing to rise.

Holy donuts.

He'd have to pack up and leave the country if he dropped that teacup.

With concentration usually reserved for algebra, he took the cup and saucer from her.

"Thank you, I—"

Suddenly, a voice tore through the room.

"Oksana, get upstairs!"

Yasmine had appeared in the doorway, looking exasperated. From what Declan had seen so far, disapproval mixed with a dash of exasperation was her natural state of being.

Both he and Oksana jumped at the sound of her bark. He bobbled the cup and nearly batted the saucer in his attempt to steady it. At the last possible second before tragedy, he hooked the cup by the handle, preventing it from sliding off the saucer. The hot liquid inside sloshed on his fingers. It felt like a baby volcano had spit up on his hand.

"That was close," he said through gritted teeth as the tea roasted his flesh.

Oksana stared at him, her hands over her open mouth.

"Are you okay?" she asked.

Yasmine, still glaring, didn't seem to appreciate the situation.

"Oksana—" she pressed.

Oksana huffed. "I'm *coming.*"

Declan put the cup and saucer on the counter and eased his hand away.

"I'll, uh, leave this here when I'm done?" he asked.

The maid paused, but Yasmine remained in the doorway, waiting with her hands on her hips.

Oksana nodded.

"Thank you. Tell me what you think later," she said before hurrying past Yasmine and out of the room.

The head maid remained to squint at Declan.

"No *fraternizing,*" she said, shaking a scolding finger at him.

He realized she thought he was flirting with Oksana.

"It's a tea thing," he explained, motioning to the cup.

She frowned and left.

"You wouldn't understand," he mumbled, grabbing a paper towel to dab the scalding liquid from his hands and pants.

He checked to be sure Oksana wasn't returning, dumped the tea, and slid the cup and saucer to a safe corner. He didn't want to risk dropping the precious cup and didn't have time to wait for the tea to cool.

He checked his watch.

Ed's family would arrive any second, and he hadn't had a moment of peace to plan his gentle interrogation.

Or have a second cup of coffee.

He strode to the lobby, where he found two women—one older and one middle-aged—standing at the unattended front desk.

"Hello, I'm the manager, Declan. Are you Ed's family?"

They turned at the sound of his voice and nodded.

"I'm his daughter, Janice, and this is my aunt Alice, his sister," said the younger of the two.

He nodded and shook their hands. "Nice to meet you, though I'm sorry for the reason. I'll take you to Ed's room."

They followed him to the elevator and gathered inside at his prompting.

"We're so sorry for your loss," he said as they rode the car upstairs.

They nodded. "He was happy here," said Alice.

When the elevator opened on the third floor, Declan motioned for them to step out so he could follow. They seemed to know the way, which was good because he'd been so distracted by the impromptu tea seminar he'd forgotten to double-check the room number.

They led him to Ed's room, and he used the master code he'd memorized the day before.

"They said they'd provide us with some boxes?" said Alice as they entered.

Declan smiled.

That would have been a nice thing for Dana to mention...

"Oh, um..."

"Here they are," said Janice, pointing to a stack of boxes and a tape gun on the floor beside Ed's bed as they entered.

Declan nodded.

Whew.

He grabbed a flattened box.

"I'll tape one up for you while you gather?"

They agreed, so he picked up the flat cardboard and tape gun and constructed a box as the ladies meandered around the room, plucking items from shelves and drawers and gathering them on the bed.

"Ed was such a wonderful part of our community. He'll be greatly missed," he said between the horrific ratcheting of the tape gun.

Inside, he groaned. Everything out of his mouth sounded *canned*, but he couldn't think of anything else to say.

Alice cocked her head. "I haven't seen you before. Usually, it's a woman?"

"Dana. I'm new."

"When did you start?"

"Um, yesterday."

She squinted at him, and he realized his earlier comment implied he knew Ed well.

"Ed's loss was a shock, even to me—the new guy. He seemed

so *healthy*. The, uh, little time I got to spend with him."

Alice seemed to let her suspicion of him slide.

"He did seem happy, didn't he? He'd seemed so *perky* lately," she said.

Declan left the finished box on the bed. "Perkier than usual?"

She nodded. "He took up painting again, which we were so happy about—" She sighed. "Of course, we had no idea an innocent hobby would end like *this*."

Declan straightened.

Oh no.

He scanned the room for the painting.

He didn't see it.

Good.

Bernie had been smart enough not to leave it lying around. Naked geriatric Venus was probably *not* the way the ladies would want to remember Ed.

"Was there anything else? Any...*warning* there might be something wrong?" he asked.

Pawing through the drawers, Alice glanced over her shoulder at him.

"Like what?"

"I don't know. Just curious if he'd seemed, uh, *content*?"

Alice stopped searching and turned to him. She seemed...*concerned*.

He rushed to clarify.

"I like hearing stories about the residents. They all have such rich lives," he added, forcing a smile.

Ugh.

Alice stared at him like he wore a crown of bananas.

He tried again.

"I guess his death was out of the blue—"

Now he'd drawn Janice's attention. She stood with a leather shaving kit in hand, squinting at him.

"Would you mind leaving us so we can get this done?" she asked.

Declan nodded. "Yes. Sorry. I'll leave you to it."

He left the tape gun on the bed and moved into the hall with a final goodbye wave. He shut the door and leaned his back against the wall.

That went well.

So much for subtle questioning. Ed's family thought he was a babbling idiot. All he'd discovered was that Ed seemed perky before his death. The fact he wasn't sick *could* imply murder, or it could mean the old guy simply dropped dead from an undiagnosed issue like millions of people did every year.

Declan blinked at the floor, lost in his regrets until he felt a *presence.*

He glanced up to see the face of an older woman peering through the leaves of a fake potted plant at the end of the hall.

He pushed off the wall.

"Hello? Can I help you?" he called to her.

The leaves snapped together, and the face disappeared.

Declan watched for a moment, but nothing else moved.

Okay...weird...

He walked to the end of the hall to look for the woman but found no sign of her.

Hm.

He shrugged it off and took the elevator downstairs for his elusive second cup of coffee. He'd spent enough time in Pineapple Port with Charlotte to know spying was often a part-time job for retirees.

You can't gossip about what you don't know about.

As he entered the break room, air popped from his lungs as if he'd been punched. The coffee pot, which had been half-full earlier, was empty but for an insulting quarter inch of muddy liquid.

He scowled.

I should've kept the darn tea.

Not wanting to make a whole pot for himself, he left, hoping to find another pot in the main dining area. Pushing open the swinging doors to the kitchen, he spotted a full pot shining on a burner like the Holy Grail.

Score.

He poured himself a cup and raised it, pausing before it reached his lips.

The same old lady's face he'd seen upstairs peeped at him through the round kitchen door window.

He lowered his mug and looked away, hoping she didn't see him spot her.

Were his movements gossipworthy? Did Dana have spies watching his progress? Maybe Bernie wanted to keep an eye on him?

He looked at the mug.

Am I allowed to drink kitchen coffee?

He stepped forward, pretending to look at something near the door.

She didn't buy it. The woman's face disappeared from the window.

Declan frowned. He didn't recognize his new shadow, but he'd only met a few residents the day before. Judging from where her face fit in the high-placed glass, she had to be tall.

Am I being tailed by Eleanor Roosevelt?

If her past behavior was any indication, she planned on *continuing* to follow him, which gave him an idea.

He waited with his back against the wall next to the doors, too far to the side for her to see him through the porthole window. After a minute, the door creaked open, and the woman stepped into the kitchen.

"You're following me," he said.

She gasped and slapped her hand to her chest.

"You're going to give me a heart attack," she said, turning to him.

She *was* tall, as he suspected, and stout. If the manor had a football team, she'd play center.

Her brown eyes looked him up and down. Though she'd been startled, the momentary flash of fear on her expression had disappeared, replaced with something akin to *defiance*.

"Can I ask why you're following me?" he asked, sipping his coffee.

She pointed at him with a crooked finger.

"I *know* you," she said.

"I'm the new manager."

She shook her head. "No. You're with that maid. You're *detectives*."

The mug froze at Declan's lips.

He hadn't seen *that* coming.

"No, I'm the new manager," he repeated.

She lifted her chin. "No. You're *detectives*."

He stood off the wall. "You must have me confused—"

She rustled in her pocket to produce a newspaper clipping, which she thrust forward for him to inspect.

He recognized the photo. They had a copy of that same picture hanging on the wall back at the office. It featured Charlotte and him smiling at the camera and had been for an article about their new detective agency.

Whoops.

He nodded, trying to keep his expression neutral.

"They do look a lot like us—"

She rolled her eyes and lowered the clipping. "Oh, stop. I'm old, not *stupid*. I want to help."

He gave up.

"Help how?" he asked.

She pursed her lips. "I can't tell you yet."

"Why?"

"I need something from you first."

Declan smirked.

Am I being shaken down?

"Look, Miss—"

"Alma."

"Look, Miss Alma, we don't have any money—"

"*Just* Alma. I don't want money. I have plenty of money. You have to get me a *date*."

He blinked at her. "A *date*?"

She held up the clipping and pointed to Charlotte.

"Are you dating her?" she asked.

"Yes."

She grunted. "I guess you're too young anyway."

Declan bit his tongue. The woman's demeanor was youthful, but the rest of her had to be creeping on eighty.

"Can we back up a second?" he suggested. "Let's assume I could get you a date. How are you proposing you'd help me?"

She smiled. "I have information."

"What kind of information?"

"You're here about the murders, right?"

He found himself speechless again. This lady knew a lot of things she wasn't supposed to know.

"Murders?" he asked, his voice cracking.

She shook her head. "*Don't.* Aren't we past pretending?"

He sighed. "What sort of date are we talking about?"

She crossed her arms over her long beaded necklace. "An afternoon. A meal."

"Is that all?"

"Yep."

"And then you'll tell me what you know?"

"Yes. After the date."

Declan rubbed his face with the hand not holding his rapidly cooling coffee.

"I might have someone in mind for you," he muttered.

She perked. "Is he handsome?"

He took a sip of his coffee and shrugged.

"He certainly thinks so."

CHAPTER ELEVEN

"I'm probably going to die," said Mariska as they walked toward the manor's pickleball court.

"Oh, I'm definitely going to die," agreed Darla.

They both wore shorts, light scoop neck tees, and sneakers. Neither of them had packed expecting pickleball.

"Maybe this is how people keep dying here. These idiot women keep making them play pickleball in the Florida sun," said Mariska, plucking her shorts from her butt cheeks. They weren't the best fit or the best tennis outfit. She'd only brought them to wear around the room.

Darla nodded. "You might be right. Maybe we can suggest that to Charlotte and *not* play pickleball? Case over?"

"I don't think so."

To the left of the pool, what had served as a single tennis court had been split into two pickleball courts with nets on wheels that rolled on for pickleball and off for tennis.

The ladies walked onto the court, heat radiating from the asphalt through their sneakers and socks.

It was only nine o'clock in the morning.

Gretchen waited on a player's bench, flanking the court. She held a black parasol, just wide enough to offer her shade. A small audience of gray and platinum blonde-haired people gathered on the wooden bleachers—a riot of colorful visors shielding their faces from the sun.

On court one, Amanda and Muffin smacked a hollow-sounding

ball back and forth with paddles. It sounded like a crowd was opening champagne bottles one after the next.

"It looks *kind* of fun," said Darla, watching the ball fly.

Mariska nodded. "I know a couple of ladies back home who love it."

"Glad you could make it," said Gretchen as they approached her. She wore a white tennis dress, pink tennis shoes, and enormous sunglasses. A pink floral scarf secured her shoulder-length white hair.

"We don't have the paddle thingies," said Darla, motioning to the two women playing.

"We have spares," said Gretchen, motioning to a pile of paddles on the bench beside her.

She called to her lackeys.

"Ladies, let's get ready."

"You're not playing?" asked Darla.

Gretchen sniffed.

"No. I have people for that."

The practicing ladies ended their game and headed over. The players glistened with sweat but didn't seem winded.

Mariska found this troubling.

Both wore color-coordinated outfits with matching visors, wristbands, and expensive sunglasses. Darla and Mariska looked down at their cobbled-together outfits and squinted as the sun turned Muffin's sequined visor into a laser cannon.

"We need to stretch," said Darla, guiding Mariska a few feet away.

Once they were out of earshot, Darla reached for her toes and motioned for Mariska to do the same.

"We can't win this," she said.

"I can't even touch my toes," said Mariska, grunting as she folded herself in half. "Do we have to win? I thought we just had to play?"

Darla blinked at her.

"That's a good question."

She straightened.

"Hey, Gretchen?"

Gretchen cocked her head, waiting. She didn't deign to answer.

"Do we have to *win* to pass whatever test this is? We've never played before, so it doesn't seem fair to make us have to *win*."

"You have to score five points," said Amanda so Gretchen wouldn't have to answer.

Darla perked. "Oh. That doesn't sound too bad."

"How many points to win?" called Mariska.

"Eleven."

Mariska looked at Darla. "That's not great. Could be worse, I guess. We have to be half as good as them."

Darla frowned. "Great math. Too bad it isn't a math quiz."

They strolled back to Gretchen.

"Alright, how do you play this thing?" asked Darla.

Gretchen motioned to Amanda, who stepped forward, cleaning her sunglasses on her shirt.

"Do you know how to play tennis?" she asked.

The ladies nodded.

Amanda shrugged. "It's like that."

"It's like that, only not like that at all," interjected Muffin.

Darla looked at her. "Do you use that head for anything besides holding up your visor?"

Muffin's hand fluttered to her visor as a couple on the front bleacher row chuckled.

Amanda continued.

"You serve diagonally, like tennis, but you hit underhand. If you're receiving, you have to wait for it to bounce to return it."

Mariska scratched her head as a rolling drip of sweat tickled her scalp. She'd been hatching a plan to smack the serve out of the sky the second it crossed over the net.

So much for that.

"The serving team has to let it bounce once, too. After that, you don't," continued Amanda. She pointed to long boxes painted on the court on either side of the net. "That area is the kitchen."

"Ooh, I'm good in the kitchen," said Mariska.

"You can't have a foot in there when you hit the ball in the air. If it bounces first, then you can step inside to get it."

Darla took a deep breath and let it out in one long, noisy huff.

"Is that it, or should I get a pen for writing all this down?" she asked.

Amanda smirked. "That's it. We'll play to eleven, and you have to win by two. Oh, and you can only score during your service, like volleyball."

"For the love of Pete—how many rules does this stupid game have?" muttered Darla.

"Charlotte was good at volleyball," mused Mariska. "She's so tall."

She wished Charlotte was nearby to play stupid pickleball for them. She'd be good at it.

"Too bad Charlotte isn't here to take our place," said Darla. She looked at Amanda. "Can we get a practice game to get a feel for things?"

"Ooh, good question," said Mariska, smacking Darla's arm.

Amanda looked at Gretchen.

Gretchen shook her head.

"Really, you should have known how to play before you got here. It's not our fault you didn't," she said, examining her nails.

Darla poked a finger at her. "Look, you snotty snowcap, I—"

Mariska grabbed Darla's arm and tugged her toward the court.

"Stop it. We have to get through this," she hissed.

Darla tugged her arm free. "But they make me *crazy.*"

"You can make them pay for it later."

"I can? Promise?"

"Sure."

Darla nodded, placated, and Mariska worried about what she'd promised. Darla tended to follow through on threats.

Gretchen stood and put her parasol aside.

"I'll flip a coin to see who goes first. Heads or tails, Amanda?"

"Heads."

Gretchen smacked the back of her hand. Mariska never saw anything rise in the air.

"Heads it is," said Gretchen, not looking at the invisible coin. She kept her attention locked on Darla.

Mariska saw the muscle in Darla's jaw flex.

"That cheating little—"

"Get into position!" shouted Gretchen before sitting.

Mariska bumped Darla toward the court. After some confusion, the ladies took their places across from each other, paddles in hand.

"Ready?" asked Darla.

Mariska set her jaw. "*Ready.*"

From her serving position, Amanda smacked the ball underhand with a *thock!*, and the game began. Caught off-guard, Mariska swung, catching only air as the ball bounced past her.

Darla tilted back her head.

"We have to do better than *that*," she said.

Mariska frowned. "I *will*. I wasn't ready."

Amanda served again, and Darla slapped the ball after a single bounce, catching it with the edge of her paddle. The ball shot over the net at an impossible angle, and Muffin lunged but missed it.

"That was lucky," said Darla, grinning.

"Do we get a point?" asked Mariska.

Darla shook her head. "No, but it's your serve. Concentrate. Pretend you're in the cornhole finals again."

Mariska nodded. "That's a good idea."

Mariska invoked the fire she usually reserved for playing cornhole and served. The ball reached the opposite court, and Amanda returned it.

"Let it bounce!" warned Darla as the ball returned to Mariska.

Mariska did and smacked it back. She liked the *pop!* of her return as the ball hit her paddle. It sounded hollow but felt *solid.*

This time, Muffin returned to Darla, arching the ball high. Darla rushed forward but stopped a second before entering the forbidden *kitchen*. She hit the ball, bellowing with satisfaction.

Muffin jumped at the sound of Darla's roar and missed the ball.

"You can't scream like that," snapped Amanda, smacking the side of her leg with the paddle.

"Who says?" asked Darla as applause broke out in the bleachers.

Gretchen whipped her attention to the crowd.

The clapping stopped.

Mariska served. Again, they got the ball in play, though Mariska's second return barely made it over the net.

Amanda ran in and smacked it over.

With the other woman so close to the net, Mariska decided instead of aiming for the court, she'd aim for Amanda.

I am a pickleball assassin.

She crushed the ball as it cleared the kitchen. Whistling back over the net, it smacked Amanda in the chest.

"Ow!" Amanda dropped her paddle and grabbed her left boob.

"That's *rude*," she snapped.

"So are fake coin tosses and making people play games they've never played before so they can talk to people," said a smirking Darla as she gave Mariska a high-five.

Play resumed.

Despite early success, Amanda and Muffin soon outmatched the newcomers, but, taking a cue from Mariska, Darla aimed for the other team to score a fifth point.

"That's five!" said Darla as Muffin spun to take a ball to the arm instead of the face.

"Oh, thank goodness," said Mariska, bending to lean her hands on her knees. Sweat poured from her auburn curls and stung her eyes.

"You're a bunch of *cheaters*," said Amanda, storming off the court.

"*You're a bunch of cheaters*," aped Darla in a nasal voice. "That's *rich* coming from *you*."

She strode to Gretchen as Amanda and Muffin gathered their things.

"Are you making a pinot or a cabernet?" asked Darla as Mariska joined her.

Gretchen stood, scowling. "What are you talking about?"

Darla shrugged. "I mean, what else are you going to do with all your *sour grapes*?"

Mariska hooted and held up a hand to return the earlier high-five. Darla noticed too late, threw out a hand, and partially missed.

"Okay. That felt less cool," she muttered.

Mariska focused on Gretchen.

"What's next?" she asked.

Gretchen ran her tongue over her perfectly white fake teeth implants. "Usually art. But the art room is closed because stupid Ed died there yesterday."

"What a jerk," drolled Darla.

Gretchen ignored her. "We'll go to cooking next. Be in the kitchen in an hour."

Mariska gasped in horror. "One hour? It'll take me longer than that to stop sweating."

Gretchen spun on her heel and strode off, Amanda and Muffin hustling to keep pace.

"Nice job," said a man from the bleachers.

"It's about time someone taught them some manners," said another woman.

Darla smiled. "Thank you. What's your name?"

The woman bit her lip and walked away. The man had already strode off.

Darla put her hands on her hips.

"Still won't talk to us," she said. "We're *heroes*, and they won't talk to us."

"Cooking is good," said Mariska, clapping with her fingertips. "I'm a *great* cook."

Darla nodded. "We probably won't get lucky enough to have it be a pierogi contest, though."

Mariska chuckled.

"That wouldn't even be fair."

CHAPTER TWELVE

Charlotte hooked the vacuum cord and wheeled the contraption back into the hall.

Finished.

She'd done her best on the rooms but suspected Yasmine wouldn't be happy with her cleaning skills. She couldn't imagine Yasmine *happy*—with or without her lack of cleaning skills. Not on her birthday, Christmas, or even after winning the lottery...

The woman acted like she only had one smile left and didn't want to waste it. And what was up with the fit she had in Ed's room? She looked ready to cry. Maybe she burst into tears whenever she got angry. Plenty of people did that.

As Charlotte exited the room, an explosion of color flashed in the corner of her eye, and she turned.

At the end of the hall, she thought she saw a large, *floppy*, red shoe disappearing around the corner.

She froze.

No...

Only one thing wore shoes like that.

Clowns.

The skin on her arm prickled.

Clowns scared the bejeezus out of her.

She took a deep breath. She knew she had to go look around that corner, but her body didn't want to move. The manor house was stately but old and a little creepy.

Loose clowns didn't help.

Charlotte took a steeling breath and strode down the hall. She didn't run. She knew she *should* run, but something wouldn't let her move that quickly.

Shame if I missed the clown...

The mansion's hallways ran around the center rooms in a large square. By the time she reached the end of her hall, she saw only a flash of movement at the end of the next as the *possible* clown turned the next corner.

"Wait!" she called out, not nearly as loud as she could have.

Get a hold of yourself, woman.

She picked up her pace.

She arced wide as she approached the next turn, in case a clawed clown lurked around the bend, waiting to leap out and clamp onto her throat with razor-sharp teeth. She heard a ding and rounded the corner in time to see the doors on the service elevator sliding shut.

Charlotte jogged to the button and forced herself to punch it several times, but the elevator had gone. She glanced at the red numbers above the doors and saw the car descend to the first floor before bouncing back to her. She braced herself in a karate stance.

The doors slid open.

The elevator was empty.

She released the breath she'd been holding.

Whew.

If there *had* been a clown in the elevator, he'd disembarked on the first floor.

Did she see a clown?

Maybe she saw red *sneakers* that looked like floppy clown shoes because the clown boxes were on her mind.

She ran a hand over her head to smooth the flyaway hairs fleeing her ponytail.

Maybe she was delirious from inhaling cleaning products all day.

Maybe I'm losing my mind.

Between living in a retirement neighborhood and working cases, would it be *odd* if she started to lose her mind?

She was about to head back down the hall to her waiting vacuum when she spotted something sparkling on the ground of the elevator car. She stopped the doors from shutting and bent down to pick up a tiny, shiny square of red.

Confetti?

She growled at the ceiling.

Fine. I'll check.

Charlotte took the elevator to the ground floor, peeked her head out, checked for marauding clowns, and headed down the hall to knock on Bernie's office door. As usual, no one stood at the check-in desk, so she couldn't ask if anyone had seen a clown wander by.

Bernie called for entry, and she pushed inside. Apple had finished her cleaning and retired to the office. She glanced up as Charlotte entered without bothering to lift her head from her bed.

"I have a quick question for you," Charlotte said as she entered.

Bernie looked up from his desk, glasses hanging from the bridge of his nose.

"Close the door."

She did and approached the desk.

"Do you have a clown here?" she asked.

Bernie's brow furrowed.

"I don't think I understand the question?"

"Have you hired a clown? To entertain the residents?"

He squinted. "Why would they want a clown? Did someone say they *wanted* a clown?"

She shook her head. "*No*—I'm not *suggesting* you hire a clown—I thought I *saw* a clown in the hall. I only caught a glimpse as they rounded the corner, and they got into the elevator before I could catch up."

He arched an eyebrow. "They? It was a herd of clowns?"

"No, just one, as far as I saw. I just don't know if it was a *he* or a *she* clown."

Bernie shook his head. "No clowns. Not hired by us, anyway. I guess it's always possible one of the residents hired someone for a party. Elderbrook is more of an apartment building than a ward, so they're welcome to do anything they like as long as it doesn't disturb the other guests."

"Do you know anything about clown keepsake boxes?"

Bernie lifted and dropped his hands on his desk with a huff.

"Why are you obsessed with clowns?" he asked.

"I'm not obsessed with clowns—"

Terrified of them, sure, not obsessed.

Charlotte pulled out her phone and navigated to the photo she'd taken of the clown boxes. She held it up for him to see.

"Several residents have these in their rooms. I wondered why, and then I thought I saw a clown. It struck me as a strange coincidence."

She stopped, knowing how silly what she was about to say sounded.

Ah well. Too late.

"I also found this."

She held up the small square.

"What is that?" he asked.

"Confetti, I think."

He rolled his eyes. "Or any little chunk of wrapping."

"Maybe..."

Bernie took a deep breath and then let it leak out of him. "I'm sorry, all I can tell you is, officially, Elderbrook has not hired any clowns."

"Okay. Just thought I should check." She slid the tiny piece of confetti back into her pocket.

He eyed her. "Have you found anything that might explain the *deaths*? Or are we working exclusively on the killer clown theory?"

Charlotte met snarky Bernie's gaze. His condescending tone grated on her—maybe because she was fresh from being chastised by Yasmine.

Declan was better with people. She only wanted to solve the mysteries.

"We're checking into a lot of angles," she said.

Worried she sounded defensive, she forced a grin, but he noticed her irritation.

He held up a hand in mea culpa.

"I'm sorry if I sound annoyed. I know you haven't had time to find much. It's just I'm under a lot of stress. We're applying to upgrade the facility to a nursing home, and I'm afraid all this—"

His shoulders slumped, and he seemed to lose the urge to continue.

"I understand," said Charlotte, feeling less like Bernie's problem was *her*. "We'll have new information for you soon, I'm sure."

He nodded. "Thank you."

She turned to leave and then turned back.

"Oh, just for the record. Yasmine caught me poking around Ed's room and had a small meltdown. She thinks I was robbing the place."

Bernie dropped back into his chair and waved her off.

"If she brings it up, I'll handle her."

"Thank you."

Charlotte left to retrieve her cart, tucked it away, and headed for the staff locker room. Sitting on the wooden bench in front of her locker, she took a deep breath and released it. She couldn't remember the last time she felt so *tired*. The skin on her hands throbbed red and raw from scrubbing showers. It didn't help that one of the residents had cooked something splattery in their oven—that mess alone had taken an extra half hour of scrubbing.

Her arms and her feet ached.

"We keep doing undercover work like this, and I'm going to have to start working out," she grumbled.

She heard a door creak and twisted to see who it was.

Bernie's granddaughter entered from the shower, dressed in street clothes. Her hair was wet.

"Hi," she said, walking to her locker.

"Hi," said Charlotte with a little wave. "I'm Charlotte—"

"I know," said Luna, opening her locker. "I'm Luna."

Charlotte nodded. "Long day, huh?"

Luna snorted. "Always."

"Have you been working for your grandfather long?"

The girl shook her head. "No. My mother thought this would help me *find direction*." She made air quotes around the words. "Like I want to get on the maid career track."

Charlotte began to change as Luna rooted in her locker.

"So, that man who died yesterday—had you noticed anything odd about him?" she asked.

Luna grunted. "No—but I am starting to think it's weird we've lost so many people this year."

"Weird in any particular way?"

Luna paused to think. "I don't know. I mean, they're *old*, so it isn't *that* weird. It just seems sudden sometimes, you know?"

Charlotte nodded. Growing up in a retirement community, she knew better than most.

"Do you think they're getting sick? Like maybe there's a flu running through the place?"

Luna shrugged. "They didn't look sick, but maybe, I guess. I really don't know."

She closed her locker, but it didn't catch. When the door bounced open, a red ball popped out and rolled across the ground.

Charlotte watched as Luna dove to grab it and shove it back inside.

The girl looked flustered.

Charlotte tilted to get a better look in the locker. Luna noticed and secured the door, careful not to let anything else escape. She glanced at Charlotte, looking like she wanted to say something, but in the end, flashed a tight smile instead.

"See you later," she said.

Charlotte nodded. "See you later."

She watched Luna go and then turned her attention to the girl's locker.

What was she so afraid I'd see?

She tested the door, but the lock held fast. Her lock picks were no use against a combination lock. She considered prying the door open but decided it was too early in the investigation to destroy people's lockers in search of who knows what.

She stared at her own clothes hanging in her locker and decided to use the staff showers before heading out. They were bigger and— thanks to Yasmine's maniacal cleaning—*cleaner* than the ones back at their sad little motel down the street.

She'd have to hurry, though—she had a meeting with Declan, Mariska, and Darla upstairs. Hopefully, one of them had discovered more than a clown infestation.

She was about to head to the showers when something flashed on the ground near Luna's locker. She bent down and picked it up, the tiny square sparkling on the tip of her finger.

Confetti.

CHAPTER THIRTEEN

Darla and Mariska entered a large kitchen off the main dining room with little time to cool down, clean up, and change after pickleball. Inside, Darla recognized a few people from the tennis bleachers sitting around a massive oak banquet table at the back of the room.

All heads turned as they entered.

"This must be the place," she said.

"Which one again?" said a voice at Darla's elbow as she walked by the table of watchers.

She paused. She didn't know who was speaking at the table beside her but recognized the voice's *style*. It reminded her of Mariska's *sneaky voice*, a *whisper* audible to astronauts circling the moon. Whoever it was, they thought they were being quiet—probably to keep *her* from hearing.

"*The one with the flowers*," answered someone else.

Darla almost missed the word *flowers* as some third person hissed *Shh!* over it, but she felt confident that was the word she'd heard.

Flowers? Or *flours*?

It had to be *flowers,* she decided. *Flours,* as a plural, didn't make much sense unless they'd be baking some complicated bread.

She hoped designer bread wouldn't be the test. She couldn't get *ordinary* bread to puff up the way it should. Every time she tried, the loaf ended up too dense. She could crack skulls with her bread. It was more of a weapon than a foodstuff. She couldn't imagine making some complicated loaf featuring *multiple* types of flour. She'd end up serving a hockey puck.

Darla sneaked a peek at the table but couldn't tell who'd been stage whispering. To remain within earshot, she pretended to admire a stand mixer.

The table went quiet.

Dangit.

When the whispering didn't resume, she moved to the large island in the center of the room, where Mariska couldn't stop caressing the quartz countertop.

"Keep your eye out for flowers," she whispered.

"Have you seen this island? It's *enormous*," said Mariska, sweeping her hand over the stone.

Darla scowled. "Did you hear me? It could be *important*."

Mariska turned to her. Darla saw her friend's front teeth press against her bottom lip and realized she was about to repeat the F-word in her *special* whisper.

If she said *flower* out loud, everyone would know they'd overheard.

"*Fl—*"

Darla slapped her hand over Mariska's mouth.

Mariska pulled away, clearly annoyed.

"*Ow.* Why did you do that?"

Darla leaned in to whisper directly in her ear.

"Do *not* say the word out loud. It could be important, and we don't want to give away that we know it. Just keep an eye out for *flowers*."

"But what kind?" asked Mariska in a normal voice.

"Can you not tell I'm trying to be sneaky?" asked Darla, squeezing her fingers into fists of frustration.

"But why? What do flow—"

Darla grabbed Mariska's wrist.

"Will you *please* stop talking? All kinds. Okay? Keep an eye out for all kinds. I'm saying I think they're important, but I don't know why yet."

Mariska pouted. "Fine, but you didn't have to punch me in the teeth."

"I didn't *punch* you. You know how you whisper. I didn't want people in China to hear."

"Shut up."

"*You* shut up. That's my *point*."

Amanda and Muffin entered the room to stand beside them at the island as the onlookers gawked and whispered.

"I love your apron," said Mariska to Muffin, friendly and chatty as always, even with her enemies.

Darla sighed.

It's a good thing she has me. These ladies would eat her alive.

"Thank you," said Muffin.

Amanda shot Muffin a disapproving scowl and then focused on Darla.

"Muffin is the cooking champion three years running," she said.

"I am never going to get used to that name," muttered Darla.

"I can't get over this island," said Mariska, massaging the quartz again.

Darla sighed. She was going to wear the stone thin if she didn't quit it.

She eyed the side-by-side sinks in the center of the enormous island. They barely detracted from prep space. Stools sat tucked beneath an overhang on the opposite side.

Darla quickly ran her hand over the quartz.

It *was* impressive.

Her attention drew to items piled at the end of the island—mustard, lunchmeat, cheeses, spreads, pickles, and several different types of bread. Those *had* to have something to do with the contest.

Sandwiches?

What did they have to do with flowers?

Her gaze shifted to the professional-grade ovens lining the opposite wall. The largest in the center had eight burners, and a pair of stacked baking ovens stood sentry to the right side of it. The wall to the left of the large stove supported a tall rack filled with jars of spices.

"I want a kitchen like this," said Mariska.

Darla laughed. "If you turned your whole house into one big kitchen, you might have a shot. I've only seen kitchens like this in magazines."

"Well, enjoy it now because you're about to be *crushed*," said Amanda, slapping her fist into her open palm.

Darla squinted at her.

"Okay, drama queen. Dial it back a notch."

Mariska giggled.

Amanda lifted her chin and sat on a bench at the end of the room. Muffin remained with hands crossed, smiling until she registered her friend had left. She yipped and hurried after Amanda.

Darla scowled. "I don't think Muffin's cooking with all her ingredients."

Mariska agreed. "Yep. That one didn't bake all the way through."

Darla glanced at the audience, her mind whirring.

Something didn't feel right.

"She's going to cheat," she said.

"Who?"

"Gretchen, all three of them—all I know is the fix is in."

"Is this the thing with the flowers again?"

"Yes—" Darla realized Mariska had mentioned the forbidden word again and huffed.

Hopeless.

She had an idea.

"Make whatever she makes," she said.

"What?" Mariska turned to gape. "That doesn't make sense. She'll make what she's best at. That would give her all the power."

"Maybe. But look how small the audience is."

Mariska eyed the people and grunted. "There *were* a lot more people for pickleball."

"That's what I'm saying. I don't think they're here to watch. I think they're *judges*. Gretchen probably told them what Muffin's going to make, and now they know to pick *that food*."

"Why would the judges cheat?"

"Seriously? For the same reason they won't talk to us. They're terrified of Gretchen."

Mariska frowned. "Oh. Right. But—what does any of this have to do with flowers?"

Darla dropped her face into her hand and took a deep breath before looking up again.

"*I don't know.* Just try and make it harder to tell which is which, okay? Whatever it takes, copy Muffin as much as possible."

Mariska sighed. "Fine. But—"

Darla held up a hand for silence as Gretchen entered, wearing a new outfit covered by an expensive brown and pink retro ruffled apron.

Amanda leaped to her feet, and Muffin followed suit.

"Which one of you is going to cook?" Gretchen asked, pointing from Mariska to Darla.

Mariska raised her hand. There'd never been any doubt she'd be the one to cook if only one of them were permitted.

"I will," she said.

"Fine. Muffin will cook for us."

Muffin smiled, and Gretchen motioned to the people sitting at the banquet.

"These are our judges."

Darla shot a look at Mariska.

See?

Mariska nodded.

Darla scanned the judges' faces.

Had they been talking about which entry they were supposed to choose? Like Mariska, she wasn't sure what *flowers* had to do with a cooking contest—at first, she'd assumed maybe it was something about the gardening competition that awaited them later—but she was glad she'd thought to put the word in Mariska's head, just in case.

Even if it then spilled out of her mouth a hundred and fifty times.

Maybe the plates had flowers on them?

Gretchen continued. "Judges, I'm going to ask you to leave the room to protect the integrity of the blind judging."

Darla snorted.

Integrity. I bet.

The small group stood and filed out of the room. One of the ladies waved goodbye as she left. She seemed sweet.

If they were a potential jury, Darla would definitely pick her.

"These are your ingredients," said Gretchen, sweeping a hand over the items piled at the end of the island. "You can use anything you find in the kitchen, though."

"In the refrigerator?" asked Mariska.

"Yes."

Mariska pointed at the racks near the stove.

"Those spices?"

"Yes."

"What about—"

Gretchen's eyes flashed. "*Anything in the kitchen.*"

Mariska nodded. "Got it."

"You have half an hour to make the most incredible sandwich possible. Any flavor, as long as it can be called a *sandwich.*"

"Is a taco a sandwich?" asked Darla.

"What about a hot dog?" asked Mariska. "Or a wrap?"

Gretchen huffed. "*I don't know.* You can take your chances if you want. The judges will decide which is the most delicious, and if they don't think it's a sandwich, that's your problem."

Darla patted Mariska on the back and sat with Gretchen and Amanda on the bench.

"Shouldn't we leave, too?" she asked, eyeing the women beside her. "So *we* don't interfere?"

Gretchen shook her head without looking at her. "We have to keep an eye on *your* girl."

Darla frowned. "And I'll keep an eye on *yours.*"

Gretchen pulled out her phone and brought up the timer app.

"You have half an hour."

She raised her hand.

"On your marks, get set, *go!*"

CHAPTER FOURTEEN

As soon as Gretchen screamed, *"Go!"* Mariska moved to the end of the island to rifle through the ingredients on the counter. Muffin didn't hesitate, either. She grabbed a loaf of round Italian bread, lunch meats, a jar of olives, peppers, capers—

Mariska gasped.

"You're making a muffuletta!" she said.

Muffin nodded.

"Don't *fraternize*," barked Gretchen from the bench.

Muffin glanced at her, looked back at Mariska apologetically, and focused on her sandwich.

"Muffin's muffuletta," muttered Mariska.

Darla had been right. Even Muffin's choice of sandwich was a hint to the judges.

Muffuletta it is.

Mariska chose a loaf of bread similar in texture to the one Muffin picked, though the shape wasn't the classic round used for a muffuletta. It could work since they'd have to slice the sandwich for the four judges anyway. She could round it then.

She cut her oval-shaped crusty bread horizontally, creating two halves—cradles awaiting ingredients.

Mariska stared at the bread, thinking about a way to take her sandwich to the next level. If this was Muffin's signature dish, how could she beat it?

Luck hadn't abandoned her. She knew a muffuletta was a cold-cut sandwich with olive salad because Bob loved olives. She'd made similar meals a million times on *sandwich-for-dinner* days.

Unfortunately, there wasn't much she could improve about lunchmeat—they shared access to the same packages. The only place she could shine was the olive salad.

Mariska threw open cabinet drawers until she found metal bowls and pulled one out. She added red wine vinegar, salt, pepper, and a touch of sugar to create a pickling liquid.

When Muffin seemed most engrossed with her cooking, Mariska added half a teaspoon of jarred Calabrian chilies to her pickling liquid to give it some *zing*.

That'll either win it or bury me.

When she finished, she put the jar of chilies into the cabinet where she'd found the metal bowl so Muffin wouldn't see it in the refrigerator and try the same trick.

No one mentioned there were rules against *hiding* ingredients...

She grabbed a knife and coarsely chopped green and Kalamata olives, cauliflower, carrots, capers, and garlic before dumping them into her pickling liquid.

While that sat, she made a neat pile of meats ready to slap on the bread so she could pickle the relish for as long as possible. She layered thinly sliced capicola, ham, Genoa salami with peppered edges, and fat and pistachio-speckled mortadella. She arranged it on the bread and then lifted the meat stack as a single unit to set it aside on a cutting board.

She eyed Muffin's progress. The competition had made her olive salad from jarred ingredients rather than pickling fresh.

Ha ha!

That had to be an advantage, didn't it?

Mariska added provolone and Swiss cheese to her meat stack.

"What else, what else..." she muttered to herself, scanning the pile of ingredients for inspiration.

"Ten minutes, Mariska," called Darla. "Get her! You can do it!"

Mariska flashed a smile and glanced at the clock on the wall. She didn't want to cut her timing too close—she worried Gretchen might cut the countdown short to catch her off-guard.

She drained the pickling liquid from her olive salad and mixed the whole mess with olive oil before slathering it on both sides of her bread. Shifting the blanket of meat and cheese on top of one side, she pressed the other half of the bread on top.

She ticked off the list of things that made recipes delicious on her fingers.

Tangy, salty, sweet, creamy, spicy, crunchy...

She had all those things.

It felt like her sandwich had *everything*.

She saw Muffin grab a plate. It didn't have flowers on it.

So much for that theory.

To be safe, she grabbed a plate from the same stack and cut her sandwich to mimic the look of Muffin's.

She compared the plates and sandwiches. They looked almost identical. If pressed to describe the differences between them, the only obvious dissimilarity was the shape of the bread, which wasn't something she thought the weasels would have warned the judges about ahead of time.

"Did you *forget anything*, Muffin?" called Gretchen.

Her words sounded very pointed.

Very *purposeful*.

"A garnish, perhaps?" added Amanda.

With one minute left, Muffin gasped.

Darla jumped to her feet and pointed at Muffin, yipping like a panicked terrier.

"This is it! They're doing it!"

Mariska watched Muffin slide a small tray from beneath a carton of eggs sitting in the back of the refrigerator.

She scowled.

What's that?

The tray held something colorful. She strained to get a better look and gasped when she saw a collection of petals.

Flowers!

Her mind stalled. Why would Muffin have flowers in the refrigerator?

She sucked in another breath as the answer lit in her mind's eye like Broadway lights.

Edible flowers.

That was it. That's what Darla heard the judges talking about.

Someone told them to pick the sandwich with the edible

flowers.

Gretchen counted down the clock.

"Five..."

Muffin flipped open the plastic tray holding her flowers, and Mariska lunged forward to grab a handful.

"Four..."

Muffin squeaked and stared at her with wide eyes full of horror.

"Good idea," said Mariska, adding a few to her plate. In the same motion, she slid her plate farther down the island, out of Muffin's reach.

"Three..."

Muffin looked at Gretchen, who motioned to the flowers.

"Just do it," hissed Gretchen.

Muffin looked at the flowers, looked at Mariska's plate, and looked back at Gretchen.

"But—?"

"Two..." said Gretchen through gritted teeth. Her counting slowed as she made time for Muffin to snap out of her confusion.

"Just do it!" echoed Amanda.

Muffin jerked to life. Her hand shot out to snatch flowers, which she threw onto her plate like rolling dice.

"One...*Time!*" shouted Darla, preempting Gretchen's count by a millisecond.

Mariska and Muffin stepped back from their plates.

Red-faced with fury, Gretchen picked up the plates and walked them to the table where the judges once sat. After setting them down, she reached for the flowers on Mariska's plate.

Mariska had been ready for the move. She stepped beside the woman.

"Don't you touch my plate," she growled.

Gretchen flinched, startled to find Mariska hovering over her. She scoffed and returned to the bench to exchange a pointed look with Amanda.

"I'll let the judges know it's time to come back in," said Amanda, taking her cue and moving for the door.

"Oh, no, you don't," said Darla, stepping in front of her to block her path. "First off, let's put these like this."

Darla shifted the sandwich plates so they sat stacked on the table from the bench's point of view instead of sitting side by side.

"What are you doing? What does that matter?" asked an alarmed Gretchen.

Darla smirked. "How do I know you didn't tell them to pick the one on the left or right? I *know* you didn't tell them to pick the *top or bottom*."

Gretchen frowned so deeply it looked like she'd broken her chin to do it.

"You're awfully suspicious," she said.

Darla crossed her arms against her chest. "Uh-huh. No reason I should be, right? *Flower girl*?"

Gretchen's cheek twitched.

"I don't know what you're talking about," she muttered.

Amanda attempted to step around Darla, only to be blocked again. Darla cupped her hands around her mouth and roared.

"Judges, come back in!"

The door swung open, and the judges filed in like they hadn't eaten in a month. Before they could notice the flowers on both plates and look to Gretchen for help, Darla herded Amanda and Gretchen out the opposite door.

"We're leaving," she said, bobbing around to block any attempt at communication between Gretchen, Amanda, and the judges.

Mariska and Muffin followed.

"I don't know who you think you are," protested Amanda as Darla hip-checked her through the door.

Gretchen, Darla, Mariska, Amanda, and Muffin left the kitchen and gathered in the hall.

Mariska heard Gretchen talking in a low voice to Muffin.

"*You better hope you made the sandwich of your life*," she said.

"It's not my fault—" said Muffin.

"*Shhh*."

Gretchen saw Mariska eyeing them and moved away from Muffin, who collapsed against the wall, staring at the floor with empty eyes.

Mariska touched the woman's arm.

"Your sandwich looked wonderful," she said.

Muffin smiled. "Thank you. So did yours."

Gretchen glared at Darla.

"You think we were trying to cheat," she said.

Darla glared back with one squinted eye like an angry pirate. "I *know* you were trying to cheat. I was just trying to make it harder."

Mariska tittered. She felt good about their attempt to make the contest fair. Thanks to Darla, she didn't think Amanda or Gretchen had delivered a secret message to the judges.

They'd have to wait and see.

Five minutes of collective pouting and glaring later, one of the judges called out to them from the kitchen.

"We're ready!"

The group pushed back into the kitchen. One plate sat at the front of the table—the other had been pushed to the side.

"This is the winner," said one of the ladies, motioning to the one in front.

Mariska recognized her less than perfectly circular bread.

"That's *mine*," she said, clasping her hands against her chest.

"Why that one?" asked Gretchen. She looked so angry Mariska thought her hair might catch fire.

Fear lit the judges' eyes as they realized they'd picked the wrong one.

"It had more zing to it?" said the only male judge, a pudgy little man with glasses.

Another judge agreed. "It was a little spicier."

"But not *too* spicy," added a third.

Mariska elbowed Darla.

"It was the Calabrian chilies. I learned that from Bobby Flay."

"Good call," said Darla.

Mariska nodded. "I think he puts those things in his breakfast cereal."

CHAPTER FIFTEEN

Charlotte headed to Mariska and Darla's room, where they'd arranged to meet after work. After checking to be sure no one could see her, she rapped on the door.

"Who is it?" called Mariska's voice from inside.

Charlotte saw the peephole darken.

"It's *me*," she whispered. "Let me in before someone sees me."

Mariska opened the door and motioned her inside, where Declan sat on the edge of one of the two single beds.

"You're late. Something up?" he asked.

She shook her head. "I took a shower downstairs to avoid that nightmare back at the hotel."

He perked. "Hm. That's not a bad idea."

Charlotte set down the bag where she'd stashed her maid uniform and cocked her head at an open miniature bottle of cheap champagne on the table.

"You're drinking champagne?" she asked.

"We earned it. We're *celebrating*," said Mariska, picking up a flute and tapping it against the one Darla held.

"I assume that means good things happened today?"

Darla rolled her eyes. "That's a matter of opinion. This place is crazy. There are *cliques*."

"Cliques? Like high school?" asked Charlotte.

"Worse, I think," said Mariska.

Charlotte sat beside Declan. "You're having trouble making friends?"

Mariska chuckled. "I feel like we had this same conversation in reverse with you when you were in high school."

Charlotte felt her cheeks warm and glanced sidelong at Declan.

"Were you not one of the popular girls growing up?" asked Declan, sticking out his lip to make a boo-boo face at her.

"Shut up," she said.

He looked at the ceiling, musing.

"A girl who grew up with retirees and collected books— *weird*—that sounds like a recipe for coolness—"

"Shut *up*," repeated Charlotte, playfully slapping his leg. She turned to Darla. "Let's get back to *your* problem. Are people here being mean to you?"

"*Very* mean," said Mariska.

Darla shrugged. "Normally, I'd tell these witches to take a long walk off a short skyscraper, but we have to do what they say to get permission to *talk* to people, or we can't get information for the case."

"Get *permission* to talk to people?" echoed Declan.

Darla nodded. "Ridiculous, isn't it? These three women— Gretchen, Amanda, and Muffin—"

Charlotte straightened. "*Muffin?*"

"*Muffin.*"

"Muffin's not as bad as the other two," said Mariska. "I don't think she *wants* to be mean, but she's terrified of the other two. They're *awful*. They won't let us talk to anyone until we pass their tests."

"What kind of tests?" asked Declan.

"Today, we played pickleball and made sandwiches. You try and play pickleball in this heat," said Darla.

"Or make a perfect muffuletta," added Mariska.

Charlotte shook her head. "I don't even know what goes into a muffuletta, but I'll trade you making a sandwich for scrubbing showers all day."

Mariska frowned. "No, thank you. My fingers lock up when I scrub things."

Charlotte held out her red fingers so Declan could see. He took her hand in his and kissed the back of it.

"You two are so sweet," said Mariska, mooning at them.

Charlotte took back her hand and changed the subject before

Mariska could start asking about wedding dates.

"I assume from the champagne you *passed* pickleball and muffulettas?"

Darla nodded. "We did. Tomorrow, there'll be more tests. If we pass those, I guess they'll let us talk to people."

Declan frowned. "I don't understand how they're stopping you from talking to people?"

"By telling people *they* can't talk to *us*," explained Mariska. "We can talk all we want, but there isn't much point if no one ever answers us."

"Why do the others listen to these women?"

"I get the impression they'll make your life a living hell if you cross them," said Darla.

"Maybe they're the key?" suggested Charlotte. "Could it be people are dying while trying to pass these tests?"

"We thought about that. I almost passed out during pickleball, but it's hard to imagine they've *killed* people on *purpose*," said Mariska. "Maybe Gretchen, but not Muffin."

"I think Muffin's lucky if she remembers to put one foot in front of the other," drawled Darla. "But she's right—they aren't killing people with pickleball. There *was* an audience watching us the whole time. If someone passed out, I don't think they'd all look the other way while Gretchen dragged the body off the court."

Charlotte hooked her mouth. She did some of her best thinking like that.

"Crowds aren't great at keeping secrets," she noted.

Declan agreed. "Bernie didn't say the people who died were new, either. I assume only newbies have to pass these tests."

"Pickleball was hot, but it was fun," said Mariska. "And I think the crowd was secretly rooting for us."

"If that's true, maybe that's your in," suggested Charlotte. "Maybe you can find people sick of being bullied. Maybe they'd be more willing to talk than anyone else."

Darla nodded. "We'll try and suss out a weak link."

"Other than Muffin," added Mariska, giggling.

"Of course, if those three are killing people *another* way—not heatstroke-related—and the rest of the residents know, that would also explain why they're so scared of them," mused Charlotte.

"People can be mean without being murderers, but I'll see if I can find out more about the three queen bees," said Declan. "You said Gretchen, Amanda, and *Muffin*? Does Muffin have a real name?"

"I don't know. We'll see if we can find out," said Mariska.

Charlotte looked at Declan. "If you can get me their room numbers, I can poke around."

He nodded, and Charlotte motioned to Darla and Mariska. "We've got the three bullies covered—you two see if you can find someone eager to talk about them and work on passing your *tests*."

"*Check*," said Darla.

"Anything else?"

Declan raised his hand. "I have a *teeny* complication. I caught a lady spying on me, and when I confronted her, she said she recognized us from the paper. That article they did about the new agency."

Charlotte covered her mouth with her hand. "Recognized you and me? Our cover is blown?"

"Yes and no. Alma says not only does she know who we are and why we're here, but she has information for us."

"She's on our side?"

"Yes, but there's a catch. A little blackmail. She wants a date."

Charlotte giggled. "With *you*?"

"No. I told her I was taken."

"How old is this woman?"

"Seventies. It's the new fifties."

"This is getting weirder by the second." Charlotte put a hand on Declan's knee. "Honey, if you have to take one for the team in the name of solving the case, I *totally* understand."

He smirked. "Very funny, but I offered her another option. In exchange for her insider information, I'm setting her up on a date."

It only took Charlotte a second to guess Declan's *solution*.

She closed her eyes.

"Oh no."

"Who?" asked Mariska.

Charlotte sighed.

"*Seamus*. You're going to hook her up with Seamus, aren't you?"

Declan nodded. "Yep."

"Oh no," said Darla.

"But he just made up with Jackie," protested Mariska.

Declan shook his head. "He doesn't have to *really* date this woman. He just needs to take her out tomorrow afternoon."

Charlotte reopened her eyes to look at Declan. "You know this is going to be a disaster, right?"

He shrugged one shoulder. "Granted, Seamus doesn't have a great track record, but with Alma's help, we may know everything we need to know by Saturday morning. Seamus *can* be charming when he has to be."

"Charming in small doses. You should keep the date short. Did he already agree to being pimped?"

Declan chuckled. "No, but I'm not too worried about him turning us down. He never passes up a chance to play the charmer. He loves stuff like this, and we'll have to pay for the date."

Charlotte sighed. "Anything else?"

"No. I can tell you Oksana makes her own tea blends for the residents. She did everything but pour it directly down my throat to get me to try some."

Darla perked. "That's the blonde, right? She offered us some, too."

Charlotte's brow knitted. "Homemade tea blends? Could she be poisoning people with tea?"

Declan shrugged. "Worth looking into. We need to find out if all the victims had their own blends and what was in them."

"I love tea. We didn't get our tea yet," said Mariska with a pout.

"It's coming, I'm sure," said Declan.

"But maybe don't drink it until we clear her. Keep it until we can check it," added Charlotte.

Mariska sighed.

Declan stood. "I talked to Ed's family. They said he seemed healthy—if anything, *more* perky than usual—in the weeks before he died."

"*More* perky? That could maybe imply something. Drugs? We should look into that angle, too," suggested Charlotte.

Declan nodded. "Other than that, I can only report that

Yasmine is terrifying."

Charlotte scoffed. "That I *know*. She's a clean freak—particular about *everything*—to the point I think she's obsessive-compulsive."

"I'd think that's a good trait in a housekeeper," said Darla.

"I guess. Not if you work for her. Speaking of her—I noticed Ed's room was already *perfect* first thing this morning—cleaned like only Yasmine could do it. I'd recognize her vacuum lines anywhere."

"Like she cleaned right after he died?" Declan scowled. "That does seem weird. Do you think she was trying to hide something?"

Charlotte shrugged. "That's what I'm wondering. Other than that, I saw Luna in the locker room. She was acting squirrelly about her locker, and..."

She drifted off.

"What?" prompted Declan.

She looked at Darla and Mariska.

"Do you two have a clown-themed keepsake box in here?"

"A *clown*?" asked Darla.

Charlotte twisted to scan the room. "I've seen the same clown box in a few rooms. This one."

She pulled out her phone and called up a photo of the box for the ladies to inspect.

"Recognize it?"

They shook their heads, and she fished in her pocket until she found a piece of paper, which she handed to Declan.

"I made a list of the rooms where I saw them. Maybe you can check if they have anything in common?"

Declan glanced at the list. "I'll see what I can find. We've got a lot of leads to run down. I guess that's good."

"Do you want us to ask about clowns?" asked Mariska.

"Sure, if you can find someone who'll talk to you." She licked her lips and noticed Declan was squinting at her.

"What?" she asked.

"You're not telling us something. I can see it on your face."

She bit her lip. "Only because I'm afraid you'll think I'm nuts."

"That train left the station a long time ago," said Darla.

Charlotte laughed. "Fine. I think I saw a clown. A *real* clown. Roaming the halls."

Declan laughed, and Darla wrapped her arms around herself.

"Ugh. You just gave me the shivers. Where did you see it? Did you talk to it?"

Charlotte shook her head. "I saw it out of the corner of my eye."

Darla grimaced. "The old *corner of the eye* clown. Not good."

"You have clowns on the brain because you don't like them and saw those boxes. It was probably some old biddy in crazy pajamas," said Mariska.

Charlotte shrugged. "Maybe. I went after it, but it got into the elevator before I could catch up."

She didn't mention how *slowly* she'd chased the clown.

Darla waved her hands like she was declaring a sliding runner safe on home plate. "Okay, cut it out with the clown talk. We have to sleep here tonight."

Charlotte tittered. "Sorry. Keep an eye out for it, though."

Darla's eyes widened.

"Oh, don't worry. If I see a clown, you'll hear about it."

Mariska shook her head. "You two are ridiculous. Clowns are supposed to make you *happy*."

"Except when they live in sewer drains, or poltergeist houses, or have the last name Gacy," noted Declan.

Charlotte pointed at him. "See? Clowns are the *worst,* and now our worst-case scenario is that this place is chock-full of killer clowns."

Declan laughed. "On the other hand, that *would* explain a lot."

CHAPTER SIXTEEN

Darla awoke to find the image of Mariska's face floating in the corner of the room, glowing by the light of her tablet.

She squinted at the clock.

Three a.m.

"What the heck are you doing awake?" she asked.

Mariska looked up. "I'm brushing up on gardening tips and tricks. We might need them for today."

"You had to do that at three o'clock in the morning?"

Mariska shrugged. "I always wake up around two."

Darla groaned. "How does Bob get any sleep?"

"I usually move into the living room, but there's nowhere to go here."

Darla sat up and propped her pillow to support her back. "I'll need to remember this in case we *really* end up roommates."

"Oh, shush. You *snore*."

"I do not. *You* snore."

Mariska giggled. "I know."

Darla swung her legs out of bed. "I was thinking—we should work on a backup plan in case we fail one of these tests."

Mariska lowered her tablet. "Funny you should say that. I was thinking the same thing. They're cheating. No matter how hard we try, we'll probably lose in the end."

"*Right*. Maybe we can turn the tables on them."

"How?"

"Maybe by getting the people they're ruling over to turn on them. Stage a coup."

Mariska pouted. "How can we do anything when no one will

even talk to us?"

Darla chuckled. "I know this has been especially hard on you. You'll talk to walls if there aren't people handy. Having these people here and not being able to talk to them—"

She gasped.

"What's wrong?" asked Mariska.

Darla's eyes widened. "*Donuts*."

"Donuts?"

"That's how we'll get people to talk to us. We'll buy them donuts."

Mariska blinked at her and lowered her tablet. "I think you just want donuts."

"No—well, *yes*, but I think this'll work. The lady next door. What's her name?"

"Gail?"

"When we were at breakfast yesterday, I overheard her begging the server for donuts. The lady reminded her they only have donuts at breakfast on the weekends."

Mariska snorted. "If they *always* had free donuts, everyone would be a thousand pounds. I know they'd have to roll *me* out of here in a wheelbarrow."

"Me too, but my point is she wants *donuts every day*, so we'll get her donuts."

"You think we can get her to talk that way?"

"Absolutely. That lady *wants* to talk. Remember how she looked at us the first day? She looked like she would *explode* if she couldn't talk to us. Donuts will push her over the edge. I know it."

Mariska nodded. "I saw that. She did look like she wanted to say something."

Darla stood. "I'm going to call Charlotte and tell her to bring us donuts on her way in."

Mariska looked at her watch. "It's not even four yet."

"Justice never sleeps."

"I'm not sure bribing people with donuts is *justice*," mumbled Mariska.

Darla found her phone and called Charlotte. The girl answered, sounding sleepy.

"You up?" asked Darla.

"This is the weirdest booty call ever," mumbled Charlotte.

"I need you to get us donuts."

"Now? It's three in the morning."

"It's almost four. I wouldn't call you at *three*."

"Mm. You're right. That would be *crazy*."

Darla dodged the sarcasm. "We need donuts. It's for work, not for us. A box of them. Good ones with chocolate icing and whatnot—"

"But get a mix. People like different things," interjected Mariska.

"Is that Mariska?' asked Charlotte. "She's up, too?"

"She's *why* I'm up. Make it two dozen. A mix." Darla turned to look at Mariska. "Do you think that's enough?"

"Get three dozen to be safe," said Mariska.

Darla eyed her. She knew the third dozen was for them.

Not a terrible idea.

"Get *three* dozen," she told Charlotte.

"Three dozen mixed donuts. Got it."

"And come in early. We need them before everyone goes down to breakfast."

"Uh-huh. That it? A collection of exotic fruits, maybe? A hundred M&Ms with the brown ones picked out? A Whitman's sampler with the jellies removed?"

"Just the donuts."

"Great. Good night."

"Good morning."

Charlotte hung up.

"Was she asleep?" asked Mariska.

"Maybe," admitted Darla with a yawn. "But she said she'd bring donuts early. I'm going to try and get back to sleep for a little bit."

"Must be nice," mumbled Mariska.

Darla had finished dressing when she heard a knock on the door. She answered to find a sleepy-eyed Charlotte standing there in her maid uniform.

"Here are your donuts," said Charlotte, thrusting a large box into her arms. "It's bad enough I have to clean toilets all day. Now, I'm your go-fer."

Darla lifted the lid to admire the sweets.

"They look amazing," said Mariska, peering over her shoulder.

"Don't drool all over them, and don't eat them all," said Darla as Mariska snatched the box and hustled them away.

"Why did you need three dozen donuts? Aren't they feeding you?" asked Charlotte.

Darla nodded her head toward the neighbor's room. "We need them for bribes. They only have donuts on the weekends at the buffet, and our neighbor wants them more often."

Charlotte glanced at the neighbor's door. "How many people are living there?"

"Just one woman."

"And you needed *three dozen* donuts?"

Darla shrugged. "If she doesn't bite, maybe someone else will. Pun intended."

"We need *options*," said Mariska, though Darla could barely understand her through the donut in her mouth.

"I thought maybe you were starting a side hustle," said Charlotte.

"No. Though that isn't a bad idea." Darla glanced over her shoulder. "I better get in there before she eats them all."

Charlotte nodded. "Move fast. I'm off to work. *Whee*."

Charlotte left, and Darla turned to find Mariska turned toward the corner of the room like a punished child.

"What are you doing?" she asked.

Mariska swallowed hard as she turned.

"Hm?"

A chunk of chocolate icing perched in the corner of her mouth.

Darla frowned. "How many did you eat?"

"One. But that one has my name on it."

She pointed, and Darla glanced at the half-empty box.

"There's a lot more than *one* donut missing."

"Hm? Oh, they're here. I got them ready." Mariska reached

into the kitchen and pulled out a plate with donuts stacked high. "I thought this would be prettier than shoving a box at her."

"And this way, we get to keep the box."

Mariska sniffed. "I have no idea what you're talking about."

Maybe it was the smell of the donuts, but Darla felt *pumped*. She clapped her hands and rubbed them together like she was trying to start a fire. They'd been floundering since arriving, and this felt like progress.

"Breakfast starts at seven-thirty, so let's get to Gail." Darla opened the door and held it open for Mariska to pass through, donut plate in hand. She needed both hands to carry the platter, which kept her from scarfing another donut on the way.

They knocked on their neighbor's door, and a few seconds later, the bird-boned woman answered, wearing a cheerful multicolor striped scoop neck tee shirt and blue shorts. Her short hair curled around her ears, from which enormous palm-tree-shaped earrings hung from sagging lobes.

Gail smiled as she opened the door and then recoiled before glancing down the hall, much as she had the day they arrived.

"What are you doing here?" she whispered.

Darla smiled. Maybe Gail didn't realize it, but she was already talking to them.

"Hello, we're your new neighbors," said Mariska, holding the plate not far from Gail's nose. "We brought you donuts to say *hi*."

The woman's eyes saucered.

"Oh my. They're *beautiful*." She leaned into the hall again, searching for witnesses. Mariska and Darla backed up to keep from getting headbutted.

Seeing no spies, Gail motioned for the ladies to enter.

"Come inside."

They followed her into her room, the layout of which mirrored their own. One queen bed sat in place of their twin singles. An empty daisy-dotted duvet cover lay on top.

Stuffing a duvet cover in Florida was akin to wearing tinfoil on your head to keep aliens from reading your thoughts.

Mariska set the donut plate on a small cherry dining table.

"I'm Mariska and this is Darla."

"I'm Gail, but everybody calls me Bunny," said the woman.

Her eyes never left the donuts.

Darla recognized her as one of the women who'd watched the tennis match. She'd been wearing large plastic earrings in the shape of crossed rackets.

"I love your earrings," said Darla, pleased she'd thought to say it. Mariska was the small-talk genius. If Mariska met a pile of dog droppings, she'd think to compliment their color and sheen. With a talker like her as her sidekick, Darla feared her own small-talk skills had atrophied.

Bunny reached up to feel her earrings as if she wasn't sure which pair hung there. "Oh, thank you. Can I get you tea or coffee?"

"Whatever's easier," said Mariska.

The woman toddled to her kitchen and retrieved three tea cups. She opened a small decorative tin, clipped tea from it with three snap-ball tea strainers, and dropped them into each cup before filling them with instant hot water. She moved so slowly that Darla felt herself nodding off.

"Milk? Sugar? Honey?" asked Bunny.

"A splash of milk," said Mariska.

Darla looked at her with horror. It had taken Bunny ten minutes to get the tea. The last thing they needed was to give the woman more work—they'd miss breakfast altogether.

Bunny added a splash of milk to all three cups and reached for the first with shaking hands.

"Let me get that," said Darla, leaping to her feet. If Bunny went to the hospital with third-degree tea burns, they'd *never* get any information from her.

Bunny sat at the table with them and ogled at the donuts.

"Oh no. I forgot the plates—"

She started to rise, and Darla put a hand on her shoulder.

"I've got them." She opened two cabinet doors before finding the plates and brought them to the table.

"I like the jelly ones," said Bunny.

Mariska plucked a sugar-covered jelly-filled donut from the pile and placed it on her plate.

"How long have you been at Elderbrook?" asked Mariska.

"Two years," said Bunny, chewing in slow, cow-cud fashion. Darla heard the click of her dentures.

"Do you like it here?"

Click. Click. Click.

"I *do*," she said, pausing. When she finished, she returned to chewing her first bite.

Click. Click. Click.

Darla looked at Mariska. She wanted to ask if she'd given Bunny a *trick* donut. One made of chewing gum.

A silence fell—at least until Bunny's next bite.

Click. Click. Click.

Darla wracked her brain for something small-talky to say. Coming up empty, she got to business.

"If you don't mind me asking, did you have to pass the tests those three women are making us take?"

Bunny frowned. "No. I was too old, so they grandfathered me in. Or I should say *grandmothered* me in."

She tittered and then sobered to peer into Darla's eyes.

"You can't tell them I talked to you."

"Oh no, we won't," said Mariska. "But—why is everyone so scared of them?"

Bunny took another bite and rolled her eyes.

"Oh, if you get on their bad side, they're horrible."

"Horrible, how?" asked Darla.

Click. Click. Click.

Bunny swallowed.

"Well, Ginny made them mad, and they started a rumor she was fooling around with her physical therapy nurse. One woman they accused of having her children taken away from her. She moved out."

"That's *terrible*," said Mariska.

"Everyone is afraid they'll start rumors? That's all?" asked Darla.

Bunny shrugged. "Sometimes, they have real evidence. Sometimes, they'll just Oscar-size someone."

"Oscar-size?"

"You know—tell everyone they aren't allowed to talk to someone anymore."

"Oh, *ostracize*," said Mariska.

Bunny looked at her. "That's what I said."

Mariska nodded. "Mm-hm. I just didn't hear you."

Bunny took a sip of her tea. "Sometimes, they'll ruin your things. They poisoned Kimmy's garden because she voted against them for one thing or another. All the plants died."

"*Bullies*," muttered Darla.

"Why don't you all revolt?" asked Mariska.

Bunny shrugged. "It's hard to get everyone to work as a group. Amanda and Gretchen have money. They bribe people. Some around here like getting dirty gifts. Not me."

Bunny finished the last large bite of her donut like an anaconda unhinging its jaw to finish off a wild pig.

"Another donut?" asked Mariska.

"I do like the Boston creams," said Bunny.

Mariska moved a Boston cream to the woman's plate and sipped her tea.

"This tea is *really* good," said Mariska.

Darla nodded. "It is, isn't it?"

"That's Bunny Blend," said Bunny, her chest puffing.

"Bunny blend? You made it?"

She shook her head and sent her palm frond earrings swinging. "No, Oksana makes it for me. She makes tea for everyone."

Darla coughed and looked at Mariska with wide eyes.

Mariska aped her expression as she set down her teacup with a sharp clatter. She looked at Darla.

"Is that the—uh, did Charlotte tell us—?"

Darla nodded.

Mariska eyed her teacup as if it had bared its teeth at her.

"We should probably go. We just wanted to say hi," said Darla, standing.

"You didn't finish your tea. Are you sure?" asked Bunny as she pulled two more donuts off the communal plate onto her own.

"We have to get ready for today's competitions," said Mariska, moving her cup to the kitchen sink.

"Oh, that nonsense," muttered Bunny as she slid a third donut to her plate.

"We'll leave the platter here and get it another time," said Darla.

Bunny—in the process of sliding a fourth donut to her plate—

lit up like a disco ball.

"They're *all* for me?"

"Of course. Don't get up. We'll let ourselves out." Darla moved to the door.

"*Thank you*," called Bunny as they left.

Darla closed the door behind them.

"I drank the tea," hissed Mariska as they walked the few steps back to their room.

"So did I."

"Are we going to die?"

"I don't know."

Mariska put her hand on her throat. "What are we going to do? I can't make myself throw up. I'm not good at it. I have a very strong stomach."

Darla frowned. "Me neither. We didn't have much. I'm sure we're fine, even if something is wrong with it."

"Look what I have." Mariska opened her hand to show Darla a wad of paper towels. She opened it, and Darla recognized tea leaves inside.

"You stole her tea?"

Mariska nodded. "I took the tea that was in my clip. Maybe Charlotte can have it tested."

Darla was impressed. "I didn't even see you palm that. Very smooth. Good idea. You're like a real detective."

Mariska beamed. "Thank you."

CHAPTER SEVENTEEN

Charlotte's phone rang as she put the final cleaning touches on her first room of the new day.

It was Declan.

"Hello, Mr. Manager," she answered.

"Hello, uh, room cleaner person. I have the room numbers of the three witches. Everyone's, actually. I'm forwarding you a photo of the room chart for the whole place."

"Perfect."

Her phone dinged, and she saw she'd received the photo.

"Got it. Thank you. Anything new?"

"Not yet. I'm meeting with Seamus in a little bit. That should be fun. She wants to go somewhere at eleven."

"Oh. Well, good luck. If anyone can keep your uncle in line, it's you. You're like a lion tamer."

"Ha. *Right.* A lion tamer wearing a meat suit."

Charlotte finished her call and braced herself for the rest of the day. Her next room was poor Dead Ed's—which she was *allowed* to clean today, which was good. She wanted to investigate again, anyway, and this time, she wouldn't have to worry about being caught, dressed down, and felt up.

She knew from Declan that Ed's family had stopped by. Maybe with the personal items cleared out, things left behind would tell a story.

She let herself inside to find Ed's family had removed almost everything personal—photos, artwork, books, clothing—all gone as expected. They didn't take the furniture.

Were they sending a truck for it? Should she bother cleaning it?

Maybe she should ask Yasmine...

Ugh.

Talking to Yasmine on *purpose* sounded like a suicide mission.

The sheets were already stripped, and there were no bathroom or kitchen messes to clean, so she decided to do the bare minimum and vacuum the footprints from the carpet. Yasmine would see she *tried* to clean. Good enough.

Stepping into the hall, she dragged her vacuum inside and propped the door open so no one would accuse her of stealing.

As she plugged the vacuum in, her attention drifted to the kitchen, where a plastic container of uncooked pasta remained on the counter. The family hadn't taken the food.

Hm...

Charlotte opened the cabinet doors until she found a decorative tin next to a bag of ground coffee. Turning it over, she saw someone had written *Ed Blend* on the bottom in permanent marker.

Oksana's tea.

It had to be.

She opened it to find a tea clip inside, half buried in tea leaves.

The man who'd dropped over dead *did* have one of Oksana's blends. She wasn't sure where to get the tea tested for poison, but she'd figure it out.

She took the tin into the hall, planning to stash it in her cleaning trolley. Before she could hide it, she noticed Oksana staring at her from outside one of the other rooms. Apple sat at her feet, staring, too.

"Oh, *hi*," she said.

Oksana's gaze dropped to the tin in her hands.

Charlotte glanced down.

Good grief, I'm stealing again.

"That is Ed's Blend. They didn't take it when they came for his things?" asked Oksana.

Charlotte shook her head. "No. It looks like they left all the furniture and food."

She waited. On the upside, it wasn't *Yasmine* who'd caught her stealing tea, but that didn't mean Oksana wouldn't turn her in. She wasn't sure how she'd keep her fake job if everyone thought she was a petty thief.

To her surprise, Oksana's expression softened.

"You like tea?" she asked.

Charlotte nodded. "It seemed a shame for it to go to waste."

Oksana's smile grew. "You wanted to try my tea so much you saved his. That is very sweet."

Charlotte's shoulders relaxed. Getting caught stealing was going much better this time.

"Yep—I heard about you and your tea. I was going to ask, do you think it is okay to take it? They'll probably only throw it out, right?"

Oksana nodded. "You take it. This is perfect. I was going to interview you today."

"Interview me?"

"Yes, to find out what tea I should make you. But now you can try his, and you can tell me how you would like it changed, yes?"

Charlotte waved her away. "Oh, you don't have to make me tea."

"It would be an honor. This is what I love."

"Okay. Thank you. I'll try his tea and let you know?"

"Wonderful."

Flashing a final smile, Oksana disappeared into the room she'd been cleaning. Apple followed.

Charlotte leaned against the door jamb.

Whew.

She tucked the tin deep into her cart where Yasmine wouldn't find it. *Probably.* She wouldn't be surprised if Yasmine suddenly marched down the hall with a bullhorn, declaring a surprise cart search.

She glanced at the doorway through which Oksana had disappeared. Apple was busy pulling off the sheets, which means they'd just started that room.

Hm.

Ed's room could wait. She had four rooms she wanted to search today, and Oksana had already caught her sneaking evidence out of the first. Now would be the safest time to search other rooms.

Charlotte pushed her cart toward Gretchen's room but left it parked between doors to confuse anyone looking for her. Maybe if Yasmine came to check on her and needed to knock on doors, it would give her an extra few seconds to look innocent.

She punched in her master code, slipped into Gretchen's room, and shut it behind her.

Her jaw slipped open.

What the...

Gretchen's room looked like something out of a French brothel. She slept in a king-sized gold four-poster bed with a toile yellow fabric canopy and matching bedspread.

Marie Antoinette would have been embarrassed to sleep in a bed that gaudy.

A plush velvet chaise lounge sat near the window, flanked by heavy felt curtains that would have made a lovely dress for Scarlett O'Hara if she lived in the Antarctic.

The whole room felt *heavy*. Charlotte ran her hands over the striped velvet wallpaper. The place looked shipped from Versaille.

She couldn't imagine a less *Florida* room.

"This place is as dark as her heart," she muttered, flicking on a light and opening a few drawers to poke around.

The woman had two entire drawers dedicated to scarves. Charlotte stopped to peer at a collection of photos hanging on the wall and realized *every one* had Gretchen in the forefront. One or two included other people, but most featured *only* her. Gretchen, in an open-mouth laugh, in a fur coat, with her chin held high, inexplicably dressed like a roaring twenties flapper—always peering down her nose at the camera.

Charlotte scowled.

Who hangs pictures of *themselves*?

She checked the kitchen and found no tea tins, then spotted a strangely large box of envelopes. Nothing else she found rifling through the cabinets explained why Gretchen needed so many envelopes. She didn't seem like the kind of gal with a hundred pen pals.

In the end, she slipped one into the pocket of her apron. Gretchen wouldn't miss *one*.

A bedstand sat jammed between the giant bed and the wall. In it, she found a pair of reading glasses, tissues, a pen, and a full, unmarked bottle of liquid with a dropper cap. She sniffed the contents and found it herbaceous.

Gretchen *would* notice if she took the bottle.

She had an epiphany and plucked a pen from the desk. She removed the cap and placed a drop of the liquid inside before resealing it.

Ta da.

Gretchen wouldn't notice a few drops missing or the pen, more than likely.

Charlotte moved to a fold-down desk and smiled. She recognized it. Several Pineapple Port residents had identical desks, and she knew the center cubby had a hidden compartment.

She pulled out a handful of papers and removed the false bottom to find a notebook tucked inside.

Paydirt.

She flipped through the book pages, pausing several times to scan the pen scrawl.

Her eyes saucered.

Holy...

Each section had a name in large, all-caps print at the top and a dollar amount ranging from five to fifty dollars. Charlotte recognized a few of the residents' names. Under each name, Gretchen had listed gossipy dirt ranging from serious to ridiculous.

One woman had slept overnight in the room of one of the male residents. Another had a drinking problem. One had an arrest record for petty theft. Another confessed to hitting her daughter. One lost control of her bowels at lunch. Beneath many rumors, Gretchen brainstormed cruel nicknames to christen her victims, circling the ones she liked best.

On a second page following each name, Gretchen listed ways that person could be annoyed, blackmailed, or otherwise tortured. She'd moved the garden plants of a woman, who preferred her flowers organized by color. She'd swapped food on people's plates and sabotaged exercise equipment.

The woman was a *menace.*

As Charlotte read on, she wondered if Gretchen wasn't a full-blown *psychopath.* She knew bored retirees needed hobbies, but torturing housemates? Clearly, she was obsessed with every shadowy detail she could wring from the place. The notes on how she could make her fellow residents miserable went on and on.

She'd kept less detailed notes in high school biology.

Charlotte used her phone to take photos of the book's most recent thirty pages before returning it to its hiding spot. She noticed little Greek column designs on either side of the cubby and knew those portions slid out for more hiding spots.

She found both column boxes stuffed with envelopes. The first she opened contained a twenty-dollar bill and a piece of paper with a date and name written on it. The second held a similar handmade coupon and ten dollars.

Charlotte removed the blackmail book again and compared the name to the amount listed in that person's section. The numbers matched.

She glanced back to where she'd found the box of envelopes.

That solved that mystery. Gretchen provided her blackmail victims with envelopes for payment.

What a sweetheart.

Charlotte put back everything she'd found and left the room, freezing when she spotted Apple standing in the middle of the hall with a sock in her mouth.

She waved to the dog, and the two stared at each other for a beat. Then, Apple spat out the sock and shuffled back into the room with Oksana.

Charlotte waited a moment to be sure Oksana wasn't coming. She couldn't stop thinking about Gretchen's blackmail enterprise. The woman was more of a monster than she'd thought. She got a *thrill* from making people unhappy. Charlotte guessed it made her feel powerful or that she had such an inferiority complex she needed to tear people down to feel better about herself.

It would be *sad* if it wasn't so *awful*.

She made a mental note to research more background information on Gretchen. There might be a thin line between being miserable and being *murderous*.

Charlotte glanced down the hall for a final Oksana check and jogged to the next door down—Amanda's room. She guessed Amanda and Gretchen had become inseparable due to proximity and a shared joy in the torment of others.

She punched in her code and stepped inside, happy to find the room unremarkable. Amanda's home base resembled a generic photo taken for an Elderbrook brochure. The more Charlotte looked at it, the more she thought it *was* the photo for the brochure she'd seen downstairs.

She began her search in the kitchen and again found no tea tin. If Oksana made tea for everyone, it seemed she wasn't a fan of the Terrible Trio.

She found a notepad containing grocery lists, reminders, and doodles on a drop-leaf table serving as a makeshift office space. No blackmail notes.

She found trash bags of clothing and empty hangers in the main bedroom closet. No suitcases were packed, so Charlotte chalked up the bags as spring cleaning.

Amanda's room held no secrets she could find.

She left and moved to Muffin's room, a few doors down. This room, too, seemed normal—nothing like Gretchen's ode to Cruella de Vil. She found a magazine with a label revealing the woman's real name—*Margaret Irving.*

She checked the usual hiding spots and was about to leave when she noticed a photo on the wall of Muffin and Dana, Declan's boss, their arms around each other, grinning at the camera.

Hm.

Maybe her close relationship with the manager had propelled her to become Gretchen's flunky. She could see Gretchen finding her useful.

Charlotte used her phone to take a snapshot of the photo and walked into an unoccupied hall. As soon as she shut the door behind her, Oksana appeared at her elbow.

She jumped.

"You scared me," she said.

"You're already in Muffin's room? But that is on my side of the hall."

Charlotte hemmed. "Hm? Oh, I was checking to see how bad things were. I thought I'd tackle the worst rooms first."

Oksana nodded as if she needed a moment to absorb the idea. "That is an interesting plan. It *is* annoying to be in your last room for the day only to find it very bad."

She didn't seem satisfied, and Charlotte realized what she'd said didn't explain why she was cleaning rooms on the wrong side of the hall.

"Oh, and I was going to clean one for you as a surprise. Payback for the future tea," she added.

This new information seemed to release Oksana from her suspicions, and she grinned.

"You do not have to do that. I love making the tea. I told you."

Charlotte nodded, pleased her impromptu cover story worked. Oksana patted her arm.

"You do your own rooms only," she said.

Charlotte nodded. "Will do."

She watched Oksana return to work and huffed a sigh.

Whew.

She returned to her next room. The name on the door said Alma.

Alma.

That was the name of Declan's lurker.

Perfect.

It wouldn't hurt to sniff around Alma's room.

She entered to find the place neat to the point of boring. The decorating wasn't modern but had a comfortable feel—more mid-century than yard sale chic. An antique typewriter sat on a small desk in front of the window, and on the wall above it were several framed articles and a black and white photo of a tall woman holding a notepad and pen as if she were interviewing the man beside her at the scene of some fracas.

Charlotte assumed the intrepid female reporter to be Alma herself.

She found another clipped news article on the kitchen table—lying there as if it had been waiting for her. This recent piece featured a photo of Declan and herself smiling in front of their new offices.

Beneath the article, she found a sticky note with two words and a smiley face.

Hello, Charlotte. ☐

Charlotte snorted a laugh.

What a cheeky monkey Alma was.

CHAPTER EIGHTEEN

Darla and Mariska stepped out of the elevator into the lobby on their way to the garden competition.

"I'm going to ruin these clothes," said Mariska. "The clothes I brought for being sloppy I already used up at tennis."

Darla nodded. "I didn't bring enough sporty clothes either. I didn't know we'd be competing for our lives."

They passed the small Elderbook gift shop, *Manor Mementos,* in the lobby, and Mariska stopped to peer inside. This time, the shop was open.

Mariska wandered inside.

"Where are you going?" asked Darla.

"I want to look around."

With a huff, Darla followed her and scanned the place. No one manned the register. On the counter, she noticed a display of natural supplements promising extra energy and held up a bottle for Mariska to see.

"We should get some of this stuff to give us pep for the gardening."

Mariska rolled her eyes. "Jackie took some of that stuff once and said it made her heart race."

Darla studied the label. It had a blue border, and plants adorned the center, winding and growing around the words *Miracle Elixir— All Natural.*"

"It says it's *all natural,*" she reported.

Mariska flipped through a rack of tee shirts. "So's cocaine. Doesn't mean I want to take it."

Darla's nose wrinkled. "Is it?"

"It's made out of poppies or coffee or cocoa beans or something. I saw all about how they make it in one of those awful movies Bob watches."

Darla shrugged. "Hm. You learn something new every day."

The label came loose and slipped off the bottle, causing Darla to bobble it just as Dana appeared.

"Hello there—I didn't hear you come in. Did you want something?" She noticed Darla fumbling to put the bottle down. "Those are great. All natural and gives you a real *spark*."

Darla settled the bottle back in its display spot.

"No, I don't think—"

Dana put her hand to the side of her mouth as if she were sharing a secret. "They're on clearance. I can actually offer you an additional twenty percent off—"

Darla considered this. She hated to turn down a super sale.

"No, thank you," she said after a moment. "Even if it is all-natural, you never know about drug interactions and whatnot."

The woman blinked at her.

"Drug interactions?"

Darla nodded. "Yep, even natural things can—"

"*Darla*," barked Mariska, holding up a large tee shirt with the Elderbrook Manor logo on the back. "We should get these."

Darla held up a finger, asking Dana to hold.

"Do they have our size?"

"I don't know, but we should get a huge one to wear over our clothes to keep them clean."

"Ooh, that's a good idea—"

"They're thirty dollars." Mariska grimaced and rehung the tee. "I guess I don't mind getting my clothes a little dirty."

Darla nodded. "Me neither. We should hurry." She turned to Dana. "I'm sorry. We have to be somewhere stupid."

Dana was staring at the bottle in her hand and looked up to shrug and smile. "No problem. Come back any time."

She took the collection of bottles and moved them behind the counter while Darla watched.

"You had a good point," she said. "Better safe than sorry."

Darla nodded. "Yep. I'm going to go get my butt kicked *au*

naturel now."

Mariska gave the tee shirts one last look of longing, and the pair headed outside.

"Thirty dollars for a tee shirt?" whispered Darla as they headed for the garden.

"Not on my watch," agreed Mariska.

A small group of chattering people had gathered at the edge of the community garden, much like they had for the tennis competition. One woman held a large umbrella she used to cast a shadow big enough for her friends to gather beneath.

At the end of the garden, a folding table held two bags of potting soil and two empty planters. On the opposite side stood four people with pads of paper and pens in their hands.

"They must be the judges," said Darla.

Mariska agreed with her deduction.

The conversations quieted as gazes turned toward the manor to watch Gretchen, Amanda, and Muffin arrive. Amanda wore pink gloves and a gardening apron covered with tiny potted flowers. Over her shoulder, she carried a gardening bag stuffed with tools.

"I guess we know who pulled the short straw for this competition," said Darla.

"Looks like it's only one of them again. I guess I should do this one, too?" asked Mariska.

Darla nodded. "You're the better gardener. Shoot. I'm starting to realize how useless I am."

"Maybe they'll have a lock-picking contest."

Darla perked. "I would *totally* win that." She eyed Amanda. "Were we supposed to show up with tools and gloves?"

"I don't know. Where would we have gotten them?"

"If they were at the store, we could probably get them for three hundred dollars," drawled Darla.

Mariska laughed. "Maybe they'll give us some?"

Darla grunted. "Sure. Because they're such generous, wonderful people."

Gretchen picked a spot where she'd be visible to everyone and raised her hands.

"Thank you all for joining us on day two of The Gauntlet," she said with a flourish.

Darla and Mariska looked at each other. That was the first time they'd heard they were competing in a *gauntlet*.

A smattering of light applause rippled through the crowd.

"Today's competition will be Marla—"

"*Darla*," corrected Darla.

Gretchen rolled her eyes. "Ugh. That's even worse."

Darla stepped forward, but Mariska grabbed her shoulder and tugged her back.

"*Temper*," warned Mariska. "Remember, this isn't for us."

Darla growled.

Gretchen cleared her throat. "As I said, this competition will be *Marla* versus ten-time garden competition champion—*Amanda*."

Again, the crowd sprinkled them with unenthusiastic applause.

"I'm going to *kill* her," grumbled Darla. Her brow knitted. She'd been so angry about Gretchen's attitude she hadn't realized what the monster had said.

She straightened and pointed to Mariska.

"It isn't me, it's *her*. She's the gardener."

Gretchen shook her head. "I'm sorry. It has to be you this time because she made the sandwich. You have to alternate."

"Who says?"

Gretchen leaned forward and smiled.

"I say."

Darla held Gretchen's unwavering gaze and then turned to Mariska.

"I can take her," she said.

Mariska nodded. "Sure you can. It's just plants and dirt."

"No, I mean, *I can take her*. Please let me kill her."

Mariska frowned. *"No."*

"Come on. You never let me have any fun."

"Sorry. Someone has to watch over you. For some reason, it's my lot in life."

Darla chuckled. "I don't know. Frank ruins a lot of my fun, too. You two are neck and neck." She turned to eye the garden. "What am I going to do? I don't know anything about gardening."

"Just do your best. I'll help if I can. I'll use hand signals or something."

Gretchen continued with her announcements.

"The competition will be *creative potting*. On this table, we've provided pots and soil. Whoever creates the best-potted plant design wins."

Darla stared at the squat, wide-rimmed planters on the table. Next to each sat a bag of soil. No tools. No plants.

"Do I get tools?" she asked.

"Did you bring any?" asked Gretchen.

"*No.*"

Gretchen crossed her arms against her chest with a smug smile. "Then I guess not."

Darla glowered. "Was I supposed to bring my plants, too?"

Gretchen waved a hand toward the large community garden. "You can use any plant in the garden."

"Terrific." She looked at Mariska. "I hate dirt."

"You'll be fine. Find a theme—"

"No conferring with your partners," snapped Gretchen.

Mariska glared at her.

"Maybe *I'll* kill her," she mumbled.

If Gretchen heard, she didn't show it. She motioned to the table.

"Take your place. You have half an hour on my mark."

Amanda set her bag beside one of the pots, and Darla stood behind the other station.

"Oh, there's one rule," added Gretchen. "No *copying*. The copier will be disqualified."

"What keeps *you* from cheating?" asked Darla.

"Um, the fact that we don't *cheat*," sneered Amanda.

"Voting is anonymous," added Gretchen.

Darla exchanged a look of dismay with Mariska. Gretchen had learned from her mistake in the kitchen. They'd be making their creations in front of everyone, and the judges would be too frightened *not* to vote for Amanda, anonymous voting or not.

Gretchen opened her parasol. Muffin leaned toward her to steal some shade, and Gretchen tilted the umbrella away to leave her wanting.

Muffin pouted.

Gretchen raised her hand. "On your marks, get set, *go!*"

She karate-chopped the air, and Amanda bolted down the

garden's center aisle. Neat, grid-like paths crisscrossed the area, making it easy to reach individual growing patches.

Darla followed her, shadowing as Amanda pulled a spade from her apron and squatted to dig up a small group of yellow flowers.

The woman squinted up at her.

"No *copycats* this time," she hissed.

Darla grimaced. She'd hoped to absorb some pointers, but Amanda was right. If she watched her every move, she'd copy without meaning to do it.

Clever of them to add a no-copying rule.

Darn it.

Darla wandered deeper into the garden, searching for inspiration. The pots weren't very big. She knew she had to think *small*.

Or maybe one *big* flower?

She stopped to gawk at a sunflower as tall as her.

Is that a thing? Giant flowers in a tiny pot? Maybe it would be cutting-edge?

The extent of her gardening at home was calling a local kid to come weed.

She wiped her brow and looked from the sunflower to the pot and back again.

Nah.

A giant flower in a tiny pot would look *crazy*.

She reached the end of the garden and was about to plunge back in when she noticed footprints leading from the garden's edge into the preserve behind the manor. The prints came from something *not* human and not *small*.

They looked a little like pointy flowers.

Tipped with claws.

"Are those *alligator* tracks?" she said aloud to herself.

She decided not to find out and hustled back into the expansive garden. Feeling safer fifteen feet away from the gator prints, she squatted to consider a clump of bright green. Whatever it was, it was a pretty color, but she suspected it was lettuce.

Nobody said anything about creating a vegetable garden.

A tiny snail slid along one of the broad leaves. She touched its mottled spiral shell, hoping it would give her luck.

"Too bad you're not a plant. Your shell is pretty."

Her head cocked to the left.

Hm.

She'd never beat Amanda at her own game.

Maybe she could change the playing field?

Darla plucked the snail from the plant and searched for more. When she'd found four of the slimy house-toters, she carried them back to her pot and placed them inside.

Amanda approached with several plants, including a pair of striking orange flowers.

"That's my best gerbera daisy," moaned a woman in the audience.

Amanda ignored her.

Darla considered the garden with new appreciation. The contestants had full access to the *community* garden—which meant anything they stole *belonged to someone else.*

She decided not to steal plants. Maybe good will could win her a vote or two, though it wouldn't unless people understood her selfless sacrifice...

She lifted her chin to make an announcement.

"It might make it hard for me to win, but I refuse to ruin anyone's gardens. Y'all worked too hard on these for me to tear them up just so these idiots can run us through hoops."

She motioned toward Gretchen, and the woman's lip curled in response.

Darla didn't mind absorbing the full brunt of Gretchen's disdain. A murmur rippled through the spectators, and she saw the corners of their mouths curl with appreciation.

Score.

Now, she had to figure out how to win with no plants.

Hm.

She poured dirt into her pot, leaving two inches of the rim to slow the snails' escape. Keeping them inside was like trying to cage Spiderman—they climbed walls, and she needed to keep them in the pot for another twenty minutes.

Amanda scoffed at her snail cage and returned to the garden to steal more plants.

Darla headed for a small shed standing on the side of the

garden plot. One side of the structure received little sun thanks to a large overhang. Darla gathered a few clumps of moss and a colorful collection of small mushrooms growing in the moldy soil there. She dropped them in her pot and combed the yard for bits of bark, bright white pebbles, leaves, and twigs. Spotting a soda can on the edge of the preserve, she gasped like she'd found a loose diamond. She snatched the can and carried it to her workspace.

On the way back, she noticed Mariska watching her with some interest.

"You *do* understand the contest, right?" she asked.

"Yes."

"You haven't picked or planted a single flower."

"I know. I'm going in another direction."

"But—"

"No coaching," snapped Gretchen.

For once, Darla was grateful to hear Gretchen shush them. Mariska was giving her angina.

Mariska huffed and mouthed the word *flowers*, pointing to the garden with her eyes wide.

Darla shook her head.

Boy, she loves saying flowers.

She turned away and decided she'd gathered enough to get started. Working with the dirt-filled pot as her base, she constructed tiny homes from the twigs, bark, and leaves she'd collected. She used the moss as turf to give the homes cheery front lawns. Miniature stone paths built from pebbles led to dead-leaf front doors. She built retaining walls to separate the properties using dirt and gravel and used a row of twigs to simulate a fence.

"Good fences make good neighbors," she mumbled to the snails as she placed one in front of a twig house and another on the opposite side of the fence. They stayed put, for the most part. Luckily, she'd found some lazy snails and not lizards. The anoles around her property back home were speedy little suckers.

When Amanda jogged into the garden to search for more plants, Darla glanced up to see her in the preserve gathering reeds.

Ooh. Bad idea, honey.

She stopped fussing with Snail Town, torn about warning her foe. Didn't the jerk see those alligator prints? How could she *miss* them?

Of course, that was one way to win.

Let a gator eat the witch.

Amanda left the preserve and reentered the garden, saving Darla from her crisis of conscience. As she stooped to uproot another person's hard-earned flowers, Darla's gaze settled on Amanda's collection of tools, most of which remained sitting on the table.

Hello there...

She borrowed Amanda's sheers and cut the aluminum can she'd found into a curvy strip to place in the dirt, shiny side up, to simulate a stream running past her snail town.

She stepped back to admire it, grinning.

That is some clever stuff right there.

She found some sandy dirt to shake around her Snail Town diorama to give the landscape variation. She liked the contrast of the light sand and pebbles against the dark dirt. Punches of green from the moss exploded like a party.

She found some small plants resembling tiny trees and planted them in a row alongside the cobblestone driveway she'd created for one snail property.

That one was a *fancy* snail. Maybe the mayor.

With one last dive back into the community garden, she found a few plants covered in tiny flowers and took a smattering to create gardens in front of her snail homes. The few flowers she stole wouldn't hurt the plants at all.

"One minute left," said Gretchen.

Darla scattered her flowers and stepped back to admire her handiwork.

Not bad.

Was Snail Town what the judges were looking for? Maybe not. She hadn't followed the rules, which alone might mean she'd lost, but she couldn't help but be a little proud.

"That's adorable," said Mariska, peering over her shoulder and into the pot.

Darla grinned.

"It is, isn't it?"

"Time!" screamed Gretchen.

Amanda took a step back and wiped her sweaty brow. Her pot

was beautiful, if predictable. She'd done an excellent job of mixing colors and heights with her selection of stolen flowers.

Thief.

Gretchen thrust a hand into her pocket and pulled out poker chips.

"Judges, I'm going to give you each a pair of chips—one red and one blue. Amanda is blue team, Carla is red."

"*Darla*," said Darla through gritted teeth.

Gretchen doled out the chips and produced an old purple Crown Royal bag to hand to one of the judges.

"Confer among yourselves and then put the chip representing the winner into the bag." She lowered her chin to glare from beneath her brow at the five judges. "I'm sure you'll make the right choice," she added.

Darla scowled.

Nice touch.

The judges wandered to the table to examine the pots.

"Think we have a chance?" asked Darla.

Mariska clucked her tongue. "I would vote for you; I'm not scared of Gretchen."

Darla nodded. That was the problem. All the judges *were*.

The judges wandered away to huddle in a circle. They didn't talk as much as Darla hoped they would. She'd thought maybe, if they *really* thought about it, she might win—but it looked as if they would do what Gretchen expected of them.

"The idea that this is fair is *ridiculous*," she grumbled.

Mariska nodded, wringing her hands.

The judges dropped their chips in the bag and stuffed the others in their pockets. The one who'd held the bag returned it to Gretchen, and they exchanged a look.

Darla felt her hope drain.

Gretchen slipped her hand into the bag and pulled out the first chip.

"Blue," she said, holding it up for all to see.

She placed it on the table and pulled a second.

"Blue."

Darla shook her head. "It's going to be a rout."

Gretchen pulled a third, and her chin tucked at the sight of it.

"*Red?*" she squeaked, glaring at the pack of judges.

"You got one," said Mariska, smacking her arm with the back of her hand.

"*Ow.*" Darla grinned. "I did, didn't I?"

"Another red," growled Gretchen, pulling a fourth chip. She stared daggers at the judges as she reached for the fifth.

Mariska yipped. "You're going to *win.*"

Darla watched Gretchen pull the final chip. Before she could see the color, she saw the tension in Gretchen's shoulders release.

Dang.

"*Blue,*" announced Gretchen, holding the last chip up in victory. "The winner and still champion is *Amanda.*"

The crowd's applause sounded like the pitter-patter of a light summer rain on a metal roof.

Amanda raised her hands in victory.

"We lost? What does that mean?" asked Mariska.

"It means you're *out,*" said Gretchen, tossing the final blue chip on the table.

She turned and strode away.

"I thought the snails were cute," whispered Muffin before jogging after Gretchen.

Amanda, smirking, took her creation and followed the others.

Mariska looked at Darla, her brow scrunched. "We're *out?*"

"Blackballed forever," said Darla. "I'm sorry."

Mariska reached out to snare Darla in a giant Polish grandmother hug.

"Don't you apologize. That garden should have won."

"I think so," said one of the judges.

Darla pulled from the hug in time to see a judge wink at them. The others started back to the manor, too frightened to admit they were the other red chip.

"Thank you," she called to them.

A few of the spectators approached.

"Thank you for not tearing up my garden the way they did," said one elderly woman.

"I love how you're standing up to them," said another. "I'm room one-fifty-six. If you ever need anything, you let me know."

She patted Mariska and headed back to the manor arm in arm

with the older woman, who'd been happy not to lose any more flowers.

"That was nice," said Mariska, watching them go.

Darla nodded and started toward the garden. "Follow me."

Mariska blocked the sun from her eyes with her flattened palm. "Where? I want to get out of the sun."

"Just follow me."

Darla led her to the back of the garden. She didn't need to point out the gator tracks—Mariska spotted them immediately.

"Are those alligator feet?" she asked.

Darla nodded. "They have to be, right? The weird thing is, Amanda came back here and walked right into the preserve."

"She didn't see them?"

"It didn't look like it. And look at the size of them. They're *enormous*. How did she *not* see them?"

"Maybe she has bad eyesight?"

"Maybe. I wanted to show you, so I knew I didn't imagine them."

Mariska shook her head. "You didn't. Can we go now?"

"Yep—but it *is* weird that she didn't see them, isn't it?"

Mariska shrugged. "I guess she was too busy kicking our butts."

Darla scoffed. "She didn't win. They had the judges in their pockets, as usual."

Mariska elbowed her in the side. "Not all of them."

Darla snickered. "Nope. Not all of them."

They exited the garden, and Darla took a moment to place Snail Town on the ground next to the plants so her residents could return home.

"Slime away home, little losers," she told them.

With a sigh, she joined Mariska to head back to the manor.

"What will we do now that we lost?" asked Mariska.

"Easy," Darla grinned at her. "We'll stage a *coup*."

CHAPTER NINETEEN

When Declan arrived to check in with Dana, her door was open, but she was nowhere to be found. He hovered near her desk and pushed through papers stacked there, looking for anything interesting. On the wall, he noticed a room chart with names.

Bingo.

He took a photo with his phone and forwarded it to Charlotte.

Check!

That was one thing off his list. He didn't even have to clean rooms. He'd *definitely* snagged the better undercover job for this case.

He checked the room numbers against the chart and wrote down the names of the people who had clowns in their rooms. Unfortunately, their names alone didn't tell him much, and he wasn't sure how to connect any dots between them.

He looked out the window and noticed Dana at the back of the community garden.

Hm.

She sure liked walking around the garden in the morning.

As he watched, she plunged into the nature preserve backing the property and disappeared into a clump of trees.

He scowled.

What the heck is she doing back there?

Whatever it was, it would keep her away for a while. He took the opportunity to rummage through her desk, searching for anything that might give him more information about the residents.

He found brochures and printouts from websites about Morocco—it seemed Dana was going on vacation after she left the manor. He also found folders in a large filing drawer—one dedicated to each resident—but inside each, the papers were nothing more sinister than permission forms for various activities. Ed had hypertension and couldn't do anything too strenuous, which argued his death might have been due to ill health. That was something. He took a photo of the sheet.

As he poked around the office, he kept one eye on the island of trees. Ten minutes later, Dana reappeared with something in her hand. He couldn't be sure, but they looked like shoes. He assumed she wore more robust shoes when she walked around the overgrown preserve.

She walked through the community garden, leaned down to switch shoes, put her other pair in a bag, and continued toward the manor.

A few other people seemed to be milling near the garden. Maybe walking around the garden area was a big part of everyone's day at Elderbrook.

He scanned the office to ensure he hadn't left any evidence of his search.

Time to go.

He left Dana's office and wandered into the breakfast room to make idle chitchat with the residents. He moved from table to table, introducing himself as the new manager.

"You're *who*?" asked one of the ladies, squinting up at him from her table after he introduced himself.

"Declan Bingham. I'm going to be the new manager," he explained.

"Dana's leaving?"

He nodded.

She seemed pleased.

"Are you going to miss her?" he asked.

She scowled at him. "No. She used to be nice, but lately—" The woman sighed. "She's been letting Gretchen and her group get away with murder."

"*Murder*?" He lowered his voice. "*Actual* murder?"

The woman cackled. "No. My goodness. I'm just saying. *Something* should be done about them—the way they bully the rest of us, but she won't do anything."

He nodded. "Would you like to set up a time that we could talk about this?"

Her eyes widened.

"No. No. I've said too much already."

"But—"

She waved him away. "Leave me to my breakfast."

Declan smiled and took a step back. It seemed that's all he'd be getting from her.

He introduced himself to a few more residents before finding one with a name that matched one of the names on his clown box list.

"I've been thinking about some new activities for the residents," he mused to her. "What do you think of performers? Like comedians or *clowns*, for example?"

The woman's eyes darted away, and she walked away without commenting further.

He let it go and moved on without better luck. Clowns weren't the easiest thing to weave into a conversation. He couldn't ask anyone about the boxes directly because there was no reason he should know about what they had in their rooms.

He stepped away to call Charlotte.

"Hey, what's up?" she answered.

"Just an update. I snooped around Dana's office and didn't find much. She was back in the preserve, so I had time for a pretty good look."

"In the preserve? Why?"

"No idea. I can tell you I found out Ed had hypertension that kept him from activities."

"So that could have killed him?"

"That's what I'm thinking. I chatted up some people at breakfast and had one woman act weird when I asked about clowns."

Charlotte chuckled. "Maybe because *you asked about clowns?*"

"Fair enough, but I think I sneaked it in pretty smooth, and her reaction felt like something more."

"Okay, I'll keep working the killer clown angle on my end. Anything else?"

"Another woman mentioned Dana doesn't seem interested in cracking down on Gretchen's crew, but she balked at the idea of talking to me about it formally."

"They're terrified."

"Seems like it. Maybe Dana is, too, and that's why she *doesn't* do something about them."

"You think she knows what Gretchen's up to?"

"Seems like she should, doesn't it? They aren't shy about testing Mariska and Darla out in the open."

"True."

He sighed. "Or maybe Dana has her eyes on leaving and doesn't care. I found brochures for Morocco in her desk."

"That's a good point. Why make trouble for yourself when you're leaving?"

"Right—" Declan saw familiar faces headed his way. "I see Darla and Mariska. Got to go."

He hung up as a sweaty Darla and Mariska approached.

"Go for a morning jog?" he asked.

They didn't seem happy.

"We lost the planting contest. That means we didn't pass the tests," said Mariska.

"What does that mean?" he asked.

"It means Gretchen isn't lifting the ban on talking to us."

"But don't worry. We're going to stage a revolt," added Darla.

He blinked at her.

Right. No reason to worry about a *revolt*.

"Is there anything I can do to help? Gather pitchforks, maybe?" he asked.

Mariska reached into her pocket to produce a wad of paper towels. "Before I forget, this is a sample of Oksana's tea if you want to get it tested for poison."

He took the soggy mess from her. "Where did you get it?"

"We used donuts to get into our neighbor's room—"

He nodded. "Like people do."

"—and she gave us her blend of tea from Oksana."

"Did you drink any of it?"

"Most of my cup," admitted Mariska.

"Me too," said Darla.

"And how do you feel?"

They looked at each other and spoke in stereo.

"Fine."

"And *she* had some?"

"I see where you're going with this, but who knows? It might be slow acting," suggested Darla.

He nodded. "Okay. Thank you. If you need anything for your revolt, let me know."

Darla grinned. "Thank you. We're going to plan it now, over some coffee."

"And donuts," added Mariska.

They headed to the elevator, and Declan looked at the wad of wet tea in his hand.

What am I going to do with this?

He walked the blob to his car and returned to stand on Elderbrook's front porch, checking his watch.

Seamus was late.

He'd called his uncle the night before to see if he'd be willing to be Alma's arm candy. As expected, he'd agreed. Seamus *loved* playing undercover. He also loved any excuse to talk to people. Dead and buried, he'd chat with the corpse in the grave next to him.

Declan heard Seamus' junker rumbling up the road before he saw it pull into the parking lot. His uncle exited the creaking vehicle, and when he slammed the door shut, Declan lost a bet with himself when the thing didn't collapse into a pile of parts.

Seamus strode forward, his barrel chest balanced precariously on his bandy legs. He stood a few inches shorter than Declan, his graying hair still thick into his sixties.

"Hey, Boyo," he said, swaggering to the porch.

"That *car*," said Declan, shaking his head.

"Hm?"

"You can't take Alma for a date in that thing."

Seamus glanced over his shoulder.

"I've never had any complaints before."

"Have you had many second dates?"

He grunted. "Fair play. Does *she* have a car?"

Declan sighed. "You can take mine."

He clapped his hands together. "Problem solved. Where's my date?"

Declan held up his palm. "Slow your roll. We need to talk. Did you clear this operation with Jackie? I'm getting flack from Mariska and Darla for even suggesting you for the job, so I'm warning you now—you won't keep this a secret once the ladies get together."

"I cleared it." He sniffed and stuffed his hands into his pockets. "Sort of."

"What do you mean, *sort of*?"

"I told Jackie you needed my help. I wasn't terribly specific about the nature of the job."

Declan frowned. "Jackie *will* find out, and Charlotte and I won't lie for you."

"Aye, I'll fill her in on the gritty details later. I needed to get out of the house first. There's a difference between going to a job *knowing* you'll be pimped and finding out after you've arrived." Seamus leaned in and winked. "Plus, if she's a real looker..."

Declan rolled his eyes. "She's close to eighty. I know you like older ladies, but I think that's pushing it."

He frowned. "You're a terrible pimp."

"Because I'm *not a pimp*. All you have to do is go on a *platonic* date."

"That's what all the pimps say. Next thing you know, I've got my boxers around my ankles—"

Declan gritted his teeth. "Seamus, I swear to—"

"Oh, calm down, Boyo. It's all in fun. Where is she?"

Declan eyed him.

"Is that what you're wearing? A tee shirt?"

Seamus turned and pointed to his back.

"Ah, but it's me own bar's tee. I just had them made. What do you think?"

Declan eyed the design. It featured a buxom mermaid wearing a bikini top made from tiny sea shells and a slogan. *Set Sail for Anne Bonny's Bar—We've Got the Booty You're After!*

Declan hung his head and pinched the bridge of his nose.

"I'll find you a shirt."

"Why? If she sees I'm a successful businessman, she'll love me all the more."

"She's not looking for a husband. She wants *companionship*. Plus, I think we have different definitions of the word *successful*. Last I heard, The Anne Bonny was barely breaking even."

He grunted. "She won't be lookin' at me books."

Declan sighed. "Look, all you have to do is be charming."

"Not a problem. I *ooze* charm."

"Ew. Don't say *ooze*."

Seamus scratched at his scruffy beard. "What's the mission? The endgame? What info do you need?"

Declan squinted. He'd hoped Seamus would shave. He forgot *look nice* to Seamus meant *put on a clean tee shirt*. He should have been more specific.

"Find out what she knows about the deaths around here. She said she'll spill after the dance tomorrow, but I wouldn't mind finding out sooner."

"Deaths? Not *murders*?"

"We don't know if they're murders yet. That's what we're here to find out."

"You think *she's* killing people?"

"Alma? No." Declan paused. "Actually, I never considered that." He shook his head. "No. That doesn't make any sense. Why would she ask for a date so she could confess?"

"She hasn't confessed yet. Maybe she's toying with you. Maybe she wants one last kill."

"Who? *You*?"

He nodded. "I'll have to stay on my toes."

"Like I said, she's old. I think you'll be okay." He reconsidered and added, "Maybe, don't eat anything she gives you. Not even tea."

"You think she'll poison me?"

"I don't think she'd do *anything*, but if she is our killer, she isn't wrestling people to the ground."

Seamus sucked at his tooth, and Declan motioned to his tee.

"Can I *please* talk you into changing your shirt? Can you try and look like a gentleman?"

Seamus glanced back at his car. "Tell you what—I've got a shirt in the car. I'll put it over this so it's still handy in case I need to impress her."

"Fine. I'll take it. Did you bring flowers like I asked?"

"Oh, yep." He put up a finger and jogged back to his car. After rustling inside the vehicle, he returned with a second shirt and a coffee mug filled with sagging pansies.

Declan scowled at the familiar mermaid logo on the mug.

"Is that from your bar, too?"

He nodded. "Nice, eh? I got two dozen of them for a song."

"And are those the pansies from the city's beautification pots? The ones they put around the lamp posts outside your place?"

Seamus winced. "You remembered them, huh?"

Declan rubbed his face with his hand. "I give up. She'll either love you or hate you."

Seamus nodded. "They usually do. Always one of those two."

"Follow me. I'll take you to her."

Declan fished in his pockets for his car keys and handed them to his uncle as he led Seamus through the lobby and down the hall to Alma's first-floor room.

"Be good. Be *nice*," whispered Declan as he knocked.

"I'm always nice," grumbled Seamus.

Alma answered, wearing a blue summer dress adorned with stitched yellow flowers. Her grey hair was swept into a chic chignon, wisps framing her face.

Declan smiled. "Alma, this is my uncle Seamus."

She eyed Seamus.

"Seamus?" she confirmed.

The object of her scrutiny bowed and answered with a thick Irish accent.

"Aye, 'tis I—directly from the Emerald Isle."

Declan groaned.

Here we go.

Alma's eyebrow arched.

"Did you ever find them?" she asked.

Seamus straightened, his brow furrowing.

"Find what now?"

Alma crossed her arms against her chest and smirked.

"Your Lucky Charms?"

Declan barked a laugh. He hadn't seen that coming.

Seamus chuckled and pointed at his date.

"I like this one. She's a pistol."

Alma turned her attention to Declan. "You don't happen to have a Jewish one, do you?"

Declan shook his head. "I'm afraid this is the only model I

have."

"I guess he'll do." She eyed Seamus again. "Is that what you're wearing?"

Undaunted, Seamus held out his hooked arm to her, and she slipped hers through.

"Come with me, Lass, to delights untold," he said, leading her down the hall.

Alma looked over her shoulder at Declan, and he gave her the thumbs up. "He's friendly. Think of him like a big sloppy dog."

She allowed Seamus to lead her outside to Declan's waiting car.

"He's an *idiot*," mumbled Declan as he watched them drive away. "But friendly."

CHAPTER TWENTY

After finishing her second to last room, Charlotte received a message from Darla requesting she come to their place. She didn't mind the break and headed up.

"What's up?" she asked as Mariska let her in.

"We lost the plant contest," said Mariska.

"*I* lost," added Darla.

Charlotte flopped on the edge of the bed.

"Bummer. Oh well. It was bound to happen with those three plotting against you."

The ladies nodded.

"We're working on an alternative plan. A *revolt*. We haven't figured out the details yet," added Darla with a little more grit in her voice than Charlotte felt comfortable about.

"Well, that's not terrifying or anything," she mumbled.

"I gave Declan some of our neighbor's tea from Oksana for testing."

"I've got some, too. How do you know it's Oksana's tea?" asked Charlotte.

"Gail told us. We were over there with the donuts."

"We *drank* the tea," added Mariska, looking grim. "Declan pointed out we weren't dead, but it doesn't hurt to have it tested?"

Charlotte nodded.

"Anyway, as soon as we have a donut break, we'll be back on the case. Did *you* find anything new?"

As Mariska spoke, she motioned to a box of donuts, and Charlotte rose to tear a chunk from one.

"I found out Alma—the one who followed Declan to get a date—is pretty sharp. She left me a message in her room because she knew we'd snoop around once she was on our radar."

"Sharp enough to be a killer?" asked Darla.

Charlotte shook her head. "I don't think so. I'm hoping she'll have the information as promised, though. Having an insider who's been here for all the deaths is nice. Who knows—we might get lucky."

"What about that sneaky girl with the locker?" asked Mariska.

"Luna? I haven't seen her today."

"Did you check her locker?"

"No, it's locked. It's a shackle combination lock. Not something we can pick."

Darla scoffed. "Speak for yourself."

Charlotte stopped chewing the second chunk of donut she'd stolen. "You know how to open a combination lock?"

Darla rolled her eyes. "Of course I do. My boyfriend in high school robbed lockers all the time."

Mariska clucked her tongue in disapproval. "Did you *ever* date anyone *nice*?"

Darla glowered at her. "I'm married to the sheriff. Doesn't that make up for some of it?"

Mariska shrugged. "I guess."

Charlotte swallowed her donut. "Can we get back to the locker? Could you see if you can open it now? There shouldn't be anyone in there."

Darla shrugged. "Sure."

Mariska frowned. "I'll stay here and draw up a plan."

"Maybe you could list all your goody-two-shoe boyfriends while I'm gone," drawled Darla.

Mariska scowled at her. "Sorry if my boyfriends didn't *teach me to break into lockers*."

Darla scoffed. "Sorry if mine didn't *bore* me to death."

"Okay, simmer down," interjected Charlotte. "We're all on the same team here."

Darla stuck her tongue out at Mariska, who replied in kind. They both giggled.

"Okay, let's hit the road," said Darla.

Charlotte gave up pretending she wouldn't eat the donut she'd been picking at and snatched the last of it before heading out the door. She didn't regret it. After all, they'd be leaving Mariska behind in the room with the last donuts, so she'd never see them again.

"Did I tell you about the alligator?" asked Darla as they rode the elevator down.

That snapped Charlotte from her donut thoughts.

"Alligator?"

"I saw alligator footprints at the back of the community garden heading into the nature preserve area."

Charlotte grimaced. "That's not good. Someone could go to water their daisies and end up dragged into the swamp."

"Amanda was there, too. She walked right into the weeds during the gardening competition. I don't know how she didn't see the prints. They were huge."

Charlotte swallowed the last of her donut. "You said the back of the garden?"

Darla nodded.

"Declan said he saw Dana walk back there this morning."

"Into the weeds?"

"I think so. I can't imagine why she'd need to be back there, but I better tell Bernie he needs a fence before he starts losing people even faster than he already is."

The doors opened, and they walked to the locker room. After ensuring the room was unoccupied, Charlotte pointed out Luna's locker.

"It's that one."

Darla moved to it and spun the lock a few times.

"The key is *pressure*. You tug on the shackle until you feel it catch, and then add five to that number."

Darla scowled as she worked, her lips a tight, thin line.

"Eleven. Remember that," she said.

"And you do that for the next two?" asked Charlotte.

"For the next, but the last one, you try every possibility until you get it."

Darla worked in silence for five minutes while Charlotte kept one eye on her and one on the door.

"*Got it*." Darla flung open Luna's locker door.

Excitement ran across Charlotte's shoulders as Darla stepped back to reveal the locker contents. Luna's street clothes hung from a hook inside. A backpack sat wedged at the bottom, and Darla yanked it out to set it on the bench. When she unzipped it, white sparkly fabric burst from the pack as if it had been springloaded.

"Is she Tinkerbelle?" asked Charlotte, pulling out the sparkly fabric. She held it up to find it jumpsuit-shaped.

"It looks like—"

Darla nodded, pulling a giant red shoe from the bag. "We found our clown, or Luna is a real weirdo."

Charlotte put the costume on the bench and dug into the bag. She produced the red ball she'd seen rolling across the floor.

"It was a *nose* I saw, not a ball," she said, putting it aside. She pulled a small notebook from the bag to find the pages filled with dates and numbers.

"It looks like a schedule. The last date is in about half an hour today, and there's a number—*one-fourteen*—a room number, I bet."

She looked up to find Darla nodding at her with a serious expression and the red ball clamped on her nose.

Charlotte giggled. "I think you have something on your face."

Darla shrugged. "I don't know what you're talking about."

Charlotte plucked the ball from Darla's nose and dropped it into the bag. "We better get this back—"

The locker room door swung open.

Darla and Charlotte twisted to find Luna in the doorway, eyes wide, gaping at them.

"What are you *doing*?" she shrieked at the sight of her stuff.

Charlotte glanced at the backpack in her hand. There was no way to pretend they hadn't broken into the girl's locker.

Luna lunged forward to grab her costume and bag.

"What are you *doing*?"

Charlotte grimaced. "I'm sorry. You were just so secretive about your locker—"

Luna gritted her teeth. "Bernie didn't hire you to investigate *me*."

"But that's just it—I don't know that *until* I investigate you."

"Why were you hiding clown stuff?" asked Darla.

Luna held their gazes for a beat as if she were trying to decide if she wanted to answer. Finally, her shoulders slumped.

"My mother hates it. She sent me here to get my mind off

clown school, but I love it. It's what I want to do."

"And you perform for the people here? Without her knowing?" asked Charlotte.

The girl nodded. "Mom thought she was distracting me, but she only gave me a place to practice." She straightened with what looked like pride. "I've gotten a few paying gigs, too. I'm making a little money on the side."

"Does Bernie know?"

Luna's pupils circled with white again.

"No. You can't tell him. He'll tell Mom."

Charlotte shook her head. "I won't tell."

"And you can't let Gretchen and her group of jerks know. They'd blackmail me."

"They'd blackmail *you*?"

"Probably. Anybody. *Everybody*. They do whatever they can to make people unhappy. That's why the others *need* me. I make them happy."

"That actually sounds nice," said Darla.

Charlotte looked at her, and she held up her hands.

"I mean, I don't know about *clowns*—"

Luna noticed and looked at Charlotte.

"You don't like clowns?"

Charlotte shook her head. "Not a fan."

Luna set down her pack. "I have a party right now. Come check me out? It's in room three-oh-nine. I know some people don't like clowns, but I swear I'll change your mind."

"That's just down the hall from us. Maybe Mariska and I can swing by," suggested Darla.

Charlotte nodded.

Better you than me.

"And you?" asked Luna.

Charlotte shook her head. "No. I *would*, but I have to get back to work."

Luna sighed. "Stupid Stephen King. *It* ruined it for us good clowns."

Charlotte tried not to think about how Luna had worded *us good clowns*. She said it like she knew there *was* a whole faction of evil clowns roaming around somewhere in their greasy face paint and—

"Charlotte?"

Charlotte snapped from her thoughts.

"Hm?"

"We should go?" said Darla as Luna continued to pull the pieces of her costume from her bag.

"Oh. Yep." She started for the door and then turned back again. "Luna, one thing. Do you have something to do with the clown trinket boxes I saw in the rooms?"

Luna smiled. "I gave them out as party gifts to remember me by when I go. I filled them with sugar-free butterscotches; if they bring them to a performance, I refill them. They love it."

Charlotte nodded.

That solved one puzzle, though she still didn't know if Elderbrook had a killer, and she'd *never* solve the puzzle of why some people liked clowns.

Darla's attention snapped to Luna.

"Will there be butterscotches at *this* performance?"

CHAPTER TWENTY-ONE

Seamus led Alma to the passenger side of Declan's car and tucked her in before jogging around to his side.

"Ready for your adventure?" he asked, reversing the vehicle.

She didn't respond, but he caught a glimpse of her rolling her eyes.

Looks like she might be a tough nut to crack.

He wasn't worried. He'd cracked harder.

He reached the end of Elderbrook's driveway, took a deep breath, and turned on his right turn signal to send them towards town.

Time for a little humor.

"So, a bagel, a cucumber, and a banana walk into a bar—"

"Turn *left*," said Alma.

He looked at her. "Hm?"

"You have your right turn signal on. Turn *left*."

"But the restaurant I picked out for us is *that* way. You have another one in mind?"

"Not exactly. Turn left."

He shrugged and pressed on the gas. "I can do that. You have a place in mind?"

"I do. And please don't finish that joke."

"You've heard it?"

Alma sighed.

Seamus shrugged.

"So, how do you like that place we came from?" he asked.

"I like it fine."

"Good. That's good." Seamus nodded. Something about Alma made him nervous. "I have a bar," he blurted.

"A bar of soap?" She snorted a laugh. "I doubt it."

He side-eyed her.

Feisty.

"What? You didn't notice I smell like a summer's day?" he asked.

"More like an *Irish* spring," she muttered, but he caught her chuckling to herself.

"Ah, look at you. Very funny. You noticed me accent."

"It's hard to miss."

"Aye. I'm from Ireland—"

"I mentioned. I used to be a reporter. I remember things."

"Aye? Well, put this in your story. Now I'm in America, and I own a bar. The sort where people drink good Irish whiskey."

"Wonderful. I *love* inspiring immigrant stories." She pointed. "Up here past the food store, make a right, and then your next left.

Seamus squinted where she'd pointed. He didn't see a restaurant. He saw a collection of strange, brightly painted structures.

"You want me to take you to the mini golf?"

She beamed at him. "*Aye.*"

Seamus shrugged and did as he was told. He pulled in, parked, and jogged around the car to open Alma's door. He attempted to help her out, but she pulled away from him.

"I can get out of a car."

He nodded and stepped back as the tall woman unfolded from the seat. Together, they strolled to the check-in booth.

"You're good at this game, then?" he asked.

She shrugged. "Should we wager on it?"

Seamus smirked. He didn't know much about mini-golf but felt confident about his skills against an old lady.

"We can play for lunch, but I warn ye, I've got quite the appetite."

"Deal. You're buying *here*, though."

"Fine." He paid the teenager manning the booth and collected their putters and balls.

"Can I trust you to keep score?" he asked, handing her the sheet and pencil.

"I wouldn't have it any other way," she said.

They strolled to the first hole, and Seamus made a grand flourish.

"Ladies first."

Alma set down her ball and knocked it up a ramp into a tiki head's mouth. Seamus moved around the totem to see the ball spit from the back of the tiki's head and roll an inch from the cup before stopping.

Hm.

"Not bad," he said, placing his ball on the starting mat.

Alma grinned. "Beginner's luck."

He thought she looked a bit smug.

He lined up his putter and gave the ball a thunk. It missed the ramp but shot wide enough that it went around the tiki head, leaving his ball feet from the hole.

He cursed under his breath.

She tapped in hers, and he lined up his second shot, his tongue hanging from the side of his mouth as he concentrated.

His ball sank into the hole.

"Ha, there we go," he said, stooping to retrieve them both. "Yours was prettier, but mine got where it was going."

She nodded and strolled to the second hole.

"So, tell me what you know about these murders," said Seamus.

Alma looked at him, eyes wide but amused.

"No foreplay?"

He barked a laugh. "We're adults. We know why we're here," he said as she knocked her ball through an arched hole drilled through the bottom of a surfboard. Her ball went directly into the hole on the other side.

Seamus grunted as Alma whooped and stepped back to let him take his turn.

"I don't know that any of the deaths have been murders. I don't jump to conclusions," said Alma.

Seamus smacked his ball. It missed the hole, hit the surfboard, and rolled back to an inch from where it started.

He pouted at Alma, and she giggled.

"You didn't see that," he said, trying again. This time, he targeted the hole, and the ball grazed the edge of the cup on the opposite side before traveling a foot past it.

"Blast it!"

He stormed to the opposite end and looked at Alma.

"Keep talking. Distract me from this horror."

She chuckled. "I'm afraid I don't have proof for you. Conjecture, sure, but like I said, I deal in facts."

Seamus hit his ball and came up short before tapping it in on his fourth try.

"Here's a fact for you. I'm one behind."

"*Two*," said Alma, noting the score on the card.

He wagged a finger at her. "I told you you didn't *see* that first one. That was *practice*."

She shook her head. "I told you, I deal in facts, and the fact is, *there is no practice*."

He sighed as they moved to the next hole.

"If you don't know about any murders, what am I doing here getting my Irish ass handed to me?"

Alma laughed and lined up her shot.

"There are a few things I know that might be helpful."

She knocked her ball up the side of a tiny volcano and into the hole.

Seamus gaped.

"I know one fact. You're a *witch*," he said. "Some kind of *golf witch*."

His ball rolled over the volcano and down the other side into a fake lava field.

"Those three horrible women—Gretchen, Amanda, and Muffin—there's something going on there. I think Amanda has something on the manager, Dana."

"Why's that?" asked Seamus. He sank the ball and hooted in celebration. "You can't shake me," he added, handing her the ball.

She smirked and moved to the next hole to knock through fake palm trees. The ball stopped six inches from the cup.

"I heard them arguing. It's got something to do with the preserve."

"Preserves? Jelly? Jam?" asked Seamus, taking his turn. He clipped the side of one tree, which rolled his ball two feet from the cup and left it obstructed by an oversized fiberglass seashell. He swore under his breath.

"The *nature preserve* behind the manor," explained Alma, sinking her ball on her second try.

Seamus took two more swings before finishing the same job.

"But you have no idea what it's about? This beef between Dana and Amanda?" he asked as they moved to the next.

"No. Though, it might have something to do with Gretchen's business. She's blackmailing half the place and demanding protection money from the other half."

"You?"

"No. Not me. She tried, but I set her straight."

"I bet you did," muttered Seamus as he dropped another stroke to a hole featuring a fiberglass ocean wave.

Alma smiled. "She's not the only one who collects dirt. Old habits."

"This Gretchen sounds like a bad penny. Why hasn't anyone reported her?"

"I've considered it," admitted Alma, tapping her ball around a shark fin. "But I'm reluctant to do so until I find out what she has on Dana and if Bernie is involved somehow."

"Bernie?"

"The owner."

"Ah. You can't take corruption to the top if the top is corrupted."

"Exactly. I'll end up kicked out or dead. And while dead sounds worse, you never know what you'll get when it comes to assisted living. The next home might have more problems than a team of horrible little women."

"You seem pretty spry to need assistance."

"At my age, you're always one wrong move away from a hospital or a real nursing home. I'd much rather share a place with another woman, but the friends I had lined up to be my roommates in old age rudely died before me. I was supposed to have a roommate and a dog, but instead, I'm in Elderbrook, which is comfortable—for now. At least, people there will notice if I don't show up for breakfast."

"So Gretchen's a blackmailer, Amanda's up to something with Dana, and who's the third one?" asked Seamus, sinking a long putt.

"Muffin."

Seamus eyed her, and she shrugged.

"Nickname," she said. "Her real name is Margaret."

"Any dirt on that one?"

"She's not as bad as the other two. I'm not sure why she travels with that pack. She didn't used to. She used to bake us all muffins, then one day that stopped, and she started hanging around with the other two chicken hawks." Alma struck her opening shot on the twelfth hole and straightened. "I do know one thing about her that not many people know."

"What's that?"

"She's Dana's mother."

"Hm. That's interesting. So Dana's maybe in cahoots with Amanda *and* her mother?"

"Maybe. I haven't confirmed it, though."

"Well, why not, Alma? I thought you were a reporter?"

He winked at her, and she smiled.

"I suppose I've lost a step or two since my reporting days."

"But your golf game is crackin'."

She nodded. "Years of vacationing on the shore. A lot of boardwalk mini golfs."

"Ah." He sank a putt. "Anything else I should take back to the boss?"

"Maybe," she said coyly.

"Maybe? You don't trust me to show up for the dance?"

Alma lined up her next shot. "I've found it's best not to trust anyone. For instance, your accent isn't as strong as when we first met."

Seamus grinned. "Ah, faith and begorrah, ye got me."

CHAPTER TWENTY-TWO

"She's a *clown?*" asked Mariska, sipping her tea.

She'd made tea for herself and Darla using good, old-fashioned, *safe* tea bags.

There was a very low chance they'd keel over with their arms curled like dead cockroaches if they stuck to *tea bag* tea.

Darla nodded. "Yep, a bona fide clown. She's doing a show down the hall if you want to go?"

Mariska took a bite of her donut. Half her mind was on their job at Elderbrook. The other half thought a donut and tea break *every day* might be nice. She'd only have *one*, though, not like the four she'd had today.

She cocked her head.

Did I have five?

"Do you want to go see Luna?" repeated Darla.

Mariska snapped from her thoughts. "Will there be magic?"

"I didn't ask. Do clowns do magic?"

"I don't know. I imagine there'll be juggling. I'm pretty sure that's their thing."

Darla sat back in her chair. "We should go. We could win people over to our side by being part of the show."

Mariska shook her head. "I don't know how to juggle."

"I don't mean *part of the show*. I mean part of the *crowd*."

Mariska chuckled. "Oh, I thought you—"

She stopped, her jaw hanging open.

Darla straightened and peered into her eyes. "What? What is it? Are you okay? Is the tea poisoned?"

"No. I'm fine. I had an idea," said Mariska slowly, putting together the pieces of her epiphany.

"You were thinking? Did it hurt?" asked Darla, chuckling to herself.

Mariska rolled her eyes. "You never get tired of that joke."

Darla snickered. "Frank does."

Mariska leaned back in her chair to cross her arms. "We should have a talent show. Think about it. Gretchen and her group of nasties are keeping people from being themselves. They're all terrified of being singled out. We should have a talent show, encouraging people to have fun. People will love us for it."

Darla's brow knit. "Do we have talents?"

"That's the best part. *We* don't have to. Our talent is putting together the show."

Darla chewed on her lip.

"Won't that take too long to plan everything?" she asked.

"No. We'll do it tomorrow. We'll just invite people. They'll bring the talent. Done."

"Ooh, we can serve *donuts*."

Mariska pointed at her friend. "*Yes*. I'll call Charlotte and tell her to bring more donuts tomorrow."

Genius.

Before Mariska could dial, someone knocked on the door. The ladies looked at each other.

"Are you expecting someone? Charlotte, maybe?" asked Mariska.

"No, but maybe she decided to go to the clown show with us?"

Darla answered the door to find Oksana standing with a decorative tin in her hands.

"Hello, I've brought you tea," she announced, thrusting it forward.

Darla stared at the tin but didn't take it until Oksana shook it and snapped her out of her trance.

"Thank you," she said, taking the gift.

Oksana's attention moved past her to the table where their tea bags sat stewing.

"Are you drinking tea *now*? From grocery store *tea bags*?" she asked like she'd caught her husband cheating.

Mariska glanced down to spot the strings hanging from their mugs, knowing there was no way to hide their shame.

"We were," she admitted.

Oksana clapped her hands together. "*Oh.* How wonderful my timing. Let me make you a cup?"

Darla's chin dropped. "Uh—"

Oksana reached to take the tin from Darla's hands, but Darla didn't release it.

"I will make the tea?" said Oksana.

"Clowns!" yipped Darla loud enough that Oksana stepped back.

"Clowns?" she echoed.

Darla nodded. "We have a clown party to go to."

Oksana's brow knit. "A clown party?"

Mariska stood to back up her friend's brilliant dodge. "*Yes*, we were just about to leave."

"Oh. Okay," said Oksana, frowning. She glanced at the tin in Darla's hands. "You be sure to try it. I promise you you will love it."

"Yep. Will do. Absolutely," said Darla.

Oksana smiled and nodded goodbye before heading down the hall.

Darla closed the door and leaned her back against it.

"That was close. We couldn't sit there and pretend to drink poisoned tea without her noticing."

"That was quick thinking," said Mariska. "Put the tin over there, and we'll give it to Charlotte next time we get a chance."

Darla set down the tin and sighed.

"The downside is now we *really* have to go to the clown party."

Darla and Mariska walked down the hall to the designated lounge on their floor and knocked on the door.

A woman answered and, at the site of Darla and Mariska, stopped to stare at them.

"We came to see Luna?" said Mariska.

The woman glanced behind her at a group of women who'd also reined in their conversation to gawk at the pair in the hall. One shook her head, her eyes wide with what looked like fear. Another shrugged.

The woman who'd answered the door leaned into the hall and looked both ways before stepping back.

"Come on in," she said. "I don't think they'll show up for this anyway."

Darla knew whom she meant.

They entered.

A large television hung from the eastern wall of the room. Sofas and chairs had been pushed away to allow room for four rows of folding chairs. Most seats were filled.

"We better get a seat before they're all gone," whispered Mariska.

The others followed them with their eyes as they took a seat.

A moment later, before Mariska could even start chatting with someone, Luna entered wearing street clothes and entered a closet at the back. She stuck a hand out, and a woman stood to press a button on the sound system. Music swelled.

"Ooh, it's starting," said Mariska excitedly.

Darla rolled her eyes.

The closet door flung open, and Luna appeared in full costume. She wore a bright yellow wig topped with a tiny red hat, and while white grease paint didn't cover her face like some clowns', she sported large red swirls of red on her cheeks and ridiculously long green eyelashes. Red pompom balls hung down the middle of her glittery white jumpsuit, and they bounced when she moved.

"Those balls look like someone knitted them for her," said Mariska.

"I did," said a woman a row back.

"Shhhh," hushed someone else.

Luna slapped her way to the front of the room—her giant clown shoes slapping like flippers. Hidden bells tucked somewhere in the flounces of her outfit jingled as she bobbed, and she honked her nose several times by squeezing it and the dented brass horn hanging at her side at the same time.

The door opened, and all heads turned as Gretchen and Amanda slipped into the room.

Everyone watched for a beat too long.

The mood of the room darkened.

Luna's eyes widened.

"*Proceed*," said Gretchen, standing against the wall beside the door.

Amanda smirked. "Sorry we're late. Our invitation must have gotten lost in the mail."

Luna scowled and visibly steeled herself before addressing the audience with a deep bow. A smattering of light applause filled the room. She smiled and faked a violent sneeze to initiate the pulling of an endless handkerchief from her pocket. She gasped, mouth hanging open in mock surprise, as the rainbow-colored cloth kept coming—sometimes smoothly, sometimes in fast clumps—until a pair of oversized clown bloomers appeared tied at the end.

The crowd applauded as she gawped at the bloomers and pretended to be shocked.

She followed the never-ending tissue trick with the classic trapped-in-a-box mime routine. She pushed against the unseen walls, tapped the invisible glass, and pretended to wipe it clean with an imaginary cloth.

"Groan," muttered Darla.

Luna reached into a bag hanging from her side and pulled out three blue balls.

"She's going to juggle," said Mariska.

Darla nodded. "Oh, goodie."

Luna eyed the balls in her hands, her hands shaking. She tossed the first into the air with a motion Darla could only describe as *spastic*. It flung to the left, and she scrambled sideways to catch it. Taking a deep breath, she tried again, this time managing to get three in the air. No sooner did she grin with victory than one ball hit another, and both shot off in opposite directions.

"I'm uh, I'm still working on this part," she mumbled as she rushed to retrieve the balls.

Gretchen reached to retrieve a ball that had rolled to her feet. She handed it back to Luna.

"It would be kinder if I *didn't* give it back to you," she said as

Luna took it.

A few audience members chuckled. Darla saw the spots on Luna's face uncovered by paint flush crimson.

"Poor girl," she said.

Mariska nodded. "She's not very good."

Darla agreed, but she *did* feel bad for her.

Luna set the balls on the ground beside her and pulled three rubber chickens from her bag. She juggled them more successfully, squeaking each as she caught it. Buoyed by the support, she picked up the pace and lost control of one.

"Pathetic," said Amanda when the chicken hit the ground.

Luna ignored her and set the chickens aside to launch into a mock ballet routine. Every pirouette ended in a stumble. Sometimes, her legs seemed stuck in place until she moved them with her hands.

The audience shifted in their seats.

"She's losing them," said Mariska.

Darla nodded.

Rolling a cart to the front of her stage area, Luna held up a pie tin for everyone to see before pretending to pour ingredients into it. She cracked and stirred invisible eggs with an invisible oversized spoon, exaggerating her movements and offering silent commentary with her eyes and facial expressions.

Gretchen pantomimed her own exaggerated yawn and sent Amanda giggling.

Luna lifted her pie and dipped behind the cart to put it in an imaginary oven. After a loud *ding!*, she retrieved the pie, only to trip and plant her face into a *real* tray of whipped cream.

A few of the audience members squealed with surprise and laughter.

"That part wasn't bad," said Darla.

Luna tipped her tiny hat as she gave her final bow before releasing a confetti explosion to end the show.

"Terrible," said Gretchen.

"What's the point?" asked Amanda.

Darla saw Luna struggling to ignore the women. Gretchen stepped forward.

"I heard your mother sent you here to keep you out of prison," she said loud enough to be heard over the clapping.

The room went silent.

"You don't know anything," said Luna, packing away her props in the rolling cart.

"You're almost as bad at being a clown as you are at being a maid," Gretchen continued. "I wonder what Bernie would think about you *clowning around* up here. What happens if he sends you back to your mother?"

Luna straightened. Her fingers curled into a shaking fist.

Darla recognized all the signs.

The girl was going to hit Gretchen.

If she did that, Gretchen would *own* her. She'd make her life a living hell, one way or the other.

Darla leaped to her feet.

"Talent show!" she yelled.

All eyes turned to her—including Gretchen and Luna's.

"What are you doing?" hissed Mariska.

Darla held a palm to her and focused on Gretchen.

"Luna's wonderful performance inspired me. I think we should all showcase our talents. I'm sure you all have some?"

She scanned the room, and several people nodded or bobbed their heads side-to-side to imply they *might* consider themselves talented.

"Tomorrow, we'll have a talent show on the enclosed porch. *Everyone* is invited." She focused on Gretchen and Amanda again. "There will be no *judging*. This is purely for fun."

"What counts as a talent?" asked a bald gentleman in the back.

"Anything," said Mariska, standing. "Anything entertaining at all."

"Two o'clock," said Darla as people stood from their seats. "Spread the word. Come one, come all!"

People shuffled from the room, most avoiding eye contact with Gretchen and Amanda, but all were chattering with what felt like excitement.

"Staff can participate too," said Darla to Luna. "Especially staff as talented as you."

Luna smiled. "I'm still working on the act—"

"So? You can get in some practice," said Mariska.

Luna shot Gretchen and Amanda a final glare, stuffed her

chickens into the bag on her hip, and stormed out of the room.

That left Mariska, Darla, Amanda, and Gretchen staring at each other.

"Who said you could throw a talent show?" asked Amanda.

Before they could answer, Gretchen touched her friend's arm. "Let them have their little show, Amanda. Let's see how it turns out."

She left the room, and Amanda followed her.

Darla didn't like her tone.

CHAPTER TWENTY-THREE

Having had his butt handed to him in mini golf, Seamus and Alma sat in a booth at the Spice Bomb for their early dinner.

He'd be paying.

Or, *Declan* would be paying—though the boy didn't know that yet.

"Seems pretty modern for around here," said Seamus, ogling the restaurant's décor.

Alma agreed. "The food is surprisingly good, and thanks to the bold fusion cuisine and chic aesthetic, no one from the manor comes here. That's why I like it."

"You don't have any friends at the manor?"

Alma rolled her eyes. "You're making me sound like a lonely heart."

"I didn't mean it like that. It just seems like you might be happier somewhere else?"

She shrugged. "I'm fine. I'm—"

She stopped short, and her eyes darted past Seamus. Behind him, he heard the hanging doorbell jingle as someone entered.

"What is it?" he asked.

Alma scrunched her tall frame down in her seat.

"It's Bernie and Gretchen."

"Bernie—he's the owner, right? And Gretchen's the bad girl?"

Alma nodded. "Quick, switch places. They'll see me here."

With a nimble move, Alma slipped from the booth, and Seamus did the same to switch seats with her. As he sat, he saw a couple sitting on the other side of the restaurant.

"Do you have a good view of them?" asked Alma.

He nodded. "They just sat."

"Tell me everything you see. Describe their expressions."

"You're surprised they're together?"

Alma nodded. "I can't think of any reason those two should be here alone."

Seamus watched as Bernie reached across the table and took Gretchen's hand.

"I can think of one," he said.

"What? What are they doing?"

"They're holding hands."

"Really? Romantically?"

"Looks like it. They're smiling and staring into each other's limpid pools."

Alma gritted her teeth. "No wonder Bernie never cracks down on her. They're having an affair."

Seamus looked at her. "Affair? One of them's married?"

"Bernie is."

"They're talking about something."

"Can you tell what?"

"I can't hear from this distance. I'm pretty impressive, but I'm not Superman."

"I mean, do they look happy? Sad? Mad?"

"Agitated, I'd say." He nodded, happy with his description. "Yeah, I'd say *agitated*."

"We need to hear that conversation."

"Do we? Think we can get a few bucks from his wife if we snap some photos?"

He pulled his phone from his pocket.

Alma gasped. "I almost forget everyone has cameras in their phones. *Yes*—take photos. Not for blackmailing his poor wife, but take good ones."

"*Compromising*," muttered Seamus, pretending to look at his phone as he took a video of the couple canoodling on the opposite side of the restaurant.

"I'm going to sneak in closer and—"

Seamus leaped to his feet directly in a server's path—a server carrying two glasses of water on a tray. The water exploded around Seamus as if he'd been struck by a water balloon. Cold splashed on his neck and ran down his shorts as the server's tray clattered to the ground.

Everyone in the restaurant turned their attention to him, including Bernie and Gretchen.

Gretchen laughed.

Seamus scowled.

She *was* an evil thing.

He nodded to the patrons and squatted to help the server gather her tray and the two acrylic glasses. The glasses had made a racket bouncing around on the tile floor, but they didn't shatter.

Seamus sat back down across from Alma.

She glared at him.

"*Smooth*," she said.

He huffed. "It doesn't matter. They don't know me from Adam."

"They do now. You're that guy who knocked the waitress into next week."

"Okay, okay. Hold on."

He stood again and pressed the video on his phone as he sauntered toward Bernie's table, pretending to be engrossed in his phone. He made it halfway there before tripping over a woman's purse and launching himself forward as he scrambled to find his feet.

He caught himself against the wall and glanced back at the bag's owner.

"Sorry," he said, tapping the purse back toward her with his foot.

She leaned to jerk the handbag to her and set it on the seat beside her, glaring at him as if she thought she could set him on fire with her eyes.

Seamus straightened against the wall near the front door and took a few more covert photos.

He glanced back at his booth and noticed Alma had retrieved a compact mirror from her purse. She angled it to keep an eye on the Elderbrook lovebirds.

Gretchen dragged her long pink nails along Bernie's hand. Bernie responded with a chuckle, his hand enveloping hers.

Seamus wandered back to the table as the server arrived with a second set of waters and two glasses of red wine.

"I got you a pinot," said Alma as he sat. "Though having seen you operate sober, I can't imagine how smooth you must be drunk."

"Oh, I'm much better with a whiskey in me, but any port in a storm," he said, raising the red to his lips.

"Did you get anything?"

He nodded. "I took a decent video and some stills. Did you see? There's definitely something going on there."

Alma nodded, her eyes scanning the crowded restaurant.

"They came here for the same reason I did—no one from the manor comes here. Too avant-garde, too expensive."

Seamus took a large gulp of his wine. "I don't know. Right now, it seems like the *hotspot* for you people."

She chuckled. "I wonder how long that's been going on. I can't believe I didn't see them before."

"Unseemly to date a customer."

She nodded. "And that's if he *wasn't* married. I've met his wife. She's a doll."

Seamus watched as the couple's body language continued to telegraph their affair.

"I think it's a fairly new thing, judging by the enthusiasm."

"Agreed," said Alma, peering into her compact. "She's up to something. I think she's seducing Bernie to her side. She's getting blackmail material on him, too."

"Why would she need something on him?"

"She wants something on everyone, but more so now. Your friends have been shaking things up."

"Charlotte and Declan?"

"Mariska and Darla."

Seamus frowned. "So you know about them, too?"

She smiled. "*Reporter.*"

Seamus chuckled. "Yeah, well, I've worked with Mariska and Darla before. I know they can be a handful once they get rolling."

Alma squinted into her mirror. "They're talking about them now."

"Who? Bernie and Gretchen?"

"Yep. Talking about your gals. She says she doesn't like them. Wants Bernie to get rid of them."

Seamus scowled. "Gretchen said that just now? How do you

know?"

"I'm a pretty good lip reader. Comes in handy as a reporter."

He smirked. "Huh. You're full of surprises, aren't you?"

She glanced up at him.

"You have no idea."

CHAPTER TWENTY-FOUR

Freshly showered and dressed in her street clothes, Charlotte entered the lobby to find Declan and Seamus there.

"How'd it go?" she asked.

Seamus grinned. "Pretty well. She's a fun old gal, our Miss Alma. We got along like a house on fire."

Charlotte looked at Declan. "Wow. We got lucky. She's one of the few who appreciate his charms."

Declan chuckled. "Yep. And she gave him intel. She says Gretchen is blackmailing people—"

"Which we knew."

"Yes, but she thinks Amanda's up to something, too. She's seen her skulking around with Dana, arguing, and walking into the preserve when they thought no one was watching."

"The preserve? The one full of alligators behind the manor?"

"That one. And, she says Muffin is Dana's *mother*."

"No kidding? That explains why Dana doesn't stop that group from bullying the other guests." She smacked her palm against her forehead. "There was a picture of Dana and Muffin together in Muffin's room. Now I know why."

Declan nodded. "There you go. In other news, they saw Bernie and Gretchen together at the restaurant where we had breakfast. Looks like they're having an affair."

Charlotte gasped. "*No.*"

"Yep."

"Wow. That was a successful date." She reached into her backpack and pulled out the tin of tea she'd taken from Ed's room to hand it to Seamus.

"I made an appointment at the testing lab to have this checked. I'll text you the address. Can you drop it off for us?"

Seamus took the canister. "Sure thing."

"Is that Oksana's tea?" asked Declan.

Charlotte nodded and then reached into the front pocket of her bag to pull out a pen.

"There's some liquid trapped in the cap here. I need this tested, too."

Seamus took it.

"What's that?" asked Declan.

She shrugged. "Just a random bottle of unlabeled stuff I found in Gretchen's drawer. Probably nothing."

She turned her attention to Seamus.

"We'll follow you out. We need to grab some food and then get to work."

"On what?" asked Declan as they strolled out of the manor.

She grinned. "We're going gator huntin'."

After grabbing dinner, Charlotte and Declan returned to the manor to creep into the back yard under cover of darkness. They both had small flashlights, but the big moon made it easy to see as they picked their way along the edge of the property toward the back of the garden.

Something rustled in the reeds, and Declan turned toward the sound.

"Maybe I'm crazy, but I'm wondering if wading into a swamp at night because someone saw enormous alligator prints is a *good* idea."

"No worries. Everyone knows gators never eat the righteous."

He nodded. "Right. Stupid."

Charlotte pointed to the edge of the garden with her flashlight.

"Darla said she saw the prints somewhere around here...*There*."

She shined the light on the clear imprint of a point-toed giant lizard's foot.

"Definitely looks gatory," agreed Declan.

He pulled a large sheath from his waistband and drew a wide

knife from it. She gawked at it.

"Are we allowed to stab gators?"

"I think if it is between us and the gator, yes. I'm not going out there in the *hopes* of stabbing gators."

Declan took a few steps into the brush and paused.

"Do you notice anything strange about this gator swamp?" he asked, stamping his feet.

Charlotte mimicked him.

"It's not swampy."

"Exactly."

He passed her to return to the edge of the garden and squatted down to feel the ground.

"It's not soft here. It hasn't rained in a while, either."

"Meaning?"

"Meaning, why are these prints so deep? They look like they were made in soft mud, and there's nothing swampy back here at all."

He stood and strode into the underbrush again with Charlotte on his heels until they reached a wall of tangled plants.

"These are weed shrubs," said Charlotte, shining her light on the leaves. "I don't know what they're called, but I helped Darla get rid of one once."

"So?"

"So look at this. It looks like a wall of them." She bent to shine her light at the base of the plants. "Little weird weeds wouldn't grow in a hedgerow like this, don't you think?"

"You think someone planted them on purpose?"

She shrugged. "Maybe."

Declan bent one of the branches, and they slipped through. Behind the hedges, they spotted a clear path leading to an island of trees.

"Someone comes this way often," said Declan.

"They're careful to hide their trail up to the wall they planted. After that, they're less careful about making tracks."

They followed the trail into the trees.

"Any idea what we're looking for?" asked Declan, pointing his flashlight into the branches of the pines.

"I don't know. The trail's harder to follow in here without all the scrub brush. It looks a little more like a path this way."

Charlotte heard a buzzing, and Declan held up a hand. "Hold on. My phone—it's Seamus."

He answered and talked for a moment before hanging up.

"Did he get the lab results back already?"

He nodded. "Yep. Nothing poisonous. Just herbal tea—"

"Good—"

"And *herb*."

Her brow knitted. "Hm?"

Declan smirked. "There was a little plastic bag of pot hidden under the tea."

"Pot? *Marijuana* pot?"

He nodded.

Charlotte chuckled. "Why Ed, you old dog. Did Seamus ask to have that tested, too?"

Declan nodded. "He said he figured we'd want that. It might not be poisoned, but it might explain why Ed was laughing so hard."

Charlotte nodded as they made their way through the trees. "*Ah*. Good point."

A moment later, they emerged from the copse and back into the full moonlight.

"Whoa," said Declan as the moon illuminated the new landscape.

A garden, about half the size of the community garden, had been built behind the trees, well hidden from prying eyes.

To their right stood a potting station made from an old folding table, and a locker sat beneath it. Charlotte opened the box to find nothing more insidious than gardening tools inside.

"Pot?" suggested Declan.

Charlotte shook her head as she walked into the garden. "I don't see any. It's all different things. I see peppers. This looks like ginger...I'm not great at identifying plants."

"I'll help."

They moved through the garden, pointing their flashlights, until Declan made a strange grunting noise.

"What is it?" asked Charlotte.

"I think you're safe from your angle, but look over my shoulder," he said.

It took a moment to spot it, but behind him, the moonlight glinted off the face of a shiny square box strapped to a tree.

"Trailcam," she said.

He nodded. "Yep."

He approached it from behind to unstrap it from the tree, with Charlotte shadowing him to stay out of view.

"What are you doing?" she asked.

"It's a cheap camera. It may not send to a cloud the owners can access. There's a card."

"So they'd have to come get it to see us on it? They might not have seen us?"

He opened the camera and turned it off.

"Either that or the undercover portion of our operation is officially over."

CHAPTER TWENTY-FIVE

As Charlotte pushed her cart toward her first room the following day, Oksana approached her with a pen and a small notebook.

Charlotte braced herself. She didn't know who might approach them today. She didn't know who was on the other side of that secret garden trail camera. Declan had taken it, for now, to make sure no one saw them on the video card, but they'd been unable to confirm any uploads to a cloud somewhere.

Someone might be watching their feed, plotting their deaths, while she was scrubbing toilets.

Oksana raised her pen.

"Did you like Ed's tea?" she asked.

Charlotte hemmed. She, of course, *hadn't* tried it for fear of being poisoned. Even if she hadn't handed the tea off to Seamus to take to the lab, she'd been too busy running around the preserve and worrying they'd blown everything.

"I didn't. I'm sorry," she said.

"That's okay. Let me do a profile on you now."

Oksana wrote *Charlotte* at the top of the page.

"This is my tea book, where I write all the mixtures for my customers."

"Customers? You mean the residents?"

She nodded. "Yes, them and others. I give the first tin free, and if they want more, they buy for a small fee. I am not getting rich this way."

"Do you have many customers?"

"Not yet. Six. But I am proud to say everyone who had tried

my blends became customers."

Charlotte nodded. "Do you grow your own teas and herbs and whatever?"

"I do."

"Do you know about the garden in the back? Is that yours?"

"The community garden?" Oksana smiled sheepishly. "Once or twice, I have *borrowed* some ingredients from there—"

"No, not that garden. The one back in the preserve."

Oksana's forehead scrunched like crumpling paper. "There is another garden?"

Charlotte studied the woman's expression and decided Oksana couldn't be the garden owner unless she was a *fantastic* liar.

"Oksana, where is your cart?" asked Yasmine as she blew through the lobby.

Oksana nodded. "Getting it now." She looked at Charlotte. "We can do this later upstairs without you-know-who." She winked and left to get her cart.

Charlotte noticed Bernie at his office door. He glanced in her direction, and they locked eyes.

"Could we talk for a second?" she asked. She hadn't seen him lately and suspected he spent as little time at the manor as possible.

He glanced at his watch but nodded and unlocked his door to let her in.

"No Apple today?" she asked, glancing at the dog bed.

"Apple's not my dog. She's Yasmine's. She just hangs out here when she's done working."

"She is?" Charlotte had difficulty imagining Yasmine teaching Apple adorable tricks or dressing her in a maid's uniform.

He nodded. "What's this about? Find something?"

"Not yet. We've got some leads."

"Good. Great."

"Were you aware of the garden in the preserve?"

"The community garden?"

"No, beyond that. There's another garden tucked behind that group of trees behind the property."

Bernie scowled. "No. I only know the one garden."

Charlotte frowned. "That means you're not the one with a camera out there."

"There's a garden with a *camera*?"

She nodded. "It's not a swamp like I assumed. It's just land, and someone's built a garden there."

He glanced at his watch again.

"Can you show me?"

"Sure. As long as you promise to help when Yasmine chews me a new one for being late to my first room."

He chuckled. "You're on your own."

As they headed out of the office and into the back yard, Charlotte used her time with Bernie to run through some other points.

"Are you aware how Gretchen, Amanda, and Muffin bully the other residents?"

Bernie looked away. "I wouldn't say they *bully* them—"

"Gretchen and probably Amanda are flat-out blackmailing some of them."

Bernie stopped in his tracks. "Blackmailing? You can't be serious."

Charlotte nodded as they continued through the yard.

"That's not good," he said, twiddling with his mustache. "I swear, sometimes it's more like being a high school principal."

"So you had no idea?"

"*No*. Why didn't anyone tell me?"

"You're not always on site to protect them. If word got out, they can't come to you."

He snorted a laugh. "*Protect* them? You make it sound like their lives are—" He realized what he was saying and paled. "You don't think Gretchen or Amanda are *killing* people, do you?"

"We don't know yet. It's something we're looking into, though."

"Surely, if things are that bad, someone would have told Dana, and she would have told me. She's in charge of the day-to-day."

"And Muffin is her mother."

He groaned. "Do you think Dana is in on this? The blackmailing?"

"We don't know yet."

"But you think this is all related to the deaths?"

"We don't have a clear link, no. I just thought you'd like to know."

Charlotte considered telling him they knew about his relationship with Gretchen but decided against it. She didn't want anything to change while they were following patterns of behavior—not even his affair.

He rubbed at his temples. "I swear, this just keeps getting worse. Thank you for letting me know, though. I can't let a few bad apples ruin things for everyone. I'll be sure to talk to everyone."

Charlotte held up a hand. "No—*don't*. Not yet. We don't want people taking pains to hide the things—we want to catch them off guard."

"Oh. That makes sense."

His expression betrayed his concern. She imagined he wanted to solve the residents' problems *and* maybe warn Gretchen that people were on to her—but he couldn't do either without ruining the murder investigation.

Charlotte led him through the community garden to the edge of the preserve.

"See those?" she said, pointing to the alligator tracks.

Bernie's eyes bugged.

"Oh no. I need to call someone—"

"Don't bother. There's a good chance they're fake—there to scare people away."

"You know that for sure?"

"No, but they're suspiciously perfect. We'll try and get you proof before you have to make any calls."

She led him into the weeds and through the little copse of trees to the garden.

"It's here—"

They broke through the treeline, and Charlotte stopped in her tracks.

Things had changed.

All that lay beyond the trees was a mottled patch of dirt and weeds.

The garden had disappeared.

"Here?" asked Bernie, sounding confused.

She pointed at the emptiness. "This was a garden last night."

The locker where they'd found the tools and the planting table had also disappeared.

Bernie scowled. "I don't understand. How could there have been a garden *here*?"

"Someone not only pulled up the plants—they replanted *weeds* to make it look like there was *never* a garden here."

She put her hand on her hips and scanned the barren patch of ground. Someone had done a heck of a job. It must have taken them all night.

Pretty impressive, really.

She pointed to a tree. "There was a trail camera hanging from there, and over here, there was a potting station and a locker with tools."

Bernie frowned.

"Sounds like quite the production. Did you take pictures?"

"We did—" Charlotte retrieved her phone and flipped through the photos she'd taken. They were all shots of individual plants— none of the garden as a *whole*. She'd been distracted by the trail cam discovery and never thought to take the most important photo.

She never dreamed the garden would disappear overnight.

Ugh.

"I'm afraid I don't have much here. It was dark."

He scowled. "What do you think it was for? What's sinister about a garden?"

"I don't know. I wasn't sure there *was* anything sinister about it—until it disappeared. It looked like a normal garden. I know they weren't growing Ed's pot."

Bernie straightened. "Ed's *pot*?"

She nodded. "We found a small bag of marijuana hidden in a tea tin in his room."

Bernie's jaw dropped, and he shook his head.

"See? I told you. I *am* a school principal."

CHAPTER TWENTY-SIX

The workday had proved uneventful. Charlotte didn't find anything else interesting in the rooms, though she did get a call from the lab about Oksana's *Ed's Blend* tea.

It was tea.

Nothing odd about it except the marijuana that had been hidden with it. That didn't mean Oksana hadn't tampered with other blends, but since Ed was one of the people who died, it weighed heavily in favor of her *not* being the killer. At least, she was not using weaponized tea.

The liquid drops proved benign, too—a mixture of common herbs—probably some kind of energy shot.

She figured it would be safe to let Oksana know she was a big fan of the bergamot in Earl Grey. She didn't know much about tea, and the woman kept asking her what flavors she liked *all morning*.

Another persistent theme for the day was the news of the talent show. She'd overheard several residents talking about it and caught someone practicing their singing. Dana let Mariska and Darla use her copier to make flyers, which they hung on the manor notice boards.

At the end of the day, after changing out of her uniform and into her clothes, Charlotte joined Mariska and Darla on the spacious all-weather porch to find a crowd gathering at three o'clock—an hour early for the talent show.

The idea had clearly captured the imagination of the residents. Charlotte felt the buzz in the air as she and Yasmine moved furniture to allow space for a stage area and set up chairs for an audience that kept growing.

Charlotte unfolded a chair near a pair of chatting women.

"You're here early," she said when she caught them watching her.

"I came early to work up the nerve to sing," said one, a cheery dumpling of a woman. "I think this was a great idea. Everyone's been a little gray lately."

"I think we're all always a little gray," quipped the other, and the two giggled.

Charlotte smiled. "Good luck—hope to hear you sing."

She turned in time to see Mariska beaming, her chest puffed.

"I think we really hit on something here," she said.

Darla nodded beside her. "It was *my* idea, but sure."

Mariska scowled. "No, it wasn't."

"Yes, it was."

Luna appeared with sheets and a long loop of thin rope. She'd assigned herself the task of creating a makeshift curtain system that could be opened for each performer and closed while the next prepared for their big moment.

"That was a good idea," said Charlotte, staring up at the curtains as Luna tested sliding the sheets back and forth along the rope.

Luna grinned. "It helps that there were hooks here from past Christmas lights. Plus, growing up, I always set up little stages for myself, so I'm like a pro at this."

Others arrived to fill in the seats, some with requests for what they'd need to perform. After setting up chairs, sound systems, and snacks, everyone scrambled to improvise props and costumes. They had to disappoint the woman who wanted a piano but found someone with an electric keyboard to lend.

"Word on the street is you're gathering quite the crowd," said Alma to Charlotte as she arrived to claim a seat.

"We are. I don't even know if we'll have time for everyone today."

Alma scanned the crowd. "This is just what everyone needed. It might be time to pay the piper."

Finding the comment odd, Charlotte followed Alma's gaze to find it riveted on Gretchen. The queen of the terrible threesome observed the growing crowd from the dining room, frowning through the glass door.

"You have something in mind for her?" asked Charlotte.

Alma turned to her, looking coy. "Seamus told you what we saw?"

"That was his mission, to report back. Though I can tell you, he enjoyed every minute of his assignment."

Alma smiled. "So did I. He's quite the character."

"That's one word for him." Charlotte set up her last chair and straightened. "Do you have a talent for today?"

Alma chuckled.

"No. I'm afraid any talents I have aren't translatable to the stage. No one wants to see me write an article or play speed chess."

Nearby, Yasmine's attention snapped to Alma.

"You play speed chess?" she asked.

Alma nodded. "I had an old source who played. It was a great way to get information out of him."

Without another word, Yasmine left the room. Charlotte watched her go and turned to Alma.

"That was the most human interaction I've seen her have, and she still made it weird at the end."

Alma chuckled. "She's all right." She eyed Charlotte and leaned in. "I can see you don't believe me, so I'll share this with you—she lost her brother last month. It's been hard for her. Not only was he family, but she was his caretaker, and they lived together. Now she's alone."

Charlotte gaped. That information *did* change her opinion of Yasmine's chronic crankiness. She'd have to give her some leeway.

"I had no idea. I thought she just hated me."

Alma shook her head. "Don't take it personally. In fact, I find it's best never to take anything personally unless you have to. Things almost always have nothing to do with you."

Charlotte nodded and stepped out of the way as a resident clipped her shoulder in his eagerness to claim a spot. He didn't bother to apologize.

Charlotte turned the other cheek.

Rude. But hey, maybe he had his reasons.

The room was nearly full. Some picked at the cheese and

cracker spread, some sat, but it looked as if everyone in the entire manor had stopped by.

Darla stepped to the microphone at the front of the room.

"If you're planning on performing, please come behind the curtains," she announced.

A smattering of people disappeared behind Luna's sheet curtains. Charlotte spotted the secret clown dragging three folded walkers with wires wound around them. She disappeared behind the stage with them.

She had no idea what that was about.

The people who'd gone behind the curtain reappeared one or two at a time to retake their seats.

Darla and Mariska walked in front of the curtain.

Gretchen and Amanda had moved from the dining room to the porch to glare from their spot against the wall.

Muffin arrived with her cohorts but stared off to the right, away from the stage, oblivious to the world around her. Charlotte thought she looked terrible—pale, tired—as if she might collapse at any second. There were scratches on her arms, but they didn't have any pattern to imply their cause. Charlotte knew she didn't have a cat.

The microphone crackled.

"I'm Darla, and this is Mariska. We're new but happy to be here," said Darla over the speakers.

Mariska waved and leaned to the mic.

"Thank you, everyone, for coming. We're going to get right to the performers."

She peeked behind the curtains and nodded to Darla, who leaned into the microphone.

"I present to you—*The Walkerettes*!" she announced with a flourish.

Darla and Mariska moved from center stage to stand beside Charlotte at the side of the stage.

"Who knew you had a carnival barker trapped inside of you," said Charlotte.

Darla chuckled. "Everyone."

Luna used a remote to lower the room's powered shades and turned off the lights, plunging the porch into relative darkness.

"This is dramatic," whispered Charlotte.

The chattering crowd hushed and fixed their eyes forward. Luna and Oksana each took a curtain in hand and slid them back to reveal three elderly ladies, each leaning on a gleaming silver walker adorned with twinkling fairy lights.

A tittering of laughter rose from the audience, interspersed with snorts. The women on the stage wore sequin-covered leotards and sparkling headbands with large pink feathers sticking out from them.

Darla produced a phone Charlotte didn't recognize, pressed a button, and upbeat music swelled from a wireless speaker at her side.

She guessed the phone was Luna's because it had a clown-themed case.

Good thing I'm a detective, or I never would have figured it out.

The three ladies on stage sprang to life with grins. They shuffled sideways in perfect sync with both the music and each other. The audience cheered as the trio kicked like Rockettes. They created a conga line, hips swaying to the rhythm, and twirled walkers like dance partners. The middle woman lifted her walker above her head for a finale while her flanking partners performed a footwork sequence.

All in all, not too shabby—too good for them to have learned it in a few hours for the talent show—which begged the question, why *had* they learned a walker dancing routine?

Charlotte giggled and clapped with the rest of them as the music ended, and the three used their glittering walkers to return to their seats.

The curtains closed, and the light came back on.

"Wow," said Charlotte.

"That was adorable," said Mariska.

Darla stepped in front of the curtains to announce *Gail and her Creations*.

"This is our neighbor," said Mariska.

When the curtain opened again, a lone woman sat in a chair on the stage. She pulled knitting from a bag sitting on the floor at her side.

"I made this one," said Gail, holding up what looked like a crochet snowflake. "And I made this one..."

Crochet show and tell continued for close to five minutes

before Gail stood and bowed as the curtains closed, and a smattering of confused clapping ensued.

"I don't think she really gets what a talent show is," said Charlotte.

Mariska shrugged. "I don't know. That Jasmine-stitch hat she made was something else. I'll have to ask her how she did that."

Darla ran up to announce *The Spoonman* and returned to her spot against the wall.

The curtains reopened on a similar scene, but a gentleman wearing a tweed vest holding a pair of spoons in one hand had replaced Gail and her crochet.

The audience fell silent, and after mumbling something to himself, the man clicked the spoons together in a slow rhythm. The clacking picked up speed until it transformed into an infectious beat. For added flair, he rattled the spoons up and down his arm, across his chest—even against his cheek. The whole thing took two minutes, but the audience cheered with appreciation.

"I'll never eat cereal again without thinking about that," said Charlotte.

Oksana took the stage next as *The Tea Lady*. A small folding table sat beside her, covered in teapots, tea leaves, and ornate cups.

She discussed the history of her family's tea-making tradition while demonstrating the correct way to prepare a cup of tea. While not the most death-defying performance, Charlotte noticed an enraptured audience, particularly when she read the tea leaves. With every mystical word, the audience leaned in closer.

When she finished, a group of resident bird watchers presented a sketch about their favorite birds, complete with homemade hand puppets.

Again, Charlotte wondered why they'd made bird hand puppets *without knowing there'd be an impromptu talent show*. For slow bird-watching days? Did they send someone out into the shrubs with the puppets so they could watch?

Apparently, the puppets were the last straw for Gretchen.

"This is pathetic," she snapped, stepping away from the wall in a rage.

The woman using a puppet seagull to talk to a puppet blue jay fell silent on the stage.

Gretchen pointed at Darla and Mariska as if she were accusing them of being witches.

"This is *them* trying to win you all over."

Darla stepped forward, and Charlotte and Mariska tensed, readying to grab her if she tried to charge Gretchen. She didn't. Instead, she picked up an unused flamingo sock puppet and tied it around her neck like a scarf.

"Look at them trying to make you have *fun*," she mocked in a stylized Gretchen voice. "You should listen to *me* because I'm the Queen of the World."

The audience rippled with nervous laughter.

"I don't know who you think you are," returned Gretchen.

"Me? I'm Gretchen. I'm not happy unless everyone around me is miserable."

Mariska stepped forward, wringing her hands together like a toady.

"I'm Amanda. I do my master's bidding. Yes, master, you tell them, *master*…"

The audience exploded with laughter.

"That's not *me*," said Amanda, her eyes wide with horror.

Gretchen poked a finger at them. "I will *destroy* you."

She turned her attention to the audience. "I'll destroy all of you!"

Gretchen spun for a dramatic exit, only to bump into Amanda, who remained gaping at Mariska. To recover, Gretchen pushed Amanda away and flung open the dining room door.

Stumbling, Amanda caught her balance against the back of a chair, glared at the stunned audience, and scrambled to follow Gretchen into the dining room.

Muffin remained, her expression blank. After a beat, she followed the other two.

The room remained quiet, everyone staring where the trio had retreated. They turned to each other, eyes wide in shocked silence. Charlotte felt their collective fear.

They feared a burned Gretchen.

Would she release her secrets in retaliation?

Yasmine held a boxed chess set over her head.

"I challenge Alma to speed chess," she announced. In her other hand, she held a timer.

Alma twisted in her seat. "What?"

"You heard me. Speed chess. Close the curtain."

The bird puppeteers shuffled to their seats as Luna and Oksana closed the curtains.

The crowd murmured nervously until the curtains reopened. Alma and Yasmine sat on opposite sides of the same little table where Oksana had set up her tea.

A chessboard sat between them.

"Start us," said Yasmine to Darla.

Darla stepped forward.

"Let the game begin!"

Alma moved her pawn forward and slapped the timer. Yasmine replied in kind.

The slapping riveted the audience, taking their minds off Gretchen's outburst. The game's tempo quickened. Alma's Queen made a daring swoop across the board, claiming Yasmine's bishop. Yasmine retaliated by cornering Alma's knight.

The intensity peaked as Alma, down to her last few pieces, appeared cornered. She maneuvered her rook with a sudden bold stroke, trapping Yasmine's king.

"*Checkmate*," she declared with uncharacteristic giddiness.

A momentary hush fell over the crowd, and Charlotte braced herself for Yasmine's response. Then, like the sun popping from behind dark clouds, the intense expression on Yasmine's face dissipated, and she *grinned*.

Yasmine grinned.

The crowd erupted into applause.

A woman stood. "Ten years ago, I had an affair with my physical therapist," she shouted.

The crowd fell silent again as all eyes turned to her.

Another woman stood. "I stole a watch from a friend because I was mad at her."

Another woman rose to her feet.

"I pooped my pants at lunch last year."

"Who hasn't?" said someone else.

The crowd laughed.

More people stood and shared their darkest secrets with the

crowd.

No one seemed terribly shocked.

"We're *old*," said Alma once the confessions died down. "We've all seen and done it all. We're human. Let's not hold that against each other."

"And more importantly, let's not let Gretchen hold it against us," said a voice from the back.

Applause and cheers filled the room.

Darla elbowed Charlotte and grinned.

"I think this turned out to be a pretty good idea," she said.

"I know," said Mariska. "I'm glad I thought of it."

CHAPTER TWENTY-SEVEN

Declan was on his way to meet Charlotte at the talent show when he passed through the lobby and noticed Dana in the parking lot, standing at the back of her car, wrestling with something that did *not* want to fit in the hatchback.

Hm.

He changed direction and moved to the front window to watch through the sheer curtain as she swore and wiped her brow with the effort. He couldn't see the object of her frustration. It was a chunky, metallic, unidentifiable beast of a thing she seemed determined to squeeze into the back of her modest sedan.

He leaned closer to the window, squinting.

What the heck is that?

She gave the item one last mighty shove, and it shifted, sending her spilling forward into the back of the car. Bouncing back out, she slammed shut the door, wiped her forehead with the back of her arm, and huffed.

Declan stepped away from the window, hoping Dana would come back inside and he'd get a chance to peek into the back of her car.

No such luck.

With a final nod of satisfaction, she slid into her driver's seat.

Shoot.

As she pulled away, Declan took a few slow paces toward the talent show location, his mind running over objects the item might have been.

Should I follow her?

It would be hard to catch her. And whatever she was wrestling could be nothing. A vacuum in need of repair or a rental floor buffer—

Rental.

He stopped with an idea.

He looked at his watch. The talent show would continue for a while, and Charlotte didn't need him there.

He wanted to take another look at the garden.

He went out the front door to avoid passing through the back porch and walked around the manor, hurrying through the community garden and plunging into the wilds of the preserve. Cutting through the copse, he emerged at the edge of the destroyed garden Charlotte had told him about.

He strolled into the square where the garden once grew, impressed by the clever way someone had planted *weeds* where plants once grew. They hadn't hidden everything, though. He found tiller tracks in the dirt.

Dana *had* rented a tiller.

It had to be.

He worked his way back to the manor and checked the shed there.

No tiller.

Yep. That had to be it. Dana rented a tiller to destroy the garden, returning it now while everyone was distracted at the talent show. Maybe he could find the receipt for evidence—

Wait a second...

Dana was gone. She'd be gone at least another half an hour— the manor wasn't near any place she could have rented the machinery.

That meant her room was unattended.

The talent show was in full swing, and he heard applause as he rushed around the side of the building to enter through the front door.

His heart pounded. He knew he wasn't winded—all the clue-finding was *exciting*.

"No wonder Charlotte loves this stuff so much," he mumbled as he headed for Dana's office. He keyed in the master code and heard the door unlatch.

It worked.

He'd worried Dana gave herself some special code, but she hadn't—probably so the cleaners could get inside.

He slipped inside and found the office different from the last time he'd been poking around. Someone had left things in a state of disarray. He assumed it was Dana herself who'd been rifling through the file drawers, but who knew?

He noticed a black trash bag and poked through it until he found a cloth bag with two large items inside. Unwrapping it, he pulled out a pair of shoes and scowled at the bottoms. The modified soles looked like someone had nailed alligator feet to the bottom. Upon further inspection, he could tell the "feet" were rubber, but the effect would have been the same as the real thing.

Alligator prints.

Dana wanted her secret garden kept *secret*. The alligator prints deterred the average passerby, protecting her clandestine horticultural activities.

He had proof.

Now, they needed one last piece of the puzzle.

They'd need to figure out why a garden full of legal herbs and vegetables was something Dana wanted to hide.

CHAPTER TWENTY-EIGHT

Alma left the all-weather room to find Yasmine talking to a couple of female residents. The women wandered off, and Yasmine noticed her approaching.

"Good game," she said, holding out her hand to shake.

"That was a lot of fun," agreed Alma. "Why didn't you ever mention you played speed chess before?"

Yasmine scoffed. "No one cares."

Alma chuckled. "I guess not." She was about to leave but paused after recalling her conversation with Seamus.

For some reason, she'd told him things she hadn't even admitted to herself.

Not recently, anyway.

She paused and swallowed.

"Um, how are you?" she asked.

Yasmine blinked, clearly surprised to find she hadn't walked on.

"Fine."

"Just fine?"

Yasmine sighed. "I think I need to move. Not the job—my home."

"Really? Why?"

She shrugged. "Things will be hard without my brother's income. I—"

Alma put her hand on Yasmine's arm.

"Hold that thought."

"Hm?"

"*She's back.*"

She pointed her eyes over the maid's shoulder, and Yasmine turned. The two watched as Gretchen walked into the dining room. Her head was down. She held a small book in her hand.

"I know that book," said Yasmine.

Alma looked at her. "What is it?"

"It's her blackmail book. She keeps it in a hidden compartment in her desk." Her gaze slid in Alma's direction. "All these ladies think their *special* desks are unique."

Alma chuckled. "You make a habit of poking around hidden compartments?"

Yasmine frowned. "*No.* She *earned* my attention. She threatened me yesterday."

"Why?"

"I caught her trying to sneak into the new ladies' room. Looking for things to ruin them, no doubt."

Alma grunted. "She's a monster."

"Yes, and it looks like she's about to start roaring."

Alma smirked at her. "I don't think so."

Gretchen looked up and stopped.

Alma walked toward her.

Yasmine followed.

"Hello, Gretchen," said Alma.

Gretchen looked up from her book and dropped it to her side. "What do you want?"

"What do you have there?" Alma asked, nodding at the book.

Gretchen moved the item behind her back.

"None of your business, you big cow."

Alma smiled. Not the first time someone had insulted her size. She hadn't expected creativity from Gretchen.

"You're not thinking of doing anything you'll regret, are you?" she asked.

"I won't regret *anything*, thank you very much," sneered Gretchen. "I think maybe it's time I remind some of these ladies what they stand to lose."

"Do you think Leah would approve?"

Gretchen scowled. "Leah who? What are you talking about?"

"You know. *Leah.* Bernie's wife."

The snarl on Gretchen's lips relaxed.

She sniffed. "What are you talking about?"

"Do you think, if Leah found out, Bernie would take your side?"

"My side—?"

"Or do you think she'd demand Bernie got rid of you? Kicked you out of Elderbrook? Sent you packing?"

Gretchen swallowed. "He can't kick me out."

"Can't he? This is a private business. He can do anything he wants."

Gretchen scoffed. "You've got *nothing*."

"Oh?" Alma reached into her pocket and pulled out her phone. She navigated to her photos and held one up for Gretchen to see.

The blood drained from Gretchen's face until her throat glowed pale against her navy scarf.

"How did you get that?" she asked in a hoarse whisper.

"I'm a *reporter*, Gretchen. This is what I do."

Yasmine swooped in and plucked the book from Gretchen's hand.

Gretchen lunged for it as Yasmine retreated.

"*Give me that!*"

"I don't think so," said Yasmine, moving out of reach.

Alma stepped between them.

Gretchen sized her up and then shifted her attention to Yasmine.

"You're *staff*. I'll have you *fired*."

Yasmine smiled.

"I'll take my chances."

Gretchen's fists closed, and her gaze shifted from Yasmine to Alma and back again.

She huffed.

"This isn't the last you'll see of me," she growled.

The ladies held their ground without responding as she stormed away.

"I'm not sure that was the smartest thing we've ever done," said Yasmine after a minute.

Alma turned to her. "I think we'll be okay."

"Why is that?"

"Well, for one, she's *mean* but not particularly clever."

Yasmine nodded. "I can't argue with that."

"And two, I sent this picture to Bernie anonymously right after the talent show with a nice note."

She held up a photo of Gretchen and Bernie holding hands at the restaurant, and Yasmine gasped.

"What did the note say?"

"Get rid of her, or Leah gets this next."

Yasmine hooted. "You think he will?"

"I think so."

"What makes you so sure?"

"I happen to know Leah has all the money. Her family is wealthy. If he loses her—"

Yasmine finished her sentence.

"He loses *everything.*"

She laughed as Charlotte approached, her eyes locked on the book in Alma's hand.

"Is that—?"

"Gretchen's blackmail. I don't think she'll be using it." Alma handed her the book. "You take it. Maybe it'll help with your investigation."

Yasmine's brow furrowed. "Her *investigation?*"

"Thanks. I'll let you know," said Charlotte. She glanced at Yasmine. "Nice chess."

"Thank you." Yasmine took a deep breath and reached out to touch Charlotte's arm before she could leave. "Charlotte, I'm sorry I've been so hard on you. My brother died, and I'm afraid I didn't take his death well. How I treated you was *inexcusable.*"

Charlotte nodded. "I'm sorry to hear about your brother. I really *do* appreciate the apology." She smiled and held up the book. "Well, back to work."

She walked off.

"Why would you give that to her?" Yasmine asked Alma. "And what did you mean by *investigations?*"

"Charlotte's not a maid. She's a detective investigating our recent spate of deaths."

Yasmine gaped. "Someone thinks those people were *murdered?*"

"Bernie. He hired her, but from what I understand, he doesn't *know* they were murders. He's just suspicious."

Yasmine pinched the bridge of her nose. "She's not a maid? That makes the way I treated her even worse, somehow."

Alma touched her shoulder. "I'm sure she understands."

Yasmine sighed. "At least, things will be better here without Gretchen. What about Amanda?"

"She'll fall apart without her leader."

Yasmine nodded. "I hope you're right."

Alma sighed. "Even so, I was thinking—I may have overstayed my welcome here."

"*You*? No. You're not thinking of leaving, are you? You're one of the good ones."

Alma chuckled. "I don't know. I never really pictured myself as someone living in a house full of people like this. If I could find a roommate—"

Alma gave Yasmine a hard stare.

"A roommate?" echoed Yasmine.

Alma nodded. "I don't know...maybe someone who recently lost a roommate?"

Yasmine put her hand on her chest.

"*Me*?"

"If you'd be interested?"

Yasmine's jaw worked in silence for a moment.

"I *would*," she said finally. "But my place is small. I don't know if you'd like it."

"I'd buy us a new place."

Yasmine's eyes widened. "You *would*? I could sell mine, but I still don't know if I'd make enough to pay for half of a place you'd like. I don't know if I would even have enough to pay rent for long on a really *nice* place..."

Alma shrugged. "We'd work something out. I'm older than you. I might become a burden after a while. I could cover the house if you didn't mind covering *me* when the time came?"

"Mind?" Yasmine laughed. "It would be my honor. Did you have a place in mind?"

Alma pulled at her chin, thinking.

"I don't know. Someone told me about an adorable little community I thought I'd check out."

"What's it called?"

"Pineapple Port."

Yasmine smiled. "Sounds nice."

Alma nodded.

"Doesn't it?"

CHAPTER TWENTY-NINE

Fresh from returning the rented tiller, Dana sat in her car in Elderbrook's driveway and retrieved the clip from her trail camera again. When the movement notification popped up on her screen, she'd assumed it was another raccoon digging up her plants.

It was no raccoon.

She'd watched in horror as two people walked around her garden. The images were fuzzy, but she could tell it was a man and a woman.

"*Who are you*?" she said out loud to her phone.

The woman was half out of the screen. The man focused on the camera. It was dark, and he stood too far away for her to see his face.

"He sees it," she whispered.

She tried to zoom in on the woman. The video got blurrier.

She swore as the feed died. She hadn't found the camera. She suspected the man took it. The last image she saw was of him heading toward the tree where she'd hung the thing.

The pair looked like...*who*? Kind of like Declan and the new maid, but that didn't make sense, did it? Those two didn't know each other. Not as far as she knew.

They *did* get hired on the same day, though...

She'd planned on destroying the garden, but not in a single night.

Her back still hurt.

She swore and called Bernie.

"Do the new manager and the new maid know each other?" she asked when he answered.

Bernie sounded distracted. "What?"

"Declan and—whatsherface—the new maid. Do they know each other?"

"Why?"

"Because they're—" She stopped.

She couldn't say. Not when she was so close to leaving. She couldn't let him know anything about the garden.

About anything.

She glanced at the manor and had an idea.

"Are you at home?"

"Yes."

"Okay. Sorry. I thought I saw them together," she said. "I think maybe they're *fraternizing*."

"It happens," said Bernie, sounding exasperated.

"Sorry to bother you. It's nothing. I'll keep an eye on it. "

"It's fine. *Goodbye*."

She hung up and stepped out of her car to enter the brightly lit lobby and move to Bernie's office door. She heard the residents at the talent show cheering.

The halls were eerily quiet.

Looking around to be sure no one was watching, she unlocked the door with her master code and entered. Bernie didn't know, but she'd helped set up the keypad system.

She'd enabled a master combination on every door, including his office.

Stepping into the room, she closed the door behind her and flipped on the light in the windowless room. She opened his laptop but found it locked with a password.

Fudge.

She gave up on the computer and instead rummaged through his drawers. She wasn't sure what she was looking for, but she *did* notice *no* mention of Declan or the new maid in the employment files.

Strange.

Bernie had been putting her off about Declan's paperwork. Now, she knew why.

Declan wasn't really the new manager, was he?

But who was he?

Dana skimmed over financial reports, contracts, and personal letters, seeking anything recent and out of place. She found Bernie's corporate checkbook and eyed the last few checks. Nothing special—the catering company, the mortgage—she paused at a note jotted beside a missing check.

Charlock.

What's Charlock? She'd never heard of it.

That wasn't familiar.

She opened her phone and searched for the word.

The Charlock Holmes Detective Agency in nearby Charity popped up.

Ice ran through her veins.

Detective agency?

Why would he hire a detective agency?

Was he that worried about the deaths? They were *old*. It was easy to chalk the deaths up to old age. Why would he investigate them?

And why would he hire a detective agency with such a goofy name—

She gasped.

Charlotte.

Charlock.

She closed her eyes.

That new maid. *Charlotte.*

That couldn't be a coincidence.

It *was* those two in her garden.

She gasped as another thought occurred to her.

Those two new residents had showed up on the same day as Charlotte and Declan.

The same *time* even.

Mariska and Darla.

Were they *all* working for the detective agency? Were the old ladies undercover? Were the residents talking to them?

Trusting them?

She put everything back in place, crept out of the office, and locked it behind her. In the lobby, people milled. The talent show was over.

There wasn't any time left.

They were on to her. She had to *go*.

Dana took the elevator to her mother's room.

CHAPTER THIRTY

Charlotte flipped another page in Gretchen's blackmail log and frowned as Declan entered the room. She'd been sitting on the bench in the staff locker room, searching through the notebook page by page, looking for anything that might imply the manor's unusual spate of deaths were murders.

Nothing seemed to fit.

"What's that?" he asked.

"Gretchen's book o' blackmail. Yasmine took it to end things once and for all, and Alma gave it to me in case it could help with our investigation."

Declan blinked at her. "Wow. That's a good thing, right? If not necessarily for us, at least for the residents?"

Charlotte turned another page. "Yep—you know what's weird about this book?"

"The fact that a grown woman keeps a blackmail book?"

"Yes, *and* there's no mention of Dana, Amanda, or Muffin."

He shrugged. "Why would she have her friends in the book?"

"She wouldn't, but I can't shake the feeling Muffin isn't friends with them on purpose. She doesn't have the same *joie d'vivre* for torturing people as the other two. I thought for sure Gretchen had something on her. I thought she was blackmailing her to force favor with Dana."

"Hm. Well, I can tell you Dana destroyed the garden."

"You can? For sure?"

He nodded. "I just confirmed it. I saw her shoving some kind of big gardening tool into her car and went back out there to check—

there *are* tiller tracks. She rented a tiller. I caught her trying to return it."

"That's something, I guess," said Charlotte. "But we still don't know what the garden was for. Oksana's tea is nothing but tea, so even if it has something to do with her blends, there's nothing evil about them."

"Well, *wait*, it gets better. I'm pretty sure all our answers are buried with that garden."

He swiped through the photos on his phone and held one up for her to see.

She squinted at the picture. "What is that? A closet? Shoes?"

He flipped to the next photo. In it, Declan held a shoe flipped over to reveal the underside.

"*Gator feet?*" she said.

He nodded. "Yep. I found them in Dana's office. These are what I saw her carrying that time I saw her coming from her office."

Charlotte cocked her head, realizing she'd found a place for some useless information bouncing around her head.

"Bootleggers used to use cow print boots so they wouldn't leave human tracks to their stills. Similar idea."

He chuckled. "Except no one worries they'll be eaten by cows."

Charlotte stood and paced as she worked through the evidence in her head.

"Okay—so we know she owned the garden, and after she saw that we found it, she destroyed it. She wasn't at the talent show, which was weird because everyone else was."

"Because she took the opportunity to return the rented equipment."

Charlotte stopped. "Where is she now?"

"I'm not sure. If she's back, she's probably napping. She must be *exhausted*. To till under that whole garden and run around planting weeds to make it look like it had never existed—"

Charlotte nodded. "She did a great job. You can tell *something* was there, but you won't be able to for long. The Florida wilds will eat it up in a week." She squinted at him. "You said she had to be exhausted."

"Sure. It was a pretty big garden, and she's not twenty."

"So, she probably had help. Muffin looked wrecked at the talent show. She had scratches all over her arms."

Declan nodded. "Like she was up all night destroying a garden? And she's Dana's mom. Whatever that garden means, they're *both* involved."

Charlotte started pacing again. "Maybe there's a third, too. Darla saw Amanda walk back there during the planting competition, which isn't all that weird, except she stepped right over those alligator tracks like she knew they were fake."

"Was she at the talent show?"

"Yes. She looked normal…" Charlotte scratched at her head as she tried to process all the possibilities. "If Amanda knows about the garden but isn't worried about it enough to help destroy it—maybe she's just blackmailing Dana and Muffin? She doesn't really care if someone finds the garden."

"She's probably blackmailing them for whatever the garden leads to—not the garden itself?"

"Which explains why Muffin works with the other two like someone with a gun to her head *and* why Dana doesn't do anything about them. She's under their thumb, too."

Declan slipped his phone back into his pocket.

"Muffin's the weak link."

Charlotte nodded.

"We can get her to talk."

CHAPTER THIRTY-ONE

Dana knocked on her mother's door.

"Leave me alone," said Muffin from inside. She sounded sleepy.

"It's me, Mom."

After a lengthy pause, the door cracked open, and Muffin peeked out, dark bags beneath each eye and an expression so slack it looked as if she didn't have the energy to keep her face from sliding off her skull and into her lap.

Dana entered, and Muffin motioned to the kitchenette. "Can I get you something?"

Dana shook her head and sat on the edge of her mother's bed.

"We need to talk."

Muffin collapsed into her comfy reading chair.

"Those two new ladies gave Gretchen and Amanda some comeuppance, I think—" she said, looking low-energy pleased.

Dana wasn't a Gretchen fan, and she *definitely* had no love for Amanda, but having either of them irritated didn't bode well.

She didn't need it.

Not *now*.

"Those two ladies are detectives. Them, the new maid, and the new manager."

Muffin brushed a hair from her face. "Who? The handsome young man taking your place is a—?" She seemed to forget what she was talking about and then circled back. "*What* are you saying?"

"I said that man is a *detective*. So is the new maid. So are the two new residents."

Muffin's head dropped back against the chair. "I don't understand. I'm so tired."

"Let me get you a cup of tea." Dana rose and made her mother a cup of tea with the instant hot water there.

Glancing over her shoulder, she saw her mother had closed her eyes.

The poor thing.

She'd been as helpful as she could be the night before with the garden. She'd been a *trooper*.

Unfortunately, she couldn't help her anymore. She just *couldn't*. How much longer would she last, anyway? Five years, maybe? Every year, she'd become more forgetful. More dizzy...

In the end, she'd tell.

Dana had no doubt.

She slipped the bottle out of her pocket and stared at the green label.

She had to do it.

She's left me no choice.

She poured half the contents into her mother's tea. She added extra cream and sugar. Luckily, her mother liked things sweet.

She slipped the bottle back into her pocket and brought the tea to her mother. She touched her knee to wake her.

"Have the tea, Mom."

Muffin shook her head and took a sip.

"Sweet," she said, but she wasn't disappointed.

"What were we talking about?" she asked.

"I was telling you the new manager, maid, and those two new ladies are detectives. They're here because of the *deaths*."

Muffin scowled and took another sip of her tea. "It wasn't us. They can't prove it."

"*Three* of the people who died were using the bad batch, Mom. It can't be a coincidence."

Muffin closed her eyes. "But no one *knows*. How could they?"

"It doesn't matter." Dana took a deep breath. "I need to go."

"I know you're quitting."

"It's more than that. I'm going to Morocco."

Muffin's eyes opened. "Morocco? What kind of country is that?"

"It's a *non-extradition* country. That's what kind of country it is."

Muffin sat up to squint at her daughter. "I don't know anything about all that. You said we'd live together. I don't want to go *there*."

"I said we could get a place together if the elixir took off, and now that dream is dead."

"But why? It was selling—"

"Because it *killed* people, Mom."

"*One batch*. Just the green label. We fixed it. We can test it in the mini-muffins again to be sure."

Dana dropped her head into her hands.

"You just don't get it. It isn't safe."

"It is *now*. The yellow oleander was one mistake, one time. It wasn't even our fault. The girl at the plant store gave us the wrong plant."

"*We* were the ones making the elixir, and *we* were the ones too stupid to know the difference between St. John's wort and yellow oleander. You think a jury will send the teenager at the plant nursery to jail for this? Or us?"

Muffin scoffed. "No one's going to jail. It was an accident."

"It's more than the mix-up and the *one* bad batch. We didn't consider a lot of important stuff. Like *drug interactions*. How did we not even think about that?"

Muffin scowled. "What interactions? What are you talking about?"

"*Ed*. He was using the good batch, and he still died."

"That had nothing to do with us. We made sure—"

"His batch wasn't poison, but even the real St. John's Wort can cause problems. It interacts with different medications. Did you know he had hypertension?"

Muffin shrugged. "Who doesn't?"

"That's my *point*. I don't know why I never thought about it. I was trying to sell those damn bottles a *day* ago, like an idiot, trying to get rid of inventory. I should have thought about all this a long time ago. Even before the mix-up."

"They're just herbs. They're *natural*."

"It doesn't *matter*. If Amanda hadn't caught me checking on the garden and noticed the oleander, we'd probably still be killing people."

Muffin's teeth gritted. "I'm like her *slave* now. She takes half my check. You have to keep selling the bottles until we have enough money to get our own place. You have to get me out of here—"

Dana clenched her fists. "Are you not hearing me? *I'm not selling any more bottles.*"

Muffin slapped her knee. "But I can't stay here."

Dana leaned back in her chair. "No, you're right about that."

"What's that mean? You said you got a better job."

"I *lied*. I'm not quitting for a better job. I'm quitting to run to Morrocco."

Muffin gaped at her daughter.

"But what about me? You can't leave me *here*."

"I *know*. Do you know I haven't even paid for you for four months? I can't afford this place anymore. Even *with* the discount. The stress of trying to hide everything, fudging the books so Bernie can't tell you're living for free—"

Muffin took a long drink from her tea and then leaned forward to take Dana's hand.

"You can't leave me. They'll kick me out. I'll have nowhere to go."

Dana felt hot tears welling behind her eyes. She squeezed her mother's hand.

"That's what I came to talk to you about. These detectives moved up the timeline. There's only one option."

"What?"

"We start over. We run."

"To Morrocco?"

"Maybe. At first. Once things cool down, maybe we can come back and start somewhere else. Somewhere far away from here. The important part is we'll be together, right?"

Muffin stared, holding her breath. She pulled her hand away to place it on her stomach.

"I don't feel well," she said.

Dana braced herself for what she needed to say next.

I need to hurry.

"You said you don't think Gretchen knows?"

Muffin shook her head. "No. I think Amanda was afraid she'd try and horn in on the action."

Dana nodded. "That makes it a little easier," she mumbled.

Muffin heard.

"Easier, *how*?" she asked, sounding winded.

Dana pulled a familiar bottle from her pocket and held it out for her mother to see its green label.

"If Gretchen doesn't know, I only have to kill one more person."

Muffin winced and then looked up at her daughter with wide eyes.

"What do you mean one *more* person?"

CHAPTER THIRTY-TWO

Charlotte and Declan knocked on Muffin's door. No one answered.

"I guess she's still downstairs?" asked Declan, checking his watch. "It's a little early for dinner."

Charlotte nodded. "She might still be milling around with the talent show crowd. We—"

A moan came from inside the room. The two looked at each other.

"Did you hear that?" asked Charlotte.

He nodded and pounded on the door with the side of his fist.

"Muffin? Can you hear me? Are you okay?"

Another moan.

Charlotte punched in the maid's code, and they pushed open the door.

Muffin lay crumpled in the corner of the room, pale and shaky, beads of sweat on her brow.

"Help," she whispered.

"I'm calling nine-one-one," said Declan. With one hand, he put the phone against his ear. With the other, he pressed the room's emergency button.

Charlotte rushed to help the woman on the ground. She lay half-propped against a wall that looked like someone had cut a panel into it. The secret door was open, revealing a hidden compartment filled with small bottles. More bottles lay on the ground around her.

Charlotte picked up one of the bottles and recognized the label as the one she'd found a piece of on her first day of work. The brown bottle looked like the unlabeled one she'd seen in Gretchen's bedside table.

"What is this?" she asked, holding up one of the bottles. "Did you drink this?"

Muffin shook her head, and she took the woman's hand in hers.

"Are you okay? Do you have pills I can get you? Do you know what's wrong?"

Muffin shook her head again, her other hand clutching the fabric of her shirt over her heart.

"The *green* label," wheezed Muffin.

Charlotte scowled. "I don't understand?"

Muffin motioned toward the hole in the wall, and Charlotte reconsidered the bottles. The trees on the label definitely looked like the bit of label she'd found in Apple's trash pile, but these labels had a blue border.

The one she'd found was green.

"These bottles? Some have green labels, and some have blue?"

Muffin nodded. "Green. *Poison.*"

"The green labels are poison? Are you poisoned, Muffin?"

Muffin rolled to the side and dry heaved, but she nodded. She lifted a hand and then let it drop.

"Tea."

Charlotte looked at Declan, who still hung on the phone with the emergency operator. "Tell them she's been poisoned, and whatever you do, don't touch that tea up there."

He nodded. "They're on the way. Five minutes."

Muffin grabbed Charlotte's hand.

"Stop Dana," she whispered. She was growing weaker by the second.

"Where is she? What's wrong?"

Yasmine rushed into the room.

"What's going on?" she asked.

"We think she's been poisoned—probably by that tea up there. Don't let anyone touch it," said Declan.

Muffin nodded. "Amanda," she said, her eyes closing.

"Amanda poisoned you?" asked Charlotte.

Muffin shook her head. "Dana. Amanda."

"Dana went to Amanda? Is that why you want me to stop her?"

Muffin's eyes fluttered open at the mention of her daughter's name. Charlotte saw a new kind of pain in the woman's eyes.

"Muffin—did *Dana* poison you? Is she going to poison Amanda?"

Muffin's body sagged, but not before she nodded one last time. Her eyes glazed as an unnatural stillness came over her.

"Muffin? *Muffin?*" Charlotte shook the woman, but she didn't respond. She looked at Declan. "I think she's dead."

He handed her the phone. "Let me see."

Charlotte made room for him.

"I think Dana poisoned her. I think she's making a run for it and couldn't take her mother with her."

"*Dana?*" gasped Yasmine, covering her mouth with her hands.

Declan sat back. "There's nothing anyone can do."

Charlotte swallowed.

"I think she was trying to tell me Dana is on her way to kill Amanda."

Declan stood. "If she's getting rid of witnesses and we were right that Amanda was blackmailing them—"

Charlotte nodded.

"We have to stop her."

CHAPTER THIRTY-THREE

Yasmine stayed with Muffin as Charlotte and Declan rushed to Amanda's room. Declan pounded on the door while Charlotte punched in the entry code.

"Amanda! Don't drink anything!" she yelled.

She flung open the door. Dana sat across from Amanda at Amanda's kitchen table, and the two women gawped at the people bursting into the room.

Amanda held a teacup in her hand. She scowled.

"What the—"

Declan dove forward to slap the cup from her hands. As he moved, Dana rose to her feet and grabbed a vase of fake flowers sitting on the table beside her. She flung it at Charlotte, who threw up her hand to block it. By the time the object had crashed against her forearms and bounced to the floor, Dana had pushed past her to escape into the hall.

Amanda squealed at the commotion and then, just as suddenly, grabbed her stomach.

Declan steadied her as she bent to vomit to keep her from bashing her skull on the table.

"She *killed* people," croaked Amanda as Dana disappeared down the hall.

Charlotte slapped the emergency button on the wall and locked eyes with Declan. "Stay with her. I'm going after Dana."

"*She's dangerous!*" was the last thing she heard as she bolted down the hall.

Sirens wailed outside as Charlotte ran after Dana's retreating figure, already at the end of the hall. She'd run right past the elevator to take the far stairs. Charlotte felt confident she'd have no problem catching her on the stairs—

She picked up speed just as a pair of paramedics burst from the elevator, blocking her way. She had to stop dead and bend backward to keep from flipping over the stretcher they pushed in front of them.

"Which way?" asked one.

Charlotte huffed in frustration as Dana slammed into the fire door and entered the far stairwell.

"Two poisonings," she told the EMTs, spinning out of their way. "Second open door is dead. First door—Amanda—she needs help."

"What kind of poisoning?" asked one EMT as the other rushed down the hall with the stretcher.

She glanced at the stairs door.

She needed to get Dana before she got away.

She threw up her hands. "I don't know. It was in the tea. There's a man in there helping her—he knows everything I do."

Charlotte ran down the hall and slammed herself into the stairs door. She heard the first-floor stairwell door open as she passed the second, her adrenaline pumping.

Her breath came in sharp, quick gasps as she closed the distance between them. She flung open the first-floor stairwell door and saw Dana at the end of the hall, entering the lobby. The woman glanced over her shoulder to see how close Charlotte was to catching her.

That's why she didn't notice Apple.

The poor dog had been sleeping in her favorite spot—the middle of the lobby. Dana returned her attention forward a second too late. Charlotte watched her trip. She flew into the air and landed sprawled across the tile floor—sliding like a hockey puck.

Apple skittered out of the way with a speed Charlotte never dreamed the pudgy bulldog possessed.

Charlotte reached Dana as she struggled to retain her feet. She dropped onto the woman, straddling her back to pin her arms to the ground.

"Get off me!" Dana roared, bucking to dislodge her.

Charlotte pressed down as Declan came tearing around the corner. He slid to a stop and smirked.

"Need a little help?"

CHAPTER THIRTY-FOUR

Several weeks later, Charlotte and Declan stopped by Pineapple Port's Yappie Hour with Charlotte's dog Abby in tow. People in the neighborhood took turns hosting the event—an excuse for people to hang out and share some box wine while their dogs watched them get more and more giggly.

They approached a picnic table where Mariska and Darla sat, enjoying their wine in short plastic cups.

"There you are," said Mariska, leaning to hand her chubby dog, Miss Izzy, a chunk of cheese.

Charlotte chuckled. "Thank goodness you're here to feed that dog. The poor thing might fade away to nothing."

Mariska rolled her eyes. "We were just talking about you two."

"All good, I hope?" asked Charlotte, taking a seat.

Declan shared a quick hello and trotted off to get some wine for the two of them. He never minded missing a little of the local gossip—it was usually the same collection of scandals with the names changed from week to week.

"I was saying I hope you cashed Bernie's check," said Darla.

Charlotte cocked her head. "He's all paid up. Why?"

"Good. Money might be scarce. He's selling the place. I saw the listing online."

"Really? Too much drama?" asked Charlotte.

Darla smirked. "You could say that. Gretchen couldn't stand the embarrassment of her fall from grace and left—but not before she tried to blackmail one more person."

"Bernie?"

"Yep. I guess he didn't give her what she wanted, and now his wife is leaving him."

"Serves him right," said Mariska, handing Izzy half a cracker.

Charlotte couldn't disagree.

Darla took a sip of her wine. "He has a buyer, apparently, and all reports say he seems like a nice guy. *Professional*."

"That's good. The people at the manor could use a break from the drama, too."

Declan handed Charlotte a glass of white wine and sat beside her.

"Did I miss anything?" he asked.

"We're talking about the manor. Bernie's selling. Gretchen's gone. Everyone's happier."

"Amanda isn't trying to keep Gretchen's memory alive?" asked Declan.

"Nah. I doubt it," said Darla. "Gretchen was the head of the snake. Amanda will be lost without her."

"I'm surprised she didn't leave with Gretchen. They could have made some other place miserable together," said Charlotte.

Declan chuckled. "Maybe being poisoned gave her some humility."

"Not as much humility as jail will give Dana," said Darla as her miniature dachshund ran circles. She glanced down to find her ankles tied with the dog's leash.

"Turbo, for crying out loud." She untangled herself and then huffed.

"You know, we almost bought some of that poison."

Mariska's brow knitted. "We did?"

"In the store, remember? Dana was pushing it, but I told her I don't like those energy potions."

"Good thing," muttered Mariska. "All I remember are those tee shirts. I wish I'd bought one."

"She had two batches," said Charlotte. "From what I understand, the elixir was a get-rich-quick scheme for Muffin and Dana, but somehow they mixed up St. John's wort and yellow oleander and ended up poisoning some people."

"How'd Amanda find out about it?" asked Darla.

"She found the garden and spotted the mistake because she was the manor's real plant expert."

"Don't remind me," grumbled Darla.

Mariska patted her arm. "I liked Snail Town."

She nodded. "Me, too."

Declan scratched Abby's chin as she begged for snacks of her own. "The ironic part is they wanted the extra money to move away from the manor. Instead, they ended up in a worse position."

Charlotte nodded. "Amanda demanded part of their sales, or she'd go to the police. They were stuck. They corrected their recipe and changed the labels from green to blue, but it was too late. Bernie suspected something was up and hired us."

"But why did Dana kill her own mother?" asked Mariska.

Charlotte shrugged. "She was desperate to get away, and Muffin complicated her escape."

Mariska shook her head. "Terrible. And then she tried to kill Amanda, too. She'd lost her mind."

"Desperation can do that to you." Charlotte took a sip of her wine. "You two seem to know a lot about the gossip at the manor since we left. Have you been sneaking back there?"

Mariska smiled. "We don't need to. It came to us."

Her gaze slipped past Charlotte, and she nodded in that direction. Charlotte turned to see two familiar women approaching with a waddling bulldog.

"Alma and Yasmine, what are you doing here?" she asked, standing to greet the ladies.

"Alma bought Tilly's place," said Darla.

"I can't believe you didn't tell me," said Charlotte.

"We just got here three days ago," said Yasmine.

"And she had to get the house *perfect* before I could talk her into taking a break," said Alma.

Yasmine shrugged. "I like things a certain way."

Charlotte laughed. "*No*, I didn't notice. You were such a laid-back boss."

Yasmine's cheeks flushed.

Charlotte motioned to Apple, who wore a hibiscus-patterned dress.

"No maid costume today?" she asked.

Yasmine grinned. "Nah. We're off duty." She looked at Alma. "Want some wine?"

"I'll take some white," she said.

Yasmine nodded and urged Apple in the direction of the wine station.

"It's nice to have you two in the neighborhood," said Declan.

"Nice to be here," said Alma, sitting. "It's a little less exciting here than at Elderbrook, but that's a *good* thing."

"You should join the Pineapple Port newsletter committee," said Charlotte. "If you've read it, you know they could use you."

Declan shrugged. "I don't know. I thought last month's feature on the hidden health benefits of early bird specials was riveting."

Charlotte chuckled. "True. Those crack reporters *did* uncover who was hoarding all the community center's library large print crosswords."

"*Ralph*," muttered Mariska. "The man is a menace."

THE END

Keep reading for sneak-peek first chapters of other books by Amy Vansant.

Thank you—Please review on Amazon!

ABOUT THE AUTHOR

USA Today and *Wall Street Journal* bestselling author Amy Vansant has written over 30 books, including the fun, thrilling Shee McQueen series, the rollicking, twisty Pineapple Port Mysteries, and the action-packed Kilty urban fantasies. Throw in a couple of romances and a YA fantasy for her nieces...

Amy specializes in fun, exciting reads with plenty of laughs and action. She lives in Jupiter, Florida, with her muse/husband and a goony Bordoodle named Archer.

You can follow Amy on AMAZON or BOOKBUB.

BOOKS BY AMY VANSANT

<u>Pineapple Port Mysteries</u>
Funny, clean & full of unforgettable characters
<u>Shee McQueen Mystery-Thrillers</u>
Action-packed, fun romantic mystery-thrillers
<u>Kilty Urban Fantasy/Romantic Suspense</u>
Action-packed romantic suspense/urban fantasy
<u>Slightly Romantic Comedies</u>
Classic romantic romps
<u>The Magicatory</u>
Middle-grade fantasy

SNEAK PEEK
SHEE MCQUEEN
MYSTERY
THRILLERS #1
THE GIRL WHO
WANTS

CHAPTER ONE

Three Weeks Ago, Nashua, New Hampshire.

Shee realized her mistake the moment her feet left the grass.

He's enormous.

She'd watched him drop from the side window of the house. He landed four feet from where she stood—still, her brain refused to register the warning signs. The nose, big and lumpy as breadfruit, the forehead some beach town could use as a jetty if they buried him to his neck...

His knees bent to absorb his weight, and *her* brain thought *got you.*

Her brain couldn't be bothered with simple math: *Giant, plus Shee, equals Pain.*

Instead, she jumped to tackle him, dangling airborne as his knees straightened and the *pet the rabbit* bastard stood to his full height.

Crap.

The math added up pretty quickly after that.

Hovering like Superman mid-flight, she couldn't do much to change her disastrous trajectory. She'd *felt* like a superhero when she left the ground. Now, she felt more like a Canada goose staring into the propellers of Captain Sully's Airbus A320.

She might take down the plane, but it was going to *hurt*.

Frankenjerk turned toward her at the exact moment she plowed into him. She clamped her arms around his waist like a little girl hugging a redwood. Lurch returned the embrace, twisting her to the ground. Her back hit the dirt, and air burst from her lungs like a double shotgun blast.

Ow.

Wheezing, she punched upward, striking Beardless Hagrid in the throat.

That didn't go over well.

Grabbing her shoulder with one hand, Dickasaurus flipped her on her stomach like a sausage link, slipped his hand under her chin, and pressed his forearm against her windpipe.

The only air she'd gulped before he cut her supply stank of damp armpit. He'd tucked her skull in his arm crotch, much like the famous noggin-less horseman once held his severed head. Fireworks exploded in the dark behind her eyes.

That's when a thought occurred to her.

I haven't been home in fifteen years.

What if she died in Gigantor's armpit? Would her father even know?

Has it been that long?

Flopping like a landed fish, she forced her assailant to adjust his hold and sucked a breath as she flipped on her back. Spittle glistened on his lips, and his brow furrowed as if she'd asked him to read a paragraph of big-boy words.

His nostrils flared like the Holland Tunnel.

There's an idea.

Making a V with her fingers, Shee thrust upward, stabbing into his nose, straining to reach his tiny brain.

Goliath roared. Jerking back, he grabbed her arm to unplug her fingers from his nose socket. She whipped away her limb before he had a good grip, fearing he'd snap her bones with his Godzilla paws.

Kneeling before her, he clamped both hands over his face, cursing as blood seeped from behind his fingers.

Shee's gaze didn't linger on that mess. Her focus fell to his crotch, hovering a foot above her feet, protected by nothing but a thin pair of oversized sweatpants.

Scrambled eggs, sir?

She kicked.

He howled.

Shee scuttled back like a crab, found her feet, and snatched her gun from her side. The gun she should have pulled *before* trying to tackle the Empire State Building.

"Move a muscle, and I'll aerate you," she said. She always liked that line.

The golem growled but remained on the ground like a good dog, cradling his family jewels.

Shee's partner in this manhunt, a local cop easier on the eyes than he was useful, rounded the corner and drew his weapon.

She smiled and holstered the gun he'd lent her...without *knowing* he'd lent it.

"Glad you could make it."

Her portion of the operation accomplished, she headed toward the car as more officers swarmed the scene.

"Shee, where are you going?" called the cop.

She stopped and turned.

"Home, I think."

His gaze dropped to her hip.

"Is that my gun?"

SNEAK PEEK
PINEAPPLE PORT
MYSTERIES #1
PINEAPPLE LIES

CHAPTER ONE

"Whachy'all doin'?"

Charlotte jumped, her paintbrush flinging a flurry of black paint droplets across her face. She shuddered and placed her free hand over her heart.

"Darla, you scared me to death."

"Sorry, Sweetpea, your door was open."

"*Sorry,*" echoed Mariska, following close on Darla's heels.

Charlotte added another stroke of black to her wall and balanced her brush on the edge of the paint can. Her knees cracked a twenty-one-gun salute as she stood. She was only twenty-six years old but had always suffered from bad knees. She didn't mind. She grew up in a fifty-five-plus retirement community, and her creaky joints provided something to complain about when the locals swapped war stories about pacemakers and hip replacements.

Nobody liked to miss out on that kind of fun.

Charlotte wiped the paint from her forehead with the back of her hand.

"Unlocked and open are not the same thing, ladies. What if I had a gentleman caller?"

Darla burst into laughter, the gold chain swinging from her hot-pink-rimmed glasses. Another pair of plastic-rimmed glasses sat perched like a baby bird on her head, tucked into a nest of champagne-blonde curls. She sobered beneath the weight of Charlotte's unamused glare.

"Did you lose your other glasses again?" asked Charlotte.

"I did. They'll turn up."

Charlotte nodded and tapped the top of her noggin. "I'm sure."

Darla's hand shot to her head.

"Oh, there you go. See? I told you they'd show up."

Mariska moved closer, nudging Darla out of the way. She threw out her arms, her breezy cotton tunic draping like aqua butterfly wings.

"Morning *hug*," she demanded.

Charlotte rolled her eyes and relented. Mariska wrapped her in a bear hug, and she sank into the woman's snuggly, Polish-grandmother's body. It was like sitting on a favorite old sofa, rife with missing springs...and then being eaten by it.

"Okay. Can't breathe," said Charlotte.

"I'm wearing the top you bought me for Christmas," Mariska mumbled in Charlotte's ear as she rocked her back and forth.

"I saw that."

"It's very comfortable."

"This *isn't*. I can't breathe. Did I mention that? We're good. Okay..."

Mariska released Charlotte and stepped back, her face flush with satisfaction. She turned and looked at the wall, scratching her cheek with flowered, enameled nails as she studied Charlotte's painting project.

"What are you doing? Painting your wall black? Are you depressed?"

Charlotte sighed. Darla and Mariska were inseparable; if one wasn't offering an opinion, the other was picking up the slack.

"You're not turning into one of those dopey Goth kids now, are you?" asked Darla.

"*No*, it has nothing to do with my mood. It's chalkboard paint. I'm making this strip of the wall into a giant chalkboard."

"Why?" Darla asked, her thick, Kentucky accent adding syllables to places the word *why* never considered having them. Her mouth twisted, and her brow lowered. Charlotte couldn't tell if she disapproved, was confused, or had suffered a sharp gas pain. Not one guess was more likely than any other.

"Because I think I figured out my problem," she said.

Darla cackled. "Oh, this oughta be good. You have any coffee left?"

"In the kitchen."

Darla and Mariska lined up and waddled toward the kitchen like baby ducks following their mama. Mariska inspected several mugs in the cabinet above the coffee machine and, finding one, put it aside. She handed Darla another. Mariska's mug of choice was the one she'd given Charlotte after her trip to Colorado's Pikes Peak. She'd bought the mug for herself, but after Charlotte laughed and explained the double entendre of the slogan emblazoned on the side, *I Got High on Pikes Peak*, she'd thrust it at her, horrified.

Nevertheless, Mariska remained proud of her fourteen thousand-foot spiraling drive to the peak, so she clandestinely drank from the offending mug whenever she visited.

Charlotte watched as she read the side of the mug, expelled a deep sigh, and poured her coffee. That heartbreaking look was why she hadn't broached the subject of Mariska's *I Got Baked in Florida* t-shirt.

The open-plan home allowed the two older women to watch Charlotte as she returned to painting the wall between her pantry and living area.

"So, are you pregnant?" Darla asked. "And after this, you're painting the nursery?"

"Ah, no. That's not even funny."

"You're the youngest woman in Pineapple Port. You're our only hope for a baby. How can you toss aside the hopes and dreams of three hundred enthusiastic, if rickety, babysitters?"

"I don't think I'm the youngest woman here anymore. I think Charlie Collins is taking his wife to the prom next week."

Darla cackled and then punctuated her amusement with a grunt of disapproval.

"Stupid men," she muttered.

Charlotte whisked away the last spot of neutral cream paint with her brush, completing her wall. She turned to find Mariska staring, her thin, over-plucked eyebrows sitting high on her forehead as she awaited the answer to the mystery of the chalkboard wall.

"So you're going to keep your grocery list on the wall?" asked Mariska. "That's very clever."

"Not exactly. Lately, I've been asking myself, *what's missing from my life?*"

Darla tilted her head. "A man. *Duh.*"

Charlotte glowered at her. "*Anyway*, last week it hit me."

Darla paused, mug nearly to her lips, waiting for Charlotte to continue.

"What hit you? A chalkboard wall?" asked Mariska.

Charlotte shook her head. "No, a *purpose*. I need to figure out what I want to *be*. My life is missing *purpose*."

Darla scoffed. "Oh, is that all? I think they had that on sale at Target last weekend. I'll pick it up for you."

Charlotte busied herself, resealing the paint can as Mariska inspected her handiwork.

"You're going to take up painting? I'll take a chalkboard wall. I can write Bob messages and make lists..."

"I'll paint your wall if you like, but starting a painting business isn't my *purpose*. The wall is so I can make a to-do list."

Darla sighed. "I have a to-do list, but it only has one thing on it: *Keep breathing.*"

Mariska giggled.

"I'm going to make goals and write them here," said Charlotte, gesturing like a game show hostess to best display her wall. "When I accomplish something, I get to cross it off. See? I completed one project. I know it works."

A knock on the door, and Charlotte's gaze swiveled to the front of the house. Her soft-coated Wheaten terrier, Abby, burst out of the bedroom and stood behind the door, barking.

"You forgot to open your blinds this morning," said Mariska.

"Death Squad," mumbled Darla.

The Death Squad patrolled the Pineapple Port retirement community every morning. If the six-woman troop passed a home showing no activity by ten a.m., they knocked on the door and demanded proof of life. They pretended to visit other businesses, asking if the homeowner would attend this meeting or that bake sale, but everyone knew the Squad was there to check if someone *died* overnight. Odds were slim that young Charlotte wouldn't make it through the evening, but the Squad didn't make exceptions.

Charlotte held Abby's collar and opened the door.

"Oh, hi, Charlotte," said a small woman in a purple t-shirt. "We were just—"

"I'm alive, Ginny. Have a good walk."

Charlotte closed the door. She opened her blinds and peeked out, and several Death Squad ladies waved to her as they resumed their march. Abby stood on the sofa and thrust her head through the blinds, her nub of a tail waving at them at high speed.

Mariska turned and dumped her remaining coffee into the sink, rinsed the purple mug, and, with one last longing glance at the Pikes Peak logo, put it in the dishwasher. She placed her hands on her ample hips and faced Charlotte.

"Do you have chalk?"

"No." Charlotte had been annoyed at herself all morning for forgetting chalk and resented having it brought to her attention. "I forgot it."

Darla motioned to the black wall. "Well, there's your first item. *Buy chalk.* Write that down."

"With what?"

"Oh. Good point."

"Anyhow, shopping lists don't count," said Charlotte.

Darla smirked. "Oh, there are *rules*. The chalkboard has *rules*, Mariska."

Mariska pursed her lips and nodded. "Very serious."

"Well, I may not have a chalkboard, but I have a wonderful sense of purpose," said Darla, putting her mug in the dishwasher.

"Oh yes? What's that?" asked Mariska.

"I've got to pick up Frank's ED pills."

She stepped over the plastic drop cloth beneath the painted wall and headed for the door.

"ED?" Charlotte blushed. "You mean for—"

"Erectile Dysfunction. Pooped Peepee. Droopy D—"

"*Got it,*" said Charlotte, cutting her short.

"Fine. But these pills are special. Want to know why?"

"Not in the least."

Mariska began to laugh, and Darla grinned.

"She's horrible," Mariska whispered as she walked by Charlotte.

Darla reached into her pocketbook and pulled out a small plastic bottle. She handed it to Charlotte.

"Read the label."

Charlotte looked at the side of the pill bottle. The label held the usual medical information, but the date was two years past due.

"He only gets them once every two years?"

"Nope. He only got them *once*. Since then, I've been refilling the bottle with little blue sleeping pills. Any time he gets the urge, he takes one, and an hour later, he's sound asleep. When he wakes up, I tell him everything was amazing."

Charlotte's jaw dropped. "That's *terrible*."

Darla dismissed her with a wave and put the bottle back in her purse.

"Nah," she said, opening the front door. "I don't have time for that nonsense. If I'm in the mood, I give him one from the original prescription."

Darla and Mariska patted Abby on the head, waved goodbye, and stepped into the Florida sun.

Charlotte shut the door behind them and balled her drop cloth of sliced trash bags. She rinsed her brush and carried the paint can back to the shed in her backyard. Returning to the house, she surveyed her neglected yard.

Ugh.

A large pile of broken concrete sat in the corner, awaiting pickup. As part of her new *life with purpose* policy, she'd hired a company to jackhammer away part of her concrete patio to provide room for a garden. The original paved yard left little room for plants. With the cement removed, Charlotte could add *grow a garden* to her chalkboard wall.

Maybe she was supposed to be a gardener or work with the earth? She didn't feel particularly *earthy*, but who knew?

Her rocky new patch of sand didn't inspire confidence. It didn't resemble the dark, healthy soil she saw in her neighbors' more successful gardens. She huffed and returned to the shed to grab a spade and cushion for her knees.

It was cool outside, the perfect time of day to pluck the stray bits of concrete from the ground before the Florida sun became unbearable. She knew she didn't like sweating, so gardening was probably *not* her calling. Still, she was determined to give everything a chance.

She needed to clean her new patch of land, shower, and buy topsoil, plants, and chalk.

"Tomatoes, cucumbers..." Charlotte mumbled, mentally making a list of plants she needed to buy.

Or seeds? Should I buy seeds or plants?

Less chance of failure starting with mature plants, though if *they* died, that would be even *more* embarrassing.

A scratching noise caught her attention, and she looked up to find her neighbor's Cairn terrier, Katie, furiously digging beside her. Part of the fence had been broken or chewed, and stocky little Katie visited whenever life in her backyard became too tedious. Charlotte's spade struck a large stone, and she removed it, tossing it toward a pile of broken concrete as Katie dug beside her.

Dirt cascaded through the air.

"Katie, you're making a mess. If you want to help, pick up stones and move them out of the garden."

Katie stopped digging long enough to stare with her large brown eyes. At least, she thought the dog was staring at her. Katie had a lazy eye that made it difficult to tell.

"Move the rocks," Charlotte repeated, demonstrating the process with her spade. "Stop making a mess, or I'll let Abby out, and then you'll be in trouble."

Katie ignored her and resumed digging. Sand arced behind her, piling against the fence.

"You better watch it, shortstack, or the next item on the list will be to *fix the fence.*"

Katie eyeballed her again, her crooked bottom teeth jutting from her mouth. She looked like a furry can opener.

"Fix your face."

Katie snorted a spray of snot and returned to digging.

Charlotte removed several bits of concrete and then shifted her kneepad a few feet closer to Katie. She saw a flash of white and felt something settle against her hand. Katie sat beside her, tail wagging, tongue lolling from the left side of her mouth.

Between the dog and her hand sat the prize Katie wanted to share.

Charlotte froze.

One word repeated, picking up pace until it was an unintelligible crescendo of nonsense in her mind.

Skull. Skull skull skullskullskullskuuuuulllll...

She blinked, sure that the object would have taken its proper shape as a rock or pile of sand when she opened her eyes.

Nope.

Hollow eye sockets stared back at her.

Hi. Nice to meet you. I'm a human skull. What's up, girl?

The lower jaw was missing. The cranium was nearly as large as Katie and shared a similar off-white coloring.

The skull had better teeth.

Charlotte realized the forehead of this bony intruder rested against her pinky. She whipped her hand away. The skull rocked toward her as if in pursuit, and she scrambled back as it rolled in her direction, slow and relentless as a movie mummy. Katie ran after the skull and pounced on it, stopping its progress.

Charlotte put her hand on her chest.

"Thank you."

Her brain raced to process the meaning of a human head in her backyard.

It has to be a joke... maybe some weird dog toy...

Charlotte gently tapped the skull with her shovel. It didn't feel like cloth or rawhide. It made a sharp-yet-thuddy noise, just the sound she suspected a human skull might make. If she had to compare the tone to something, it would be the sound of a girl about to freak out while tapping a metal shovel on a human skull.

"Oh, Katie. What did you find?"

The question increased Katie's rate of tail wag. She yipped and returned to the hole she'd dug, retrieving the lower jaw.

"Oh no... Stop that. You sick little—"

Katie stood, human jawbone clenched in her teeth, tail wagging so furiously that Charlotte thought she might lift off like a chubby little helicopter. The terrier spun and skittered through the fence back to her yard, dragging her prize in tow. The jawbone stuck in the slats, but Katie wrestled it through and disappeared into her yard.

"Katie, *no*," said Charlotte, reaching toward the retreating dog. "Katie—I'm pretty sure that has to stay with the head."

She leaned forward and nearly touched the jawless skull before yanking away her hand.

Whose head is in my garden?

She felt her eyes growing wider—like pancake batter poured into a pan.

Hold the phone.

Heads usually come attached to bodies.

Were there more *bones*?

What was worse? Finding a whole skeleton or finding *only* a head?

Charlotte hoped the rest of the body lay nearby and then shook her head at the oddity of her wish.

She glanced around her plot of dirt and realized she might be kneeling in a *whole graveyard*. More bones. More *heads*. She scrambled to her feet and dropped her shovel.

Charlotte glanced back at her house, where her chalkboard wall waited patiently.

She *really* needed some chalk.

Made in the USA
Las Vegas, NV
03 November 2024